# Beyond
# THE END

## THE EXISTENCE SERIES BOOK 1

# THE EXISTENCE SERIES

REMEMBER
BEYOND THE END
LIES A PLACE
FOR THE ETERNAL

For more information on the series, sign up for
Tara C. Allred's newsletter at www.taracallred.net.

# OTHER BOOKS BY
# TARA C. ALLRED

SANDERS' STARFISH
UNAUTHORED LETTERS
THE OTHER SIDE OF QUIET
HELPING HELPER

# Beyond
# THE END

## THE EXISTENCE SERIES BOOK 1

## TARA C. ALLRED

First published in the US in 2020 by Patella Publishing.

This edition published in 2022.

Patella Publishing
First Paperback Edition: 2020
Second Paperback Edition: 2022
ISBN: 9780986421587

Cover design by Melissa Williams Design
Typesetting by Amanda Reid with Melissa Williams Design

Publisher's Note: This novel is a work of fiction. Names, characters, places, and incidents are either products of the author's imagination or used fictitiously. All characters are fictional, and any similarity to people living or dead is purely coincidental.

*Published in the United States of America*

*Patella Publishing*

*For Aubrey*
*who heard the story first*
*and helped bring Leilani's world to life*

# AUTHOR'S NOTE

Dear Reader,

Several years ago, a plotline began. My first thought was, "This is a cool idea. I want to read it. Someone should write this story."

Then the more I explored the characters and their experiences, the more I really wanted this storyline to exist!

I was completely unqualified for the task, but, bit by bit, I challenged myself to become that writer. Since then, I've learned a lot! It's been a giant undertaking. Meanwhile, the story has changed me in many ways.

At times, I've wondered if this series is really only for me. If so, that is grand! I love what it's done, how it's remade me, and how I now view the world.

So why share it? Each time I publish a book, it becomes a gift offered to others all around the globe. It's scary, and it's exciting. Who "the right audience is" I don't know. But perhaps there is *one* reader who will discover a wonderful change, like I did, from these characters' journeys.

The book takes place in the year 2050. Early drafts covered events that also occurred during 2028-2033. After much debate, and recommendations from test readers, I pulled out the 2028-2033 events and placed them in the short novel *Remember*. You can pick up a copy of *Remember* for free by signing up for my newsletter, or you can pick up a low-cost copy online. It is not essential to read *Remember* first.

This book, *Beyond the End,* is about Leilani's journey (the 16-year-old protagonist). She has no clue of the events that took place in *Remember*. So if you came here specifically for Leilani's story, then dive into *Beyond the End* (Book 1) and skip *Remember* (A Prelude to The Existence Series).

If you are here for the adults' journey, in addition to Leilani's journey, and want the complete experience, then may I suggest the short read of *Remember*, which is the origin story of the invention Em-Path. It shares the dynamics of those involved with Em-Path's creation. It also adds to the overall interest and complexity of The Existence Series. But again, it is not critical to have read *Remember* before enjoying *Beyond the End* (Book 1).

Either way, I hope you enjoy The Existence Series.

The rest of the books in the series are *Lies a Place* (Book 2) and *For the Eternal* (Book 3).

You are invited to experience something different. I hope what you discover is special, fun, and personally enlightening too. Even though it's been a lot of work, I'm grateful for Leilani's story.

Thank you for being here with me. Enjoy!

*Tara C. Allred*

"Life is a luminous pause
between two great mysteries,
which themselves are one."

— Carl Jung

# PART ONE

# ONE

## LEILANI

The rose and yellow sky stretched out over the horizon. The sun, still hidden below, was coming, acting as an offstage spotlight, casting an amber glow toward my family's island.

I loved this spotlight moment, the colors mixing across the sky, the light calling attention to the jutting and cutting of the cliffs off in the distance. In moments like these, the island felt larger than it was, the brilliance adding a new dimension to everything, leaving me with hope that I could make it another day living here.

My oldest brother, Clark, liked to tell me how good I had it. Me, the first born after the world ended. Technically, I was born before the world ended. But not by much. Therefore, I was always lumped into the *after* group. My sister, Caroline, was six years older than me, and the last of us born in the *before* group. A big divide between me and all my half-siblings.

Our Labrador, Huck, found me sitting on the beach. He brought a stick, commanding my attention with his wagging tail and demanding bark. I willingly succumbed to his pleadings and tossed it along the crescent beach.

From our house, I came down to this spot every morning. Sometimes to think, or to daydream of going someplace else, or just to get away.

All my other siblings were married now, living on other parts of the island. It was just me and Dad and Mom—and sometimes that was still too many people.

Behind me, Dad cleared his throat. With even greater exuberance, Huck returned the stick to him. Then Dad did his trick. He took the stick and threw it so far into the patch of trees and bushes that it would take Huck a good twenty minutes to locate the right one. Huck was a loyalist, unwilling to settle for anything other than the original stick, which meant Dad wanted this time undisturbed.

Here on Mom's errand, all three of us knew a reprimand would come softer from Dad.

I stood but didn't face him. Instead, I let the waves bury my feet in the sand while I looked toward the horizon. The sun now shone on my face.

"Hi, sweetheart," he said quietly.

At least he would talk respectfully, whereas Mom would expect blind obedience and speak to me like I was a little kid.

I gave a nod. "Just tracking the swells."

"And? What have you found?" Amid his assignment to reprimand me, he sounded pleased.

I let silence carry for a bit as I performed a count. "Four feet at ten seconds."

He let out a chuckle. "Nice job, scientist."

Instead of smiling, I closed my eyes while I waited for him to accomplish his task.

He breathed loudly. Finally, he said, "You know why I came to talk to you."

I kept my eyes closed and folded my arms. My fight with Mom began yesterday afternoon only to worsen this morning. I figured silence was my best response.

"You shouldn't have ... talked to your mother . . . like that," he said.

I opened my eyes toward the blue sky. It took a lot of willpower to hold back the exasperated huff building inside. I placed a fist against my hip. "Dad, she wants me to be like Violet and Grace. And I'm not."

His tactical silence caused me to look at him. He stayed waiting until I dropped my fist to my side.

We stared at each other. As the island patriarch, and self-appointed mediator of any family divide, he most likely was trying to choose his words wisely.

Even though Mom was wrong, he would feel obligated to side with her. However, my theory was, if he understood the full story, he'd secretly agree with me.

And, with his granddaughters, Violet and Grace, even though I was right that they were lightminded in what they thought about every day, Dad wouldn't be able to say anything unkind about them.

By the time he actually spoke, I concluded I could have done a faster job of writing his mediation script. "You don't need to be like Violet or Grace. But you do need to be respectful to your mom."

My lips pressed together to suppress the huff. Then I proceeded to give him the full story. "Yesterday after school, I was reading *The Descent of Man*—"

"I thought you were reading *The Origin of Species?*

5

"I finished it." I gave him a shrug. "So, when I returned it to your shelf, I saw *The Descent of Man* and borrowed it."

"Oh." He nodded at the ocean, but I caught the pride that spread across his face. As I'd hypothesized, the more details he had, the more support he'd give me.

So, I continued. "But Violet and Grace were at the house, and Violet said, 'Why do you read that?' So I said, 'Because I like it.' And Grace said, 'I don't get how you can even understand that stuff.' Then Violet said, 'I only read romance.' Grace said, 'I don't read.' And Violet said, 'Well, you should at least read romance, it's all about love and getting together with your man.'" I raised my eyebrows at him. "Dad. I don't want to get together with my *man.* So, all I said was if they learned how to actually read, and then think, they wouldn't need a man."

Although his mouth didn't share a smile, his eyes did. "Your mom said you said a few other words, too."

"Only after she told me to be careful what I say, and that right now I know too little about all that myself."

A half-smile came. "She just wants you to be open to falling in love. Someday."

"Like with who?" I tossed an arm toward the sea emphasizing there were no options here.

His smile left. "Right now, you're way too young to be worried about any of this."

I couldn't help it; I had to roll my eyes at him. Then, my annoyed chuckle followed. "I'm not the one who needs that reminder. I'm not the one reading to *get together with my man.*" I placed my hands on my hips and took in a large breath. Then I added, "I'm the one that would rather be out there doing something with my life, instead of hanging around those immature subadults."

"Leilani!"

I knew it. Dad would support me once he had the facts, but he would never tolerate any of us engaging in name-calling—and I was guilty.

I let out a sigh—my effort to signify my remorse. "I'm just tired of listening to Violet and Grace talk about how the only reason they are willing to learn 'stuff' is so they can be better moms and teach that 'stuff' to their children, while they stay home and take care of their herds of babies. Seriously, they talk about it all the time! And if I speak up and say I'd rather focus on doing something useful, with science, Mom gets mad at me. I said I don't want to be like her, and she said, 'What, be a mom?' And I said, 'Yes.' And she said, 'Then I might as well give myself a life sentence of despair and misery.'"

"I doubt she said those exact words."

Dad also wouldn't allow for exaggerations. Guilty again.

"There's a whole life ahead of you." He kept his words calm. "With lots of wonderful things. You have plenty of time to figure out what you want. And I think, in time, you'll find you want some of those joyful things."

I scowled at him. The reprimand was only leading us toward the bigger issue. I turned back to the water and spoke to the waves. "I want to do something good with my life."

"And you will, Leilani," he said softly.

"What I plan to do with my life doesn't involve

me staying here on this island."

He drew in a long breath. He did this every time I brought up the suffocating feeling I felt. Every day it just seemed to grow more intense.

But each time I mentioned it, he would pull in a big breath of air, and let it circulate through his lungs like he wanted to delay talking to me about my real concerns. Like he was just trying to say what I'd already heard others say: that I was lucky to be alive, and that I was lucky to have a place to live, even if it was just this island.

He shifted to look at a wave crashing against some cliffs in the distance. "You're right, Leilani. You will do something good," he said, "something great, with your life. But what you are destined for involves great things on this island."

"No." I moved to place myself directly in his line of sight. I pressed my fists against my hips. Then I tilted my head out toward the horizon. "I want off this island."

He looked past me. Finally, he said, "You already know what I'm going to say."

"How can there be nothing else out there?"

"Because there isn't. You already know this."

Again, I shifted, standing almost on tiptoe to make sure I directly met his eyes. "It doesn't make sense that this is all there is."

A movement occurred behind us. We both turned. From the brush, I expected to see Huck finally emerging with his stick. Instead, I caught the movement of a larger shadow shifting, followed by a low voice, "An excellent observation."

Dad stepped back. I peered toward the brush.

"Certainly," the voice came again, a bit louder

now, "there is more out there."

Dad gasped. A strange man emerged. He was dressed in a metallic purple suit with a nearly translucent beige button shirt that opened at the chest. A mass of blond hair, sculpted into a tousle around his forehead, jetted out toward us. In place of flip-flops, his alligator loafers treaded through the sand.

"You know there's more." The man nodded at Dad coolly.

Dad said nothing, only tilted his head to look closer at the man with his orange-tinted skin and his sharp facial lines. Then, as the man's ice crystal eyes narrowed, Dad gasped again.

"Ashyr," Dad said quietly.

"Hello, Foster."

My mouth fell open as the two stared at each other.

# TWO

## LEILANI

One hundred and eighty-nine people lived on the island. Actually, one hundred and ninety due to my half-sister Kate's recent baby boy. Every person I knew. Either they were family, which was the case with most people on the island, or the others were on the island because they had a longtime working relationship or friendship with my parents, *before the world ended.*

So, it was hard to process what I now saw: this stranger, there on the beach with his shiny suit, his reptile-skinned shoes, and the black liner around his eyes.

Even though it was rude, I couldn't pull my eyes away. And I couldn't seem to shut my gaping mouth either.

I felt a brain wave malfunction because I could only process two ideas.

He knew Dad.

And he wasn't from here.

Meanwhile, I liked his eyes. They were clear blue as the softest wave on a quiet day. But when those eyes met mine, I quickly looked away. My cheeks burned like I should be ashamed over how intrigued I was with this mystery man.

I shook off the feeling, only to spot the ink on his neck: the word *EnRapture* in fancy script running down toward his bared chest.

I looked to Dad. His head was pulled back, his brow furrowed, his stance firm but shifting back toward the house. He was tense, something I rarely see in him.

"Who is he?" I whispered, although the man was still close enough to hear.

"No one." But right as Dad said that, the man extended a hand covered in gold bangles and a large ring and stepped toward me.

"Ashyr Harmon. And you?"

"Go get your mother." Dad's firm voice shook me.

Before I could accept the handshake, Ashyr's hand drew toward his lips. "Ah, yes. Mariana. Won't she be delighted to see me?"

This was too much! I looked from this man, Ashyr, to Dad. He knew Mom, too.

"Maybe she'll invite me to stay for a bite," he said. "It was a long trip, as you know. You're not easy to find. But I figure that's all part of your infrastructure."

Dad didn't move.

"I suppose you didn't expect to see me, did you, old mate?" While Dad's eyes stayed locked on him, Ashyr's eyebrows raised like he had just won a game or something. "You're not the only one whose hypothetical invention worked out. Congrats to both of us."

My brain still felt caught in some kind of malfunction. I tried to grasp what this Ashyr guy meant while Dad turned toward me. The scowl on his face ran deep. "Go, now!"

But I couldn't move. Instead, I looked back and forth. Dad's shoulders were tight against his loose Hawaiian shirt while this stranger, in his shiny suit, shared a casual grin toward the ocean.

"Leilani," Dad's tone remained even, but the discomfort on his face was clear.

I chose one of the many questions pounding inside my head. "Which invention is he talking about?"

I caught Ashyr's grin widen. His bracelets clanged together like music as he spread his hand across the panorama beach, the ocean waves, the land behind us. "This pl—"

"Stop!" Dad interjected. "Enough."

"Dad?" Fear surfaced in my voice.

Although Ashyr's grin softened, it still hung on the corners of his lips. "Your daughter." Those clear blue eyes studied me, as if evaluating me.

I shot Dad a glance, but he volunteered nothing, only kept his eyes fixed on Ashyr.

When I looked back, Ashyr nodded at me and said, "How old?"

"Sixteen," I volunteered. "Seventeen next month."

A smile bent around Ashyr's face. "In our society, seventeen starts the integration process into adult life."

Suddenly, Dad moved fast. He stepped between me and Ashyr and planted his hands firmly on my shoulders. He met my eyes. "Get Mom, now. Quick. It's important."

It was the pressure in his hands—and the fear in his voice—that made me agree.

I hustled up the sand, but when I reached the

house's path, I turned back to see the two still standing near each other on the beach.

Whatever this was, it was *clearly* important— this stranger who seemed to have fallen from the sky.

# THREE

## MARIANA

She heard footsteps followed by Leilani's voice. "Who and her?"

As was so often the case with Leilani, the words were undecipherable.

"Excuse me?" Mariana lifted her eyes from the monitor while refusing to turn around and face her mumbling daughter.

"Who and her?" The same nonsense tumbled out.

Foster had once said, "Perhaps it's your hearing to blame." But the issue only came with Leilani, not with any of the other children or grandchildren. With Leilani, the words only made sense if Mariana turned around to watch her daughter's lips and facial expressions.

But today, she didn't feel like facing her disrespectful daughter. Instead, she tapped her stylus on the birch table and paused to look at the family photos above the monitor. A combination of images showed various stages of growth, yet the backdrop was always the same: the crescent-shaped beach and their ocean.

Her eyes settled on Zane, with his rich island tan. Then, on Caroline with her dark eyes and lashes. Her other children, from her first marriage, had never been so difficult to raise.

She'd already spoken to Leilani about the mumbling. Numerous times. But nothing changed.

"I can't understand you." She spun around to face Leilani. "Are you saying, 'Who and her?' I don't know who 'Who' is or 'her' so I can't answer that." Right after the words came out, Mariana cursed herself, her tone, the clear frustration with her daughter.

"Ashyr!" Leilani said with force.

The clear word caused Mariana's head to pull back. "Excuse me?"

"Who's Ashyr?" Leilani said distinctly.

"I don't think . . ." Against the sudden surging heartbeat, Mariana spun back to her computer. "I don't think I know an Ashyr on the island." She scanned her appointments while keeping her focus away from Leilani. In twenty minutes, she had a session with the Hill family on the south side of the island. She ran her hands through her thick hair, compliments of her father's Puerto Rican heritage, and stared at her distorted reflection on the monitor's screen while trying to regain a normal heart rate.

"And her hand man," Leilani's words mumbled out again.

Mariana spun around, fury pulsed inside, all due to that stupid name. "Is Ashyr a girl? I don't know Ashyr and her hand man!"

"Ashyr Harmon!" Leilani practically spit the words out. "Who is Ashyr Harmon?"

Mariana's hand slapped over her heart. "Where did you hear that? That name?"

"He's not from the island." Leilani put a fist

against her hip. "But you know that, don't you?"

Although her breathing wouldn't soften, Mariana tried to mask it with a sugar-coated statement. "It sounds like we have some questions for each other."

Both Leilani's fists pressed against her hips. "Why don't you go first?"

Mariana drew in a breath, determined to soften her tone that had been stirred by his name. "Where's your father?"

"Down on the beach. Talking to him."

"Ashyr?"

"Your turn to answer."

Mariana just shook her head. Foster, dear Foster, face-to-face with Ashyr on the beach.

Leilani folded her arms against Mariana's headshake. "Don't say 'no.' You asked a question, I answered. Now I ask a question, you answer. That's how this works. Who is he, Mom?"

She released a deep exhale, except some air felt trapped in her throat, as if Mariana needed a reserve, a breath to forge through this, whatever *this* was, that lay ahead. "Someone . . ." she struggled to get out the words, "just someone your father and I once knew."

"Not from the island."

She didn't miss Leilani's emphasis, a statement not a question. Still, Mariana answered as if it were a question. "Did he look like he was from the island?" her voice again sounded tense.

"He looks interesting."

Mariana clutched her head. "Oh, please don't say that."

"Maybe odd," Leilani added.

The extra breath in Mariana shot out. "Go with odd. Please go with odd!"

"He asked for you."

"Oh, hell!" Mariana threw herself against her chair. "Of course he did."

"Mom!" She tilted her head. A coy look covered Leilani's lips. "You don't cuss! How many times have you told me that?" Then, a playful smile emerged. "Is it time to wash your mouth out with soap?"

The teasing look was exactly what was needed. A memory of a little Leilani surfaced, thoughts of her childhood which offered the *why* behind all this. For Leilani, for Zane, and Caroline. For Foster and his children. And now, the *why* had continued for the grandchildren, running around the island. Choices had been made to benefit all of them.

With that clear reminder, Mariana stood; and with a thick mask of calmness, she said, "Well, if Ashyr's here, we better go find him."

\* \* \*

Electric blue spots sloshed through the coarse sand. She had always been practical with her toenail paint. Traditional. Mauve, orchid, rose, pink, and on rare, rare, occasions, bright red. But today, Mariana wore bold blue.

Caroline, who ran the island salon, had championed her mother into such bravery. And now, with each step, Mariana tracked that blue, wanting them to run to Foster, only to tromp along purposefully to appear calm for Leilani, while also trying not to stumble over the thoughts of this reunion with Ashyr.

She'd canceled her upcoming appointment with the Hills, explaining an emergency had presented itself, while her hands ran through her hair, again and again. Then she followed Leilani out into the island sun.

To at last spot him.

Ashyr, who looked nothing like the Ashyr she'd known. Once, his hair had been dark and receding. Now, he had a full head of sweeping dusty blond hair, almost the same color as Foster's, minus her husband's gray.

And his skin. Even from a distance, she could see its tight, shiny, almost polished features, especially as he stood against the sun-dried texture of Foster's.

He even looked stronger, more youthful in physique, while Foster's shoulders appeared heavy as if former burdens from the past had returned.

It was happening.

While Mariana's toes sloshed through the sand, she watched the fancy man in the suit bringing his weight to the island. And in front of her eyes, she saw the transfer, as Foster accepted, shifting it tightly across his shoulders.

# FOUR

## LEILANI

As Mom and I neared, I strained to catch snippets of Dad and Ashyr's conversation. I caught words like *destruction, epic war, pandemic,* only for Ashyr to break the conversation with, "Mariana."

His hands were pressed into the pockets of his suit coat that sparkled against the rays of the morning sun.

At first, Mom didn't meet his eyes, only nodded and said, "Ashyr." Then, she looked up, connecting with his blue eyes, and paused. I watched her closely as she stepped back. Her shoulders straightened stiffly.

I kept my distance away from the adults, finding a safe, quiet spot from which to observe. They stood like an equilateral triangle, Dad and Ashyr serving as the bottom points while Mom served as the top point nearest to me.

"I was just talking to Foster, my good mate, about how he did it." Ashyr waved his hand around the beach. "And, I suppose you did too. And I was asking when you both left us?"

Dad spoke to Mom, his voice low and firm. "I told him we left when we needed to."

"I figure you left around the time of the war. When Asia and Europe broke their nuclear pact. In case the world wasn't broken enough, between that and the awful pandemic which spread through Africa, full-fledged destruction seeping into the cells of the next generation, it was awful stuff. Is that what did it for you? Or was it the fallout of the U.S. government?

"I'm certain you weren't there for that aftermath. The federal government died, then the state governments followed. Right as the natural disasters hit. Still can't get over what happened to the East coast. Oh, and the gulf line! Region after region, it was horrific. Then, throw in the long-awaited San Andreas fault earthquake—wow! Nothing like that one. If you weren't there for the quake, you can't even imagine it. But ironically, our circle of the world, we came out okay. Other than we don't travel. Instead, we just stay in our established spot. Which works out more than fine, because we no longer need to leave our region, our home. Yet, here I am." He paused, stretching his arms out wide as if wanting to extend a hug to old friends.

My parents were frozen, paralyzed as they looked from Ashyr to each other.

Under the shadows of a nearby palm tree, I held my breath and watched as Ashyr continued speaking.

"It took a bit to get our L.A. back to a state of being functional. But we got through it. With the government no longer a resource, we formed a tribunal society. And we're actually thriving again. I mean really thriving. We're like our own little island, too." He spread his hands out wide again, but my parents only gave him an empty response.

"We're no longer part of the destruction. In fact, we're quite separate from the rest of the globe. Although, we do sometimes have visitors, seeking out a specific resource. Which shouldn't surprise you."

As unfortunate luck would have it, a quick sudden sneeze shot out of me. It came from nowhere, the type you can't stifle or delay.

Mom spun around like she'd forgotten about me. "Go home," she ordered.

I stuck my hip out and folded my arms. For Mom, who never hears me, it seemed unfair she had to hear me right then. "I'm just listening," I said.

"A beautiful sky you have here," Ashyr said, pulling Mom to turn back, only for Ashyr to give a grin that reminded me of a cat ready to pounce on a bird.

She shifted from their triangle and took a step closer to Dad. From my angle, I caught the raised eyebrow and her nod backward toward me.

Meanwhile, Ashyr spun his lush hair around as if taking in the breeze. "Do you know what today is? Such irony, the date before us." When he got no response, he continued. "Here we are on July 4, 2050. Yes, July 4th. A calendar date that used to signify Independence Day for the United States. Parades. Fireworks. Celebrations. A flag."

"Freedoms that are gone," Dad at last said.

"Yes. That country is gone. But look at your own little paradise you've created here." He spun back to face Dad. "I really want to see this place, mate. Very much want to see what's been done. What you have in the works. How you pulled it all off." His bleached eyebrows drew up, followed by another twist of a smile. "I suppose the patent's pending."

Dad lifted a stiff arm. "All of this is complicated."

Ashyr nodded while the smile remained. "I'm sure it is."

"Foster!" Mom's head nudged again back toward me.

"Sure." Dad nodded, but his face looked lost, similar to that vague absentness he sometimes conveyed when he was absorbed in one of his invention designs. "Take Ashyr up," he said. "Let's show him the place."

Mom raised her eyebrows, clearly not approving of his suggestion.

But his eyebrows raised as well, then he looked toward me. "I need to talk to Leilani," he said, low and slow.

A tight, nervous laugh came from Mom. "Good luck." Her feet moved, slow like heavy weights, one step after another, through the sand toward Ashyr. Her voice sounded guarded and angry. "Let's go."

Then she led the mysterious Ashyr up the incline toward the house. Huck met them on the path and allowed Ashyr to pet his neck. Then as if entranced by the stranger, too, he followed them.

Dad's hand touched my arm. "I need something from you," he said. "And I wouldn't ask if it wasn't important."

The burden in his voice stirred me further. "Dad." I stepped away from his touch to look at him squarely. "What's going on?"

"That's what I need from you." His tone transferred into a sound of masked softness. "Patience, dear. A lot of patience right now."

"Who is that guy?" I nudged my head toward the house, catching a glimpse of Ashyr as he stepped onto the back deck. When I turned back, Dad was watching him too.

"He's someone from our past," he said distantly. "Some things your mom and I wanted to be done with a long time ago."

Not until Ashyr followed Mom through the glass doors and they were out of sight did Dad look at me again. "For right now," he spoke calmly, "we need some adult time to settle whatever has brought him here."

When it came to Dad, I'd never had to search for it before: the difference between a truth and a lie. But at that moment, as I studied the dark blueness looking back at me, I found myself hunting. "And where did he come from?" I asked.

"It's a long story." He shifted and looked out toward the ocean. "Which is why I need you to be patient right now."

I stood tall. I used my voice to return the focus to where it needed to be. "So, you lied to me?"

"No. No, no, no." Dad raised his arms. His eyes met mine. Then suddenly, his hands pressed against my shoulders. For a moment, it seemed like he was going to give me a hug, which would not have helped things.

Instead, he kept his elbows locked. I could feel the stiffness through his hands. "We've protected you. All of this is to protect you."

"From what?"

"I'll explain it all after he leaves." He twisted back toward the house, causing his hold on my shoulders to feel even more awkward. "We just need Ashyr to leave."

I broke out of his grasp. "So, I have choices. I don't have to live on this island."

"No." He turned back and his eyes revealed a fear. "There aren't choices."

I was done with the lack of answers. I rolled my eyes and threw my hand out toward the water. "He's from somewhere. So, that's where I want to go."

He just kept shaking his head. A lost look covered his eyes. "It doesn't work that way."

"I'll find his boat," I said, determined. The fact that Dad and Mom had lied to me burned at the questions I had asked them for years. "Or I'll build a boat." My chest heaved up and down. I tried to control my voice. "But . . . I'm going to leave this island."

I wanted Dad to stop shaking his head. Then, to make matters worse, all he did was repeat himself. "It doesn't work that way."

"Because you don't want it to."

"Because it's not how it seems."

"Then explain it."

"Leilani." He said my name like he had numerous times before, when he thought I needed to calm down, to think instead of let emotion rule my thoughts. But his counsel over my "maturing" behavior, as he had once called it, seemed absolutely pointless now.

"You," he said. "Me. Your mom. Let's talk about it. All of it. Figure out what you want. What your options are. I just need you to be patient right now."

"I know what I want." The emotion rose in my voice. "I don't want to live here."

A painful look flashed over his eyes. "When you understand it all, you may change your mind." He stepped away and scanned the panoramic view of our crescent beach. "Until then, I need you to know something. Things are about to get more confusing, for a bit. Confusion, first, but then it will get better, and it will be okay. For a short time, confusion is okay." When he met my eyes again, a sadness covered his face. "I'll tell you everything, I promise. And, my dear science girl, when I tell you . . ." He gave me a somber smile. "You'll see unbelievable wonders here. And then . . . we'll talk about these other things."

His smile held a reminiscent look of our previous talks over my questions about the biological lifecycle of organisms, the chemistry that makes up human life, the reoccurring patterns found in physics. Dad had told me on numerous occasions he would never tire of talking with me about the wonders of our existence. And his look, right then, confused me, pulling at those memories, causing my head to tilt and my tone to soften slightly. "Everything?"

"Yes."

"Like how I can see more than just this island?"

His smile disappeared. "Go to Kate's house, help her out with the baby until I come. Then we'll talk from there." He reached an arm out and pulled me into a halfway hug. "Meanwhile, know it's because I love you, dear. Everything I do is because I love you."

# FIVE

## MARIANA

Ashyr lowered himself onto the couch while scanning their living space. "It's Robinson Crusoe meets H.G. Wells." He waved a hand over the room with its tropical plants, bamboo furniture, and paintings of palm trees and bright birds of paradise. "You just have to look for it." His eyes rested on her.

Across from him, she gripped the back of the rattan frame chair as he picked up the coconut shell that Foster had left on the glass coffee table earlier. With a sideways glance, he examined the embedded computerized screen. "Some drawing software. Some system, a transportation device, scooped out like a time capsule, clearly some specs at the early stages of development."

With lips pressed together tightly, she reached her hand out and waited for him to relinquish the shell. Then she placed it on a nearby bookshelf.

"I like your hut here." He smiled at her. "A thatched roof. Bamboo fences and walls. With nice underground plumbing, right?"

His smile informed her he knew more than they wished he did. Still, his eyes triggered at something from their past. So, she took his bait. "The dishwasher system is underground," she said. "You slide a dish down a chute, and within thirty seconds it appears through a separate panel, sanitized."

"You lie?" His impressed smile pulled at her own.

But as he watched her, she couldn't hold the smile. She looked away. He did, too, up toward the fan's wooden blades shaped like tropical leaves.

"Solar-powered?" he asked. "Hydroelectric? Wind-powered? All the above?"

She gave the slightest nod.

"Two decades since, Mariana. Countless exchanges with other humans, yet none remain as pure and as memorable as that memory you shared with me."

Her eyes looked to the coffee table, through the glass, to the ground.

"I keep that memory undiluted," he said.

She looked past him to the glass doors. "Here comes Foster." She dashed to meet him. With her eyes, she tried to communicate with her husband that they needed to remove Ashyr from their home.

Instead, Ashyr extended his arm against the back of the sofa and spoke to Foster. "A lot has changed, hasn't it, mate?"

All Foster gave was a nod.

"We've come a long way since that hospital garden bench. You, Foster, so broken inside after losing your wife, Haizley. And me nearly dead. Seems like an alternative lifetime ago, doesn't it?"

"Why are you here?" Foster asked.

Instead of answering, Ashyr waved his arms wide. "I believed in you. And here it is. Your new world."

Foster maintained eye contact but didn't say anything.

"So, now that I found you, mate, you know I'll be mesmerized by this tour. I'm looking forward to seeing the grounds, your magical gardens, this miracle of an island. Just finding your home has already proved most interesting."

Mariana left Foster's side to plant herself in the doorway arch which led into the kitchen. Like a security guard, there to protect the rest of her home, she folded her arms and glared at Ashyr.

"You're here because you need help," Foster said harshly.

"I came," Ashyr answered calmly, "because, I wanted to see you. And yes, I knew you could help."

"Why would we?" Mariana asked. "How can you even pretend we'd come to your rescue?"

He shifted to face her; his smile remained soft and calm. "Because it's not my rescue."

With an exhausted sigh, Foster took a seat across from Ashyr. "How bad is it?"

"Bad enough," Ashyr said.

Foster twisted around to exchange a pained look with Mariana. "I've been dreading this day."

"Let it go," Mariana warned.

But he didn't; he turned back to gaze at the coffee table, and said, "It's like there have been footsteps leading up to this. Like an approaching knock at my conscience." Without looking up, he waved a hand at Ashyr while a heavy sigh followed. "And now, here it is. The sound. The call to open up, to do whatever we need to do."

"No!" Mariana roared. Ashyr drew back. Foster straightened too.

She stared at the back of Foster expecting him to turn around. Instead, he stiffly faced Ashyr. "Explain how bad it is?"

"Why? Foster!" Mariana expelled an exasperated sigh. "You don't need to open your figurative door."

Ashyr met Mariana's eyes, but Foster did not. She looked away. Just that brief eye contact was enough, stirring so much of the past back into their lives.

"It's fixable," he said more to her than to Foster.

She let out a sarcastic laugh as her eyes danced back to his. "I'm sure it is, Ashyr."

"So, spit it out," Foster said.

"Well…" Ashyr stood and then strolled around the room. "I'm a bit mystified where to begin." He stepped onto the bamboo mat and followed it to the ornate corner table with its twine-wrapped legs, polished seashell knobs, and glass countertop. "It's been nearly twenty years since Em-Path." From the table, he reached for the family picture framed in the dried palm tree leaves. "Wow! This your whole crew?"

"Yes," Foster answered coldly.

Ashyr peered at the picture. "Ah, I see Clark. Okay, and that must be Rex. And, wow Kate sure has changed. Let's see, which one was your youngest, Foster?" He ran his finger over the photo. "Well, there's yours, Mariana. She grew up to look a lot like you. Oh, and that must be your boy too. So, let's see how many do we have here?" With his finger, he appeared to be counting. "One of Fosters. One of Marianas. Another of Fosters. Look at all these children!"

"There's thirty-one of us there," Foster interrupted.

"Twenty-nine," Mariana said quietly. "Emery and Malo weren't born yet."

He released a low tight whistle. Then he looked at both of them. "Wow! Thirty-one. So, how many grandkids is that for you two combined?"

"Fifteen," Mariana said. She knew what Ashyr was doing.

"Funny, isn't it," Ashyr's fingers ran over the rough textured frame while his eyes danced back and forth between Foster and Mariana. "Here all this, all of it began by me getting to see Clark's birthday celebration through Em-Path. And then Mariana, I got to see Zane's birth. Directly from your point of view. I still remember those moments. I've seen a lot, experienced plenty. Got lots of memories all melding together into noise. But those two memories, they don't leave me. They just stay."

Ashyr's words cut through Mariana, causing her to frown over his underlying bitterness, his hidden anger, the burning irony.

He stepped away from the corner table, back towards them, offering them a kinder grin. But he didn't release the photo.

"After you left," he said softly as if luring her back to a time when they all cared about each other. "I focused my inventions on fairness. On creating a world where we all had access to similar things. Where we weren't discriminated by statuses, by ties that others couldn't have."

But despite his tone, she still heard it, his words like a hard cookie dipping into a tea steeped in envy and resentment.

"Thanks to my efforts," he said. "Society has changed. Ever since you left, my focus has been on fairness. And I've succeeded too." He glanced down again at the photo. "But this." He waved it at them. "Your swarm of DNA populating your island—away from our broken world—it almost seems unfair."

# SIX

## LEILANI

There was no way I was heading to Kate's. She definitely would be no helpful source for answers. Not now, after I've been living on this island—basically all my life—and not even questioning what my parents had been telling me all this time.

I needed to go where I could find answers. So, I headed to my thinking place, near the pond where the goats drank, to deduce facts, to capture something solid to hold on to.

Instead, the walk over to the pond flooded me with memories. I thought of a time when I was six years old, when I'd been playing with Violet and Grace and told them my big secret. That I believed our parents were robbers and had kidnapped us.

I hadn't thought of that memory in years. But now, I remembered the firmness I once held.

As a little kid, I'd planned to run away, off the island. I even gave Violet and Grace a specific date and time. They were to pack their bags and be ready to go.

Except when I showed up, they told me they had figured I was playing make-believe.

It had been a deflating day. I'd held a grudge for

a week. But why had I thought that? As a child, why did I see my parents as imposters?

Now, ten years later, I sat with the goats as they chewed their grass, and I looked up at the sky to sift through my thoughts. My young theory must have come from the adult talk time. I remember that craving I had to listen to them, only for them all to silence quickly whenever they saw me approach. It lessened as I grew older, but as a small child, it came too often. That clamming up of their words, their discussions ceasing as soon as any of us young ones came near.

Back then, I had picked up on something. Some hidden secret that existed.

Of course, my parents weren't kidnappers. They were my parents. I looked like Mom. I thought like Dad. My brother Cormac, through the years, talked about coming to the hospital, seeing me as a newborn, before the world ended.

The sequence of events went like this. I was born. The world ended. We relocated to this island because it was the only habitable place left. And we were lucky to be alive.

That was it.

The end.

Until today—where I faced the haunting question of what was actually true.

# SEVEN

## MARIANA

She wanted to regain the family photo; yank it from his clutched hand. But as he wandered, she felt it critical to stay strategically positioned in the kitchen archway, ensuring he didn't venture further inside their home. However, when he set it on the coffee table to then sit across from it on the couch, the fury nearly combusted inside her.

He scanned the room. "Got anything to drink?"

Quickly, she dodged his eyes only to meet Foster's. At last, her husband was looking at her. However, torn opposition covered his face.

"Oh! Just go get it for him," she blurted out.

Being hospitable to Ashyr repulsed her, but the glee which spread across Foster's face over her permission infuriated her even further.

"Yeah. Sure." Foster nodded to her while masking his tone to not match the yearning so apparent on his face. Which was pointless to hide, because as soon as he shifted to Ashyr, she heard her husband's tone reveal his inner excitement. "I've crossbred some grapes here. Along with some other fruits, some pomegranates, and cranberries. I built a modest greenhouse out back. And found a new hybrid." Bit by bit, the hype in his voice kept growing, like an anxious boy leading a friend to his newly constructed fort. "The juice tastes dry like wine. And it creates a state of calmness—as if you'd just drank wine. But the juice has no ethanol content. No fermentation achieving tranquility. No yeast added. No acidic taste. Rather, what we have is a chemical structure in line with a vinegar."

"Extraordinary," Ashyr said with wide eyes.

"The juice is remarkable." Foster's body leaned closer toward the couch. "We call it Grady's Grape Juice."

The men's grins, their nods, and their talk of remarkable inventions—the incredible things happening here, that there even was a *here*—it all felt like spiders crawling on Mariana's skin. She took a step back, further into the kitchen. But she could still hear the youthfulness in Foster's voice and see the continuous lifting of Ashyr's eyes.

Right in front of her, a rhythm from the past had been stirred, causing the painful, unanswerable question to circle back: had certain events been different between them all, what would their lives be like now?

# EIGHT

## LEILANI

I wanted the truth. A determination to find it gripped me.

I left my spot near the pond and headed back over the barbed wire fence. Carefully, I slipped through it to not snag my clothes or cut my skin. When I reached the dirt path, I took off fast. If I couldn't trust my parents, then I had to hope this Ashyr guy had the answers.

Right as I neared the house, I spotted Dad coming from the front door. I darted behind a monkeypod tree. While he headed toward the cellar door, my heartbeat softened. With his head bent and his footsteps focused, he was in concentration mode. I was safe, as long as I stayed put until it was clear.

But the fact he entered the cellar meant one thing: he was bringing out a bottle of his fancy juice. Since he only shared this on special occasions, and only at immediate family gatherings, this was indeed interesting.

Once the front door shut again, I counted to sixty before I resumed my course toward the house.

I stayed in the shadows, against the east wall. Mom was in the kitchen. I could hear her opening cupboards. So, I crawled past the first open window and paused before the next, pressing up against the hut, while Ashyr's voice came from the living room.

"Excited to try this, mate."

"I expect you'll like it." Dad sounded joyful.

"And then?" Ashyr's voice boomed. "A tour of the place. Of all you've done. Of how you did it!"

I heard the cork pop. Then Dad's voice lowered as if speaking only to Ashyr while Mom kept making noise in the kitchen. I couldn't make out Dad's exact words, but it seemed he said, "Remember that day, when I first told you about . . . idea? And you said, you thought I . . . could do it."

Ashyr's voice spoke low too. "I've thought of that day often." I could barely make out the rest. "Here you did it, mate . . . a gift . . . science to defy science . . . remarkable . . . what about . . ." There was some name I didn't catch and then, "did he achieve his, too?"

Dad's voice lifted again. "Thank you, dear."

Glasses tinkled. Mom said nothing, but Dad sounded pleased. "You ready for this?" He used that same energetic voice with us when he gathered us around to share one of his latest project developments. "Enjoy your first drink," he said, "of *sensu in vino veritas.*"

Silence, followed by praises over the juice. As I strained to hear better, an idea hit me thanks to the teachings of my brother Zane. If all went well, I'd be able to use the roof trick to hear and see into the living room.

I stepped cautiously through the front door, then through the entry room, toward the stairway. Tender placement as I slid a foot along the floorboards. Mom didn't hear anything these days. But

Dad, he'd certainly catch me if I stepped wrong.

Once on the second floor, I moved into my parents' room. Then to the window—it was already open to let a morning breeze flow through the room. All I needed now was to lift the screen lightly, then step out. I did, and like the softest sound of a cat, I moved toward the skylight.

With a triumphant exhale, I sat cross-legged on the roof. But to see both Ashyr and Dad, I had to arch my back to an awkward forty-five-degree angle. And to hear them, I needed to address the roof vent. With the softest lift of my arm, I scooted back a couple of feet and lifted the cap. Like magic, their blessed voices reached my ears.

"Can I get another?" Ashyr asked. I scooted ever so slowly toward the skylight to catch his raised glass.

This would say everything. Dad rarely let my brothers have a second glass. Only on birthdays, holidays, or a noteworthy celebration. Otherwise, small amounts, due to all the prep work to get the right temperature, the right timing, the right portions of the different fruits.

But there it was: Dad pouring Ashyr a second glass. Then he set the bottle on the coffee table as if inviting Ashyr to help himself to more in the future—which seemed likely because Ashyr took a long drink before setting his glass back down.

Then Ashyr tilted his head upwards, and I hastily pulled back. Thankfully, his eyes were closed. His chest heaved up and down as if enjoying the tropical air. "Very nice," he said.

From my angle, Dad's shoulders appeared to relax again.

When Ashyr looked at Dad, he scooted forward and his fingers pressed against one another. "Now, the easiest thing would just be to show you. You know that, don't you?"

Although I couldn't see Mom, I definitely heard her grunt.

"Don't worry, Mariana," Ashyr nodded toward the kitchen. "One exchange between us does not require Foster to grow a third arm or anything. Your little paradise will remain intact. All will be well. But you really should see the improvements, the newer versions that have shaped us through the years."

Dad twisted toward the kitchen and paused as if making eye contact with Mom.

Ashyr took another drink. "Foster, you shared this with me." He raised the glass which again seemed nearly empty. "So now, let me share the great-grandchild of Em-Path with you." He lifted his head as if sending another grin toward Mom in the kitchen.

Only for his head to jerk back. I could just picture the look Mom gave him. Her disdain look that I knew too well, the one that chilled you instantly inside. Ashyr looked away, shifting further into the sofa to fix his attention on Dad. "You shouldn't have left," he said. "It grew into something much bigger than you would have thought."

"I'm guessing not bigger than what *you* thought." Mom's sarcastic tone grated against my ears. "You always said it would be big."

But Ashyr played against her well. With another tilt in her direction, he followed up with a laugh. "I did. I did." Then he motioned to his glass. "Care if

I pour some more?"

Dad nodded, even with a pleased smile. I couldn't wait to tell my brothers. They wouldn't believe it.

It was Mom who threw out the restrictions. "Only a quarter of a glass."

But Ashyr's smile seemed to go deeper, like he was more amused than bothered by her. He lifted the bottle and followed her rationing instructions. Then he took a short swallow and paused as if holding the liquid in his mouth.

"That was nice." He set the glass down. Then he spoke so low, I had to inch my ear closer to the vent to barely catch, "Okay, Foster. I'm ready. Time to share with you what you've missed back home.

# NINE

## FOSTER

Ashyr produced a silver cylinder from inside his suit coat. Its length was about the size of an eyeglass case. He set it on the coffee table and rolled it toward Foster. "I carry around a novice kit, for exchanges like this. Well . . ." he let out a short chuckle. "Actually, this particular circumstance is quite rare." Then, he produced a second tube, this one shimmering with a dark bluish-purple hue.

"What is this?" Foster asked.

"Meet EnRapture 500." Ashyr waved a hand at the cylinder he held. "Em-Path's latest descendant." He slid a thumb over a scanner in the center of the tube. From one end of the device, a red synthetic item appeared. "We made some modifications to the overall experience." He unrolled the fabric to reveal something that resembled a neoprene superhero's mask. Except, in place of holes, the eye areas were blacked out with an opaque material. "This is what everyone uses."

"Nope." Foster shook his head. "Not going to happen."

From the kitchen's archway, Mariana snorted a laugh. "Thank goodness you have some sense, dear."

He spun to meet Mariana's confirming glance only to turn back to a confused look on Ashyr.

"This is not going to hurt him." Ashyr placed the mask on the table near Foster. Then he tipped the canister over and shook it twice. Two pills fell into his palm.

Again, Foster shook his head. "No. Not after what we've been through, I can't trust your words."

"Really?" Ashyr placed one pill next to him and extended the other toward Foster. After all we've been through." He kept it extended, waiting for Foster to take it.

Foster's eyes narrowed at the pill. "I don't trust you in the slightest."

"Ouch." The hand drew back. "That hurts." Ashyr dropped the pills back into the canister's dispensing slot, one by one. "But certainly, your loss." He reached for the mask. "I mean everything is built to the highest standards. Top of the line, derived from the industry's best. And EnRapture's products set the bar for all the industries now." He rolled the mask up and inserted it back into the canister, then pressed one more button on the device before slipping it back into his suit coat. "It pretty much runs our society. So popular, it's become its own currency."

"Wow." Mariana suddenly appeared next to the coffee table. "All this time, Ashyr, and here I thought you couldn't surprise me. Yet, you have." As Ashyr grinned over the remark, she shifted to share her depreciating comment with Foster. "A Frankenstein Em-Path is now being used in place of money."

"First bartering, then coins, paper money, checks, credit cards, bitcoins, and now EnRapture."

Ashyr paused. "I told you this would change the world."

Within Foster's view, Mariana rolled her eyes and pressed her lips tightly together.

"Thanks for validating our concerns, Ashyr." Foster stood. But his eyes locked again on the silver cylinder still there on the coffee table. "Let's just do it the old way."

"Or, better yet," Mariana blocked Foster's path, "he could just tell you. Like people do. With words." She twisted to face the couch. "Exchanges made through the recapping of events through your mouth. Tell your stories using your own words, and share the *truth* of what happened and why you're here."

Ashyr gave her a half-grin. "You're funny, Mariana."

But her close presence disrupted Foster. She had never fully understood his deep fears that burned from Em-Path. But now, at last, in front of him was an opportunity to extinguish those flames.

"Just let's do this," he said, still unable to move past her. "Before I change my mind. Not your EnRapt stuff." He nodded at what was left on the table. "Do you have any of the original Em-Path, instead?"

"Because it's not like we have that stuff lying around here," Mariana said sarcastically.

With a heaved-out breath, Ashyr shifted his eyes from Foster to Mariana then back to Foster. "It's so archaic, the old way. But give me a moment." He reached for the silver canister. "Let me tweak it. With some adjustments . . ." He rolled around the canister until he flipped open a compartment revealing a small computer screen and proceeded to tap in a code. "Doubt our current generation of users even knows this option exists." Once he shut the compartment, he rolled the tube around in his hands, then used his thumbprint to unlock the canister. A plain gray goggle mask emerged. As Ashyr unrolled it, a thin pair of spandex gloves appeared tucked inside.

Foster peered down. His fingertips ached to touch the thin fabric, and his eyes hunted for signs of the synapses transfer points on the palm and finger areas. As Ashyr tenderly laid the gloves on the table, Foster never spotted these critical exchange nodes.

To hide his growing curiosity, Foster shifted his weight back, and eagerly waited for Ashyr to reveal the earbuds. But instead, Ashyr tipped the canister around and shook out a pill.

"No." Mariana stepped toward the canister.

"Please, Mariana." Ashyr's fingers curled around the pill. "Just let Foster speak in his own language. Or, rather—" Ashyr tilted his head, offering Foster a sideways glance. "Let us inventors speak in a language that will work for us."

"That's ridiculous!" Her hands flew to her hips. "That's not the same drug. It's not what Foster crafted. You have a different pill there. This is all a bunch of nonsense. And I don't want him taking it."

As if protecting them, Ashyr laid the canister over the goggles and gloves. "It's not like I'm trying to kill him."

Foster raised his palms. "Forget it." He stepped back and reevaluated his choices. "Why don't you just tell us. Like Mariana said, explain with words."

Ashyr shook his head. "My words aren't enough.

You know that. Words can't adequately express some things. It's why you built this in the first place, to give your wife Haizley, before she died, what she needed, beyond words."

"Stop!" Mariana commanded. "You're a salesman." She stepped around the coffee table, drawing closer to Ashyr. "You've shown up in our home and you're trying to sell us something that we don't want. We don't want it! So, you don't have a sale. So, you can leave."

With hands on her hips, her chest rose and fell at a rapid rate, and her eyes glared at Ashyr whose hand remained clutched around the synthetic drug alteration of Foster's work.

A definite pull of sides. A choice Foster needed to make.

He angled himself, stepping closer toward the two. "We have some Em-Path pills," he said calmly to Ashyr.

"Foster!"

He met her eyes with dread. Demons from their past. Fears they had run from. Ghosts of the future they had avoided. And now, at last, against her wishes, Foster chose to face the outcome of Em-Path. "You know where they are," he said to her. "Would you mind retrieving them?"

# TEN

## LEILANI

My heart raced. Mom was heading up the stairs toward her bedroom. In a short moment, she would spot me.

With feet planted firmly against the roof, I twisted to see a palm branch scraping against the side of the house. My brother Cormac was the fastest palm tree climber on the island. When I was twelve, he gave me some tips. Here was my moment of truth.

I slipped off my flip-flops and tucked them into the back pockets of my shorts.

I had to grab a sturdy palm frond instead of a dead one. And, I had to do it silently, without a running start from the roof.

As the seconds moved, I could practically hear Mom's feet pounding in time with my beating heart. By now, she had to be on the second floor.

So, I took two firm steps and leaped. The palm frond heaved from my weight and I clawed toward the stable trunk.

While I worked to find my breath, the tree rocked up and down from the impact. Then, I waited. A closet drawer opened, then a cupboard, Mom muttered something.

My scraped arms hugged the trunk firmly. That leap hurt. But no broken bones. As Mom kept ruffling above and Dad kept talking below, I deemed my jump a total victory.

Tightening my grip, I started to shinny down. But Ashyr's voice approached the window.

"So, really, tell me how you did it."

With the slightest rotation, I spotted the back of Dad's head and the shoulder of Ashyr. One sound and I would have eye contact with either one of them. I wrapped my arms even stronger around the trunk, pausing, while Dad shook his head and said, "Did what?"

Ashyr's hand spread wide. "How you built all this? Where we are standing right now?"

Out of breath, I felt like I would lose my grip.

Dad shifted, sliding down into the bamboo chair. "It's complicated." He sounded tense.

"I'm sure it is," Ashyr said. "This is fun, being here, you know. Yes. That day, that silly little day, when you, Brody, and I sat around sharing our most off-the-wall dream inventions. It was before we hired Mariana, wasn't it? Back in the very early days of building Em-Path. And look, your crazy dream invention came true. Mine did too. And what about Brody?" his voice dipped into a new sound, like a hunger. "What happened to Brody?"

Dad shrugged.

Ashyr shrugged his shoulder too. "You worked on this island together, didn't you?"

Dad shrugged again. I held on tight, determined to catch every one of his words. "The sale was done," he said. "We all moved on. We did what we needed to do with what you'd left us with."

"No. We were a family." The lightness in Ashyr's tone shifted. "And then, you all just up and disappeared."

Dad made no movements and offered no words. The bark cut into my skin. My muscles felt ready to give out.

"You shut us out to get what you wanted," Dad, at last, said. "And we had to figure out where to go from there."

"And," Ashyr snorted out a laugh. "Am I supposed to feel sorry for you? You all got a healthy sum from the sale. Back then, we all were taking risks. Nobody was crying when the risk-taking began. But then suddenly, you turned uber-ethical. You didn't like my deal—that Em-Path would bring regular people joy instead of just the broken and sick. It wasn't right, mate."

"That's not it." Dad pressed a palm against his forehead right as my left arm muscles quit. I leaped about four feet down, enough to make a solid sound.

I rolled into some nearby brush. I laid flat against the earth. I figured I was done for.

But Dad kept talking. "The problems with Em-Path went beyond what I could repair."

"*Foster*," Ashyr said, and I heaved out an agonized breath. That fall hurt. But I was fairly sure I didn't break anything. I remained still and breathless while I listened. "You wanted to shut the whole thing down—when it wasn't yours to stop. You forgot you were only a part of the greater whole. All four of us worked hard to create it. So, pulling the plug, like you suddenly wanted to, that wasn't an option."

I started to move out of the brush only to spot

Dad's face at the window. My heart felt like it had taken off on a 400-meter dash.

Fortunately, he didn't look down. Instead, concern covered his face.

At last, he walked away.

"I fixed your bugs," Ashyr said. "I turned Em-Path's weaknesses into its strength. You should have stayed with me, mate."

"Then why are you here?" Dad's former kindness was gone. "You're here because you need me to fix something. Am I right? You need me, don't you, Ashyr?"

My arms felt scratched and sore. Most likely, a large bruise would emerge on my leg from the fall. But I remained still while Ashyr said, "It's complicated. Like your magic land here."

The front door opened. Footsteps joined me outside. Mom was heading in my direction.

My tired body rose, ready to do a backward crab crawl to scoot away from the house, but I waited to gauge the direction of Mom's footsteps. Other footsteps moved closer toward the window in front of me. Ashyr appeared. He spoke forward, as if at me. "So. Where is he? Brody? Here on your island?"

"No," Dad said, and the front door shut again.

Dog feet. Huck was coming right at me. Mom must have let him out, which meant he would spot me and bark to play.

I crab crawled away from the house just as I heard Dad's last words.

"Brody built his own."

# ELEVEN

## MARIANA

With no eagerness to return to the men, Mariana attended to Huck's whining as if one of the grandkids were outside ready to play.

But when she opened the door, no one was on the dirt road. Other than Huck's whines, stillness came from the shed to the left, to the greenhouse on the right, to the large laboratory up the road. Still, his tail wagged back and forth, exuberance ready to explode. Perhaps he was after a bird.

She released his collar, shut the door, and turned back to hear Ashyr's disturbing laughter coming from the other end of the house.

"All that time we worked together," he said. "And here I had no idea you and Brody were such buddies."

She tightened her grip around the box and headed through the dining room, only to pause in the kitchen.

"Stress," Foster said. "Combined stress brings people together."

From her placement, she studied Foster, standing near the back door. His chin jutted out like a defiant moment was unfolding. Whereas Ashyr spoke from alongside the wall. "Well . . . I want to see Brody too."

Foster shrugged like Ashyr's request would be ignored.

"I'm good at offering deals." Ashyr stepped further into Mariana's line of sight. He folded his arms.

But Foster shook his head. "There's nothing I want."

"Sure there is." She didn't see Ashyr's grin, but she felt it as he said, "Ride with me on my invisible airship, mate. Then together, you and Brody can show me how you managed to place your islands here. In the clouds."

"Don't, Ashyr!"

Her commanding tone caused him to jump. His hand flew to his heart. "What?" While Ashyr recovered, she marched into the living room and stood face-to-face with him as he said, "Speak inventor-to-inventor with your husband? Try to stop his mind from creating?"

She glared. Then she extended the old box toward Foster only to draw it back for a further scolding. "Do not ask him to share. You know what his weaknesses are."

She spun toward the door. "Foster." With her head, she motioned him to follow her into the kitchen. As soon as possible, she wanted this Em-Path box out of her hands, but more than that, she wanted Ashyr gone, and she certainly didn't want to witness a Foster crazy enough to go down Ashyr's poison-filled rabbit hole.

She stopped about halfway near the sink, close enough to keep Ashyr within visible range but far enough from earshot.

"Looks like you found it," Foster said softly, his eyes focused more on the box than her.

"We need him to leave," she said firmly.

"That's why I'm doing this," he said softly. But when he finally looked at her, he appeared distant, as if very much lost somewhere in the past.

"Have you been drinking more of that?" She pointed into the living room, at the abandoned bottle on the far end of the coffee table.

"Just those two glasses," he said. But when he turned back to the living room, rather than looking at the bottle, it seemed he faced Ashyr.

Still, even from her distance, Mariana could see the bottle's contents were nearly three quarters gone. "Stop drinking it. And remember, nothing good will come of this." She handed him the Em-Path box. "He can't show you anything that will help. It won't lessen your guilt. Or free you. What's done is done. All that's left . . ." She spat out her last words for Ashyr to hear, "is for you to get him out of here."

Ashyr's hand flew to his chest. "Mariana. I bet Brody's wife would treat me better than this."

"He's a manipulator," she hissed at Foster. "You know that as well as I do."

"What's Brody's wife's name?" Ashyr asked from the living room, his eyes watching them both. "Sunny, isn't it? Ah, yes, it's something like Sachi, but she goes by Sunny. Does she still live up to that name? Living in the clouds, enjoying the sun in closer proximity than the rest of us common folk."

She reached for Foster's hand and yanked on it to pull his ear closer. "Remember how you once said I was your voice of reason. If that's true, then listen to me! Just get him off our island. I can't say it enough—and you know as well as I do—nothing good comes from dealing with him. Nothing! So, don't let his sweet talk or modified memories pull you in. Just do what you need to do so we can be done with him—for good."

A small twitch tugged at Foster's lips, and an expression of teasing filled his eyes. "How far do you want me to go—to get rid of him?"

"I'm serious, Foster. We need to be done with him."

"Well." A grimmer expression crossed Foster's face. "This . . ." he raised the Em-Path box, "seems pretty extreme. But it's my effort to speed things along."

"No." Ashyr picked up his glass and approached the wine bottle. "It's Sunny who's sweet." His grin widened at Mariana as he poured himself another drink. "She always liked me. Same with Brody, until you two turned him against me." He swallowed the juice and made his way back to the couch.

Then he tossed his hair back as if such implants had changed him into something decent. As if he now was an equal to Foster—which was such a lie. Ashyr never had any of the talent or goodness that made up Foster. And no crop of hair implants or a fancy suit or an artificial youth would change that.

"They have a son too. But you know that," he said.

She pressed her fingers into Foster's hand, pulling him closer in her attempt to block Ashyr from her view while speaking loud enough for him to hear. "Leave it to him to find a way to get drunk on your *safe* drink."

"Don't worry," Ashyr announced. "I'm not

drunk, just extremely happy right now. Just glad to see my friends again."

She heard him stand. "You should have some of this." He appeared in the kitchen arch with one of his horrid grins. "Might calm you down." He extended the bottle toward her. "Help all of us be more clearheaded as we talk about what's next."

Stepping past Foster, Mariana blocked Ashyr from proceeding further into their home. "Ashyr!" She grabbed the bottle and motioned him back to the couch. "Just sit." Her other hand balled into a fist. "Sit. And understand, there is no *next*."

# TWELVE

## FOSTER

Mariana huffed at him. "Do whatever you're going to do." She shrugged her shoulders then left Foster alone with the Em-Path box in his hands.

As soon as he opened it, the complicated times of the past would spill out. Still, this needed to happen.

He shook the box, listening for the earbuds, the goggles, the medicine bottle with the freeze-dried pills. He'd gone to all the trouble to freeze-dry the pills, like he always somehow knew he wasn't yet finished with Em-Path.

Once he returned to the couch, Ashyr scooted over, making room for them to sit side by side, as the two had done during their very first experience with Em-Path. Twenty-two years ago, there on a bench in a hospital garden, Ashyr dying of cancer, Foster mourning the loss of his first wife from the same cancer. Together, they had shared his invention. One moment which had led to all this.

He avoided Mariana's eyes as he opened the box and handed Ashyr the left-handed glove. Then he withdrew the medicine bottle, opened the lid, and shook out two chalk-white pills which he placed on the coffee table. Next, he pulled out the earbuds then set them back in the box. "We don't have access anymore to the app for the ambiance sounds or the visual stimulus."

Ashyr laughed as he reached in to pull out a pair of the goggles. "The modern stuff addresses all that, it's all built in. You sure you don't want to use it?"

"Ashyr!" Mariana's voice from behind made Foster jump. "He's doing it, all right."

Again Ashyr reached into the box and pulled out a pair of the earbuds. Then he slipped one into his ear. "For what it's worth, I don't much care for the audio stimuli. Stopped using it long ago—but it's always nice to have these around to block out other incoming distractions."

Foster twisted around and met Mariana's eyes. Her arms were folded and pressed against her chest. "If you're wondering, yes, I'll keep quiet. And yes, I'm staying," she stated. "And yes, I think you are a fool."

He pulled in a breath then gave her the smallest headshake. "I can't explain it, I just . . ."

"For science," she mocked him.

"For science," Ashyr said loudly. His body shifted into place. He looked forward while he inserted the other earbud then pulled the goggles over his eyes.

"Yes." Foster looked from Mariana back to the box on the coffee table. "For science," he said softly, then retrieved a pill off the table and swallowed it.

# THIRTEEN

## LEILANI

I kept trying to shake free of Huck. I tried Dad's trick numerous times of throwing the stick into the brush. I'd take off running, and within like seconds Huck would appear, stick in his mouth, obstructing my path.

The tail kept wagging. When I tried to tell him not now, he would whine.

I tried to pass, and the whine hinted at a full launch of barks.

More attempts of throwing the stick to ditch him.

More failures with him back in front of me, stick in mouth.

A couple of times I got close to returning to the house, but Huck's face appeared. His grumble toyed with a bark, like at any moment he would alert the adults to look out the window to see me.

I had to get rid of Huck.

So, I changed strategies. Throwing the stick up the road, I moved as fast as I could toward Violet's house. Her younger brother would play with him. That seemed like the best solution under the circumstances.

With each throw, I heard the adults' words echo in my mind.

*Em-Path.*

*EnRapture.*

Each step along the dirt road made the march grow: *Em-Path. EnRapture. Em-Path. EnRapture.*

Dad's creation. Mom working alongside him. Ashyr a part of all this—of them—a huge life they lived before this—this island they built.

They built an island.

My legs felt weak as Huck dropped the stick at my feet.

My parents built an island!

# FOURTEEN
## YAM

## Travel log

July 3, 2050

3:15 p.m.

*You called it. You said it would be a girl that got me in trouble. And it was.*

Yam paused, not ready to capture more of his thoughts. Especially with the mental strain of intentionally trying to avoid the words *Baba, Mum, parents, home,* or *help.*

Tightness grew in his breath. His heart quickened.

Moments earlier, tucked in a safe corner of the room, he'd applied the band-aid-like stickers underneath his ears. Swiftly, he'd unfastened the elastic that held the bun at the top of his head so hair covered his ears. Underneath his hair, he rubbed at his nearly shaved scalp and cleared his thoughts in preparation for this communication.

Focused. No unintentional words filtering in to alert Baba. Instead, the FID, the Fluid Interface device, logged his nonverbal words in a digital file.

A non-concerning check-in.

Now in haste, he removed the stickers. He had shared enough.

No lies. Yet.

And he wouldn't lie.

He was an honest person. A good son. Integrity was one of the best character traits he aspired to.

But the mere thought that he had carefully worked to leave out the truth kept Yam's heart racing.

He pressed his head against the wall. The corner he crouched in was small, but removed from all the surrounding mirrors, since each mirror seemed to hint that someone was watching him.

The youth correction officer had called it a holding room. But it felt like a cell, even if it did have a couch, a sink, and a water closet.

Yam closed his eyes. But he couldn't shut out the image of the corrections officer's face. Dark eyes, beige skin with tattooed diagonal lines pointing toward his mouth, placing all the focus on the words that came out.

"You've been reported! You must speak to someone from the council."

The girl, Aria, stood close. "He didn't touch me," she said strongly while pointing at Yam.

The officer's eyes showed no mercy. "You both are coming with me."

Behind the scene they had created, a chain of drone cars waited. Yam scanned the park. The group of youth watched from the basketball court, close enough to either help or hinder Yam's escape if he chose to run.

Then the officer tapped at the taser strapped

to his side. The longer Yam delayed, the more his options dwindled.

The girl's head leaned toward Yam. "Just let me do the talking," she whispered. "I can get us out of this."

He held to those words as he followed her toward each of their single-passenger drones. A final choice in a series of decisions that had led him here. Sitting. Waiting. Feeling trapped in this holding cell.

# FIFTEEN

## LEILANI

I cut myself once quite badly while trying to open a coconut the wrong way. Mom said I went into shock as I watched the blood run down my hand.

She took me to our little island clinic where I got four stitches. It hurt.

But it was the shock I remembered now while the ground stared back at me. The dirt seemed to tell me it had a history, something I knew nothing about.

More memories came as Huck nudged the stick into my view. While picking it up, I thought of a school project Dad helped me with when I was a kid. We built a model of the island. It had a waterfall and a pump that cycled the water back through. $H_2O$ flowing up, waterfalling down, running along the river, out to a little sea, then reverting through it all again.

The class loved our mini replication. It looked so real.

Until those Saco cousins started horse playing near it, pushing each other. Pedro collided into it. The island toppled, crashed, and shattered. Water, plaster, dirt, little glued sticks, and miniature plants went everywhere.

I hated Pedro that day. I still do.

Dad tried to reassure me it was fixable. But we never fixed it: this model of the island that he knew too well.

My life was not at all what it seemed.

I commanded myself out of the shock, determined once again to get back to hearing more of what Ashyr might share.

I dashed the rest of the way up the hill. Huck loved chasing me. He even forgot about the stick as we reached the door.

It was Violet who greeted us. "Will you take Huck?" I asked.

Before she even said, "Yes," I shooed him into the door. Then I took off running again.

"Leilani!"

I turned back while my feet kept shuffling backward. Violet had her fingers wrapped around Huck's collar. "What's going on?"

"I'll explain later. I think it's really important. News that's going to blow your mind."

"Okay. You better come tell me."

And right then I knew I loved her. She was my closest friend. "I will. I promise."

Then I took off again, sprinting as fast as I possibly could.

# SIXTEEN

## YAM

### Travel log

July 3, 2050
3:58 p.m.

*The girl's name is Aria. She met me, or rather she found me, two years ago, right before I headed back to the warehouse during a supply run. I reported the incident at the time. At that moment, there were no issues.*

Yam slid off the FID. All it would take was silently thinking Baba's name and a transmission would go through alerting him to Yam's situation.

Against the wall, he closed his eyes and thought through the events, working backward in his mind. What had happened, what had led him—after these years of safely being discrete, skillfully moving under the radar—to end up here now?

Before Aria, he hadn't talked to anyone. Certainly not the residents, the youth, anyone except those he did a transaction with, then he always followed the approved script. Bit by bit, he shuttled items from his two-passenger drone to the trailer at the warehouse. Then once full, he hooked up the trailer to the helipod and he headed home.

*Get in. Get out. Do the business that needs to be done.* Just as Baba had taught him. *Don't dawdle. And never talk to the people other than for necessary transactions.*

Since age fourteen, he had been deemed old enough to do these runs solo, without Baba, as long as he followed all the rules.

But one time, Aria had spotted him and said hello. An innocent hello!

Something he had done had her curious enough to follow him straight up to the roof of the hardware building, where Yam was only a few yards from his drone. Had he just made it there first, before she had stopped him, he could have been flying back to the deserted warehouse district. Then no story. No continuation of events with Aria to land him in his current situation.

Now, he kept justifying why he didn't need to notify Baba and Mum. If it became necessary, he would at least use the FID to tell them his supply run was behind schedule. Then, once home, he'd share with Baba the details of his mistake.

Until then, he'd work with Aria to get out of here.

And then, no more mistakes. Nothing to collide their world with Ashyr's.

# SEVENTEEN

## ASHYR

As the memory exchange began, the images came through slowly, as if Foster was extremely inexperienced. Such irony. The creator offering slow sluggish images like watercolors bleeding together.

Ashyr had seen more captivating intros during training sessions with the youth compared to this.

Eventually, the blurs of colors began to take shape into a large warehouse the size of a small city. There were pumps, valves, water tanks, air handlers, and lots of gadgets. The area was labeled "The Technosphere."

Mariana walked with him. "You are going to be amazed," he said. Her smile back seemed to say she did not doubt him.

They climbed a metallic ladder up through a thick hole of volcanic rock until their heads appeared in an atrium of nature.

Mariana gasped. The blurred lines of the memories disappeared, replaced by rich sharpness, clean beauty. Incredible detail surrounded Ashyr.

Admiration. Pure, undiluted awe!

Within Foster's memory, Ashyr stood in a ginormous atrium of vines, trees, and flowers. Lots of flowers. Hibiscus. Plumeria. Jasmine.

Sweet, crisp, beauty.

Birds flew overhead.

A centipede worked its way through the dirt.

"As a kid," Foster said to her, the pride so apparent in her eyes, "I studied everything I could find on Biosphere II. It was completed clear back in 1991, and I figured if they could make it almost work, why not fix their error and then embrace the possibilities. It just seemed so feasible, a sustainable giant paludarium. And then make it transportable, so it can go wherever it's needed. And here it is."

She reached for his hand. "Here it is."

He felt the tenderness of her bones, the warmth of her skin, the rose-colored fingernails cradled against his hand—the only problem was the hand belonged to Foster, not Ashyr.

The memory changed. Mariana now stood next to Foster on a lookout tower surveying further progress. Foster was lost talking, while Mariana seemed transfixed on his words.

"When I was twelve, my science teacher predicted we were the generation that would see it all end."

Again, the hand holding, and then Ashyr noticed the belly bump, the pregnancy, the gestation period of Foster and Mariana's creation.

Foster kept talking. "Back then, we were at a crossroads. The teacher said we could own our place on the planet, and that meant there could be hope. But it had to be a global responsibility. And if we didn't own it, and never found ways to work together and support one another, we would lose our future. We would find peril instead. And here we are."

Such Foster—focusing on the doom and gloom.

"I had a teacher that said . . ." Mariana spoke with a lightness, a hope, a softness that made Ashyr hunger for her even more. "'Human ingenuity is what will devise an answer to our current problems. If we are to make a difference for the new generation, this is the time for innovation, creativity, and fresh perspectives.' And that is what you've done, Foster. You've worked to create a solution."

Ashyr had done that too. He had a new generation, a better way of life, due to his innovation and creativity. Fortunately, the memory shifted, breaking away from the two's verbal intimacy.

Except, where Foster led him only made the experience worse.

Mariana hunched against a palm tree. Her body was in pain. Her breathing shallow.

"Not yet," Foster was saying.

"Not yet," she repeated, in a pained cry. "I'm not having this baby here."

"The boat is on its way. We will get you back."

"I shouldn't have come." She sounded like tears were near due to the pain. "I just wanted to see for myself how close we are—how it's nearly ready."

Foster touched her, caressing her arm. "When you're ready, when the baby's ready, the island will be too."

She gave the softest of smiles. Ashyr felt a sickening disgust over what Foster chose to share. Years ago, during the early days of Em-Path, such intimate family moments of Foster's fatherly life, of Mariana's intimate mothering moments, were a fascination. But now, with Ashyr's trained EnRapture mind, such old-fashioned ways felt like acid rain.

More dangerous than good.

One father, one mother, working to bring a child into existence. Such a small selfish group, hoarding their own procreation ritual of building a single unit of human life. Instead, they could expand their efforts, they could embrace opportunities to offer so much more.

Foster spoke strongly, "Just breathe."

She tried.

"Take a deep breath."

She tried again.

Foster just kept talking. Like words would make the boat arrive faster and stop Mariana's deep and apparent pain.

"This air you breathe right now," he said, quick and eagerly, "it's part of the ecosystem of our island. Think about it."

She nodded, a half-smile there on her face.

"Our breaths will fill the air and connect us."

She squeezed his hand and kept nodding.

"Together," he said, "with the plants, we, all of us, we will be working to keep this bottle of life living."

Her smile grew stronger.

"Breathe," he said again.

She closed her eyes and did.

"That breath you just took in, think about all that's in that breath. Perhaps some $CO_2$ from me, standing here right next to you. Maybe some carbon from the Pacific Ocean nearby. It's there to connect with us too. Keep breathing. Think about our breaths. We get to take a portion of the ocean, the life and oxygen that it brings. Then think about the carbon we have here in this soil. Carbon as far back as the dinosaurs. So, now exhale that breath on our island. If God's willing, that carbon in that breath will continue, and someday that carbon is going to be present in the breath of your great-great-grandchild."

She opened her eyes. More smiles. Calmness settled around her while a chime was heard off in the distance, signaling the boat's arrival. She hugged her large belly and said, "I hope so."

At last! A new scene emerged. A soft red hue appeared across the horizon. Peach. Pink. Then a redness. Followed by baby gray tones. A magnificent sunset. Except, it wasn't.

Darkness emerged as if dusk, sweeping over the midday. All sound stopped.

From Foster, the retelling of events came out in a state of silence, like slow-action movie frames. He called out to the group which surrounded him, directing the people toward his great invention.

He spoke into his radio. He blasted out a pre-programmed message. He looked at the clock, noting the time when the world broke apart.

Soon, over a hundred people had boarded a boat. Men, women, and children sped toward an island out at sea which was covered by a secured dome.

From there, a submarine waited, shuttling trips down into the output chamber. From the output chamber, residents entered the belly of the island, the "technosphere" where an array of equipment supported the land above. Then the people were escorted quickly to the upper level with its lush environment.

Once all the residents were accounted for, Foster

stood near Mariana with all their children close at hand, a newborn babe in his arms. Then a battalion of underwater missiles ignited, forcing the large dish upwards into the heavens.

From their horizon, they watched the redness, the darkness, and smoke covering the eastern skies. Mother Earth groaned.

A message beeped through Foster's radio device. *Bon Voyage,* from Brody. In the distance, Foster watched the other smaller island ascend as well.

He messaged back, *We actually did it!* Then Foster breathed in the grandest breath of his life.

# EIGHTEEN

## FOSTER

*I am an equalizer.* Foster heard Ashyr's voice within his mind.

*Usually, I talk less. In fact, talking isn't really encouraged during an EnRapture experience, but I feel you need some clarification, some instructions.*

A gigantic red flower, like a lily, burst open and the stigma danced forward. Then Foster descended forward into the open petals. The movement, the colors, the sensations pulsing from Ashyr's neurons, along with the interception of Ashyr's voice unnerved Foster. This was not Em-Path at all!

A strong, creamy, spicy scent filled Foster's lungs, taking his mind to a sudden longing, an uncomfortableness, a sense of needing to take control, but not wanting to stop this.

Nothing bad had occurred. Just a large flower, opening wide, Foster feeling the softness, the silkiness, as pollen danced around him from the stamen to the pistil. Monk chant music pulsed along with the dancing, stirring an exotic intrigue. His breathing heightened with the rhythm, becoming one with the movement surrounding him.

In and out. In and out. A cadence flowed inside

and outside him. The environmental senses impacted him tremendously, making him want this exchange to end. To find control again. But another part of him desired to continue forward while his breathing grew stronger, deeper, the rhythm around him intensifying.

The realization that Ashyr could do this with his mind, create such a real presence within Foster while simultaneously taking in the memory Foster was sharing with him, this feat needed to be celebrated. In a sense, Ashyr was a genius.

A small nag, like a tiny biting midge, nipped at his mind, pricked at his heart, and tattled to his senses this was not Em-Path. Not at all the purpose of its creation. Not what he'd ever wanted it to be.

True, the exchange wasn't leading Foster any closer to understanding the truth. He still didn't know why Ashyr had come. What he needed from Foster. Rather, this was Ashyr's elaborate ploy to create a show-and-tell while stimulating, manipulating, and evoking passionate chords within Foster.

Signature Ashyr—stirring a confusion along with a hunger for more. Presenting lies filled with enticement, intrigue, and entertainment. Divided, Foster wanted to shut his mind off to this display while also feeling a desperate thrill to embrace such extremes.

At last, a shift happened. The chants faded. The intense red petals softened toward a new visual scene. Foster's breathing shifted, too, as he tried to place himself over what was happening around him.

He stood in a wide-open grassy field. An enormous black pot rested in the center of his view. Birds chirped. Butterflies fluttered. The pot suddenly swelled. Huge golden bricks filled its chamber until the bricks overflowed to the ground.

*I had four goals with EnRapture.* Ashyr's voice returned. *All of which have been achieved.*

A large red band of color shot out from the gold-producing cauldron.

*First, I created a product that brings happiness and enjoyment to others.*

A large yellow band of color shot out into the sky from the pot aligning itself alongside the red band.

*Second, I offered this product to a society that was ready to embrace it.*

*See, Foster, the world, the nation, our state, our region, all of it had faded into new. A new frontier to build what was best for the people.*

Replacing the meadow, Foster now stood in front of a large screen, and images like movie clips blasted in front of him. Twenty images at a time, sharing news of destruction, turmoil, pandemics, natural disasters, loss of human life, the Earth groaning with sadness. It was more than Foster could take in, but right as the effects, the fears, the weight, and heartbreak of this destruction seemed to nearly consume him, Ashyr shared one final image: a bird's-eye view of the tumultuous shaking along the San Andreas fault line.

*The earthquake blocked our community in. I mean, there were treacherous ways in and out, but overall, as I said, we became our own island. And with A.J. positioning me in the way he had, before his death, I had a chance to be a founding father of this new land.*

The meadow was back, and in place of the screen, images floated around like large bubbles swaying easily through the sky. Coming and going, happy human faces, one after another. The more faces that appeared, the more these happy faces' physical features shifted into a less traditional look, more of a hybrid of gender, ethnicities, race. A different breed of society, many features altered, except for their continuous smiles which began at the lips and grew until it reached their eyes.

*It was an extraordinary opportunity to begin again, to learn from the past, identify what had not been working, why our former society had become so broken. Then start anew, finding solutions before the old problems resurfaced.*

The bubbles disappeared, the focus back on the caldron, a new color shooting up, a green band which joined the others.

*Third, I created equality.*

*A brilliant solution only made possible through the gift of EnRapture.*

Through similar floating means, scenes of action, adventure, extreme sports, high-end foods, extraordinary amounts of money, fast cars, and more drifted past Foster until only one bubble-like image remained.

This image paused directly in front of Foster then just stayed. It was an image of Leonardo da Vinci's *Vitruvian Man,* the male physique along with his duplication of both arms and legs, the alteration of positions to fit inside the circle and square shapes.

Except in Ashyr's shared image, surfer shorts

covered the man's private anatomy. Either Ashyr was trying to be funny or he wanted this renaissance figure to have some commonality to Foster's younger identity.

*Everyone in our society has an outer persona.*

The figure became animated, the arms and legs shifting, morphing together, then separated again.

*And we have built what we call accessories. These enhance, change, modify, remove, or blend with the current body to further enhance one's experience.*

In quick succession, the arms, hands, legs, feet, and head of the figure moved, rapidly changing positions to strike loud, voguing stances.

*Skin color, ethnicity, gender, age, every aspect of one's appearance is modifiable.*

The figure stopped moving. Its skin flashed through whirls of tones, like a crayon line-up from the darkest brown, to tan, to beige, to ivory. Facial features shifted too: a long face, a round face, strong cheekbones, chubby cheeks, wrinkles around the eyes followed by baby-skin smoothness.

*These are surgical modifications—but the point is, we have the means to make all this accessible. So people can choose who they want to be, how they want to look, it's their choice in creating their own identity. Biological traits no longer limit them. They control their destiny.*

More modifications continued on the figure, a rapid succession of a large Adam's apple, facial hair, the surf shorts transforming into a flowing skirt, the bare muscular chest covered up with a bikini top, suddenly that top filling with unnatural cleavage, followed by a tie whirling around the neck, knotting into place, the tie's tail getting lost between the breasts' canyon.

Foster felt queasy again. Uncertainty. Confusion. Another divide occurring within his feelings.

*But here is the interesting thing,* Ashyr continued. *Because of EnRapture, no one cares about another outer persona, not like before. Instead, the focus is on how desirable their inner persona is. It's about what they can offer another in wish fulfillment through EnRapture. In our society, people modify their outer persona with the goal to enhance their inner experiences. They seek the maximum sensory experience so they can then share what they have seen and felt with their partner, offering wish fulfill-ment that goes into the wild, extreme, and limitless.*

The family photo of Foster and Mariana reappeared, except all their children were blurred out. The focus remained sharp and bright on Foster and Mariana.

*What you two saw as Em-Path's weakness has turned into EnRapture's strength. We encourage creativity, variety, eccentricity. Reality holds no necessary place within these exchanges. New ideas, stronger action, heightened adventures, the more "wowed" a user is the greater the partner is rewarded by a numerical value given to the partner through a registry that tracks each exchange.*

*The system encourages more and more EnRapture exchanges, a deeper desire to build the registry and be sought after by the most desirable users.*

The meadow returned, and a large blue band shot out from the cauldron, joining the other colors in a tight spectrum.

*Fourth, I created fairness for everyone.*

*By the time I reached this goal, it was already there, right in front of me, what everyone in our society wanted.*

*See, by removing the inequalities that had been plaguing our former society, I found the underlying cause of such problems.*

In place of the meadow, a plain piece of snow-white paper filled Foster's view. A drawing unfolded. A house appeared, the style close to a five-year-old artistic level with its triangular roof and windows which were drawn on both sides of the framed door.

*For years, we've lived under the hierarchy unit of families.*

The drawing continued as Ashyr listed out the roles.

*Father, Mother, Brother, Sister, Siblings, Children—a small group attached under one establishment.*

*This is outdated and problematic. So, an update was needed.*

*What I found was once we created fairness for families—once we all were a part of the same unit with no family advantages among us—then we truly had a fair society.*

Darkness surrounded Foster—thick, heavy, opaqueness. Only his audio sense was fed—whisperings, two voices, one clearly Ashyr's, the other higher-toned in pitch.

Foster could barely make out the words.

*It's all done within the lab.*

*Let's free up women.*

*Let's not leave men out.*

*Or leave anyone out for that matter.*

*Remove the restrictions caused by gender.*

*Create a fairness for all.*

In the darkness, Ashyr spoke again to Foster. *We did it. We grow our babies from embryo to newborn within the lab.*

*Children are produced without placing a physical strain on the woman, removing that singular mother-child connection, expanding it to include all. Now everyone is part of the wonder.*

Slowly, a scene opened, a woman with dark curls on her left side and green-dyed spikes on her right side sat across from Ashyr at a table with barstool-raised chairs in a penthouse living room. Her eyebrows resembled streaks of thick tip permanent markers that rose as she spoke, her voice matching the voice Foster heard in the darkness. "You want life to offer experiences that are fair to all, well, here you go. If a man can't carry a child, why should a woman be able to? If a woman wants to not birth a child, why does she have to go through such biological efforts to prevent this? It's an unfairness. So, we remove it. Eliminate the discrepancy. Just as you've been saying, with all this, life can be fair. Everyone can be treated the same."

*Her name is Serena.* Ashyr spoke to Foster, pausing on the woman's face. *She is now my business partner, after A.J.'s death. Once I took sole ownership of all this, she entered, and she's brilliant.*

The scene in the penthouse living room continued, Serena and Ashyr's heads bent down over tablets, holograms whirling around them, drafting paper spread out, ideas flowing. Foster only caught snippets and phrases.

*Lab produces the babies, hit puberty, required, a donation.*

*Sperms collected and stored.*

*Eggs collected and stored.*

*Young men. Young women. Train them early, prepare them for EnRapture.*

*After the collection, eliminate unfair opportunities. Remove disadvantages. Maintain fairness.*

Then the words became clear. Serena said, "It's all there, Ashyr—it's just a few steps away for this to be fair for everyone. And you can do this."

"I see," Ashyr said, "after we collect, we remove gender."

"It's just an accessory now. It can come and go as anyone wants it to."

# NINETEEN

## FOSTER

He jerked his gloved hand away from Ashyr's grasp. A searing headache shot through Foster.

"Why did you do that?" Ashyr clutched his head while his gloved hand remained extended. "Finish this, Foster. You shouldn't have been able to break free."

"No!" Foster pressed his fingertips into his temples. Inside his skull, it felt like a clash of freefalling neurons smacking against brick walls, repeatedly.

"Why did you give us an old prototype one?" Ashyr's breathing was jagged. "The modern stuff, you'd never be able to break the connection like that! You of all people should know . . ." But his words dwindled off as he now pressed both palms against his head.

Foster tried to speak, but words couldn't form.

"I'm not sure I can control the nausea." Ashyr leaned down between his knees. "Where's your toilet?"

By applying deeper pressure into his temples, Foster, at last, found the pain bearable. Words finally came. "I want to know what you did!"

Ashyr gave a faint headshake, while his head

rested near his lap. "About what?" He gasped for a breath. "I'm still flocking through your flying bottle ecosystem. Right now, do you control your flight . . . or are we just floating like a satellite now? I didn't catch that . . . mate."

"Why would you sterilize people?"

"I didn't." Ashyr lifted his head, then his entire body pressed into the sofa. His breathing came out tight. "It was a choice. Everyone had a choice."

Foster's face dropped. "But you did it."

"Foster," Mariana called out. She stood above him, her eyes dashing between him and Ashyr. "He did what?"

Ashyr heaved forward as if vomit might transpire.

"Ashyr!" Mariana said. "What do you need?"

Slowly, he rose and wiped the sweat from his forehead. "That was horrible, Foster."

"It's exactly what you once did to me," Mariana said hotly. "Breaking the connection before the exchange is through."

"What you did . . ." Foster stood, too, pacing himself away from the couch, closer to Mariana. His headache, although wretched, paled against his racing heart. "To others! That's horrible!"

Ashyr looked from Mariana then back to Foster. His hands dropped from his forehead to his side. His shoulders rolled back. Then, he stuck his chest out as if ready for a fight. "Really? Why should you have a happy, simple life, an easy family life, with the woman you picked, when the rest of us don't get that—I don't have what you have. I don't get a woman like Mariana, or kids like Clark or a little Zane, Jr., and now your joint Leilani. It's not fair, mate. It's wrong. So, I helped build a plan that provides equality, a fairness to all."

From across the back of the couch, Mariana faced Ashyr, her head slanted as if she'd misheard. "What did you do?"

He gave her a square look. "As far as family goes, we're all the same now. Everyone has the same family unit."

"It's a mockery," Foster said.

"It's fair," Ashyr said.

"How?" Mariana's face flushed red. She stepped to Foster's side and reached for his hand, pulling it close to her, as if the two of them together could withstand this horrifying news.

"It was family segregation," Ashyr said. "But it's gone. We removed the traditional, and now there's no longer separation with someone having more or less than another. We're all the same no matter who anyone is."

"This is wrong," Foster said.

Ashyr shrugged. "I don't think most people see it as you do."

"Really?" Mariana's eyes grew huge. "Are they normal human beings?"

"See!" Ashyr threw up his hands. "A statement like that, that proves you have bias, that you separate people based on their family status. It's unfair. Both of you have biases that alienate the rest of us who don't fit into your traditional, perfect family idea."

Foster and Mariana exchanged a confused look. Then Foster turned back. "No, Ashyr! Before, there was order in the world, but this—this is chaos!"

# TWENTY

## YAM

### Travel log

July 3, 2050
4:30 p.m.

*I'm doing fine. I've been waiting for over ninety minutes now. I think Aria is being held in a neighboring room. We are going to speak to someone from the council. Together.*

*I'll be fine. Once we talk our way out of this, I'll be heading back soon.*

*I'll be okay. And . . . I hope Aria will be too.*

Yam quickly removed the stickers. The more time that passed, the more he wanted to cry out to Baba, to notify him of the situation. One word, one cry of his name, and Baba would come.

But what would he do?

There were certain things Baba couldn't do, requirements they'd agreed upon. Still, no matter what was decided, one thing was for certain: if Yam ran into any trouble, Baba would rescue him.

Even if this was Yam's mistake.

But if this continued to escalate, it would be

like telling Baba he couldn't trust Yam. That Yam couldn't manage these runs by himself.

He didn't want to fail. Not at this. Not at anything.

And he didn't want to lose the freedom that came with these runs, especially the scavenger runs.

He closed his eyes to leave the holding cell, to revisit that parking area when Aria had first appeared. She had asked him questions—then talked over herself, letting her own words fill in the answers. It was comical at first, cute, in a way. It reminded him of his sister.

During that first encounter, she held no threat. In fact, Yam had found little alarm in the situation. He even had told Baba as soon as he got back, and Baba had followed up with, *"Be careful."*

That was it.

Yam let his mind slip deeper into that memory. Other than a few scattered parked drones, the place had been empty. From a neighboring building, the monorail zipped past. Other drones in the distance weaved around buildings. And then he heard, "Who are you?"

He had spun around to see her: dreadlocks drawn up like felt yarn in colorful strands of black, blue, and orangish-brown. Over her glasses was a flashy EnRapture eye mask with the blackened eye portions cut out. It was bright red with cat-eye angles and streamers which tumbled down like ringlets alongside her hair.

From her short shorts, Yam noticed her long copper-skinned legs which led down into lime green, canvas, slip-on shoes. A long-sleeved, skin-tight, maroon shirt with a lime green, frilly, short sleeve camisole covered her top. In fact, the frill covering seemed too tight around a certain area.

Not that Yam should have noticed that. But these people all dressed as if to call attention to specific parts of their body. Some statement that needed to be made. Yam just assumed he had identified the girl's statement.

She didn't ask him again who he was. Rather, she answered the question as if he'd asked. "I'm Aria. Third batch born under the Ashyr Order. I like colors. Thanks to a colored pencil set I had as a kid, I make it a point to craft clever names for my colors. Like my shorts, they are *Water You Up To?* Get it? Blue, water, what are you?"

She drew her mouth up. Her glasses and cat-eye EnRapture mask also lifted.

Yam snorted a brief laugh.

"Oh, you like that." She took a step closer. "I have more. My skin is currently toned to *Caramel Latte*. My mask is *Hot Tamale*, and I like to practice wearing a mask, so I do. And my top, it's *Lime All Yours*. Which, when you have an exchange with me, it'll all be in color. Bright colors. So, remember that, okay?"

Yam stepped back. Under no conditions, ever, ever, would he agree to an exchange. Baba wouldn't allow it. And Yam, even if he could bypass Baba, held no desire. Zero desire. Less than zero. A negative amount of desire to try EnRapture.

"I won't," he said firmly, stealing a sideways glance to gauge the distance to his drone to get out of there.

"What do you mean you won't?" Her cat-eyed smile had fallen, but her eyes gave him a tender question back.

"I don't believe in that stuff."

As soon as the words came out, Yam knew he had made a mistake.

"What stuff?"

But she didn't let him struggle through an answer. Instead, she started sharing the names of the colors in her hair, only for Yam to cut her off, to excuse himself to get out fast. On that journey home, he determined he would not slip up again.

But, in time, he did.

Otherwise, he wouldn't be waiting here in this holding cell.

# TWENTY-ONE

## YAM

### Travel log

July 3, 2050
5:02 p.m.

*Starting to wonder if they are planning to keep me for the night. If they do, I will need to connect. But I am not concerned at the moment. Aria said she knew how to talk us out of this. So we should be just fine. I think I've already mentioned that.*

*One more hour. Then if someone doesn't come, I will determine the next steps to take.*

The longer the delay, the more Yam had time to think. The more Yam thought, the more critical this mess became.

Over and over he kept returning to Aria's words. *Just let me do the talking.*

Easy enough.

He had no desire to talk.

Something about all this made it seem like she had dealt with a correction before. Maybe, for her, this was no big deal.

Even though he was getting better at managing

his output thoughts, Yam didn't want to slip up. So, as soon as he'd finished his check-in log, he removed the device stickers again.

For now, he would just keep waiting. And crafting his words wisely each time he logged in.

To manage the growing fears, and his awful boredom, Yam continued to remember back.

It was true. The first time he'd met Aria, he told her nothing. Just like he had relayed to Baba.

But the following time, six months later, during his next supply run, as odd luck would have it, he ran into her again.

She couldn't have been waiting for him. But it almost seemed like she was.

He was out on the main street, the monorail track directly above, drones flying overhead, people moving around him on foot or in the scooter lanes. It was rush hour, a small segment of the day where EnRapture experiences were on hold and everyone was on the move to get to their best destination. Yam liked this time the least: the crowds, the noise, the sights, the fears of standing out even while knowing he wouldn't. Not among the number of people bustling along, quickly doing what they needed to get done so they could get ready for their next EnRapture experience.

Amid all of it came her voice, "I've been looking for you."

She stood there dressed in short shorts again, another tight spandex long-sleeved top, and another snug camisole. She also wore two belts: one attached to her shorts, the other twisted in an uncomfortable looking way around her waist.

"I can't seem to find you among any of the youth

centers," she said. "When were you born?"

Before he felt pressure to say anything, she answered her question once again in her own way. "I already told you I'm third batch born. And if you're first batch, have you heard the latest news? It was just announced. Two collection cycles are required for each female born in the first batch, and then they will be the first to graduate. Can you believe it?"

She waited, looking at him, expecting a response, so he gave her a brief shrug of the shoulder: a cautious expression that could be translated into he couldn't believe the news she had just shared instead of that he had no idea what she was talking about.

Fortunately, she kept right on talking. While he walked, she stayed next to him.

"So, are you going to ask me why I'm wearing a second belt?"

He glanced over at her, noting her long, slender, flawless legs, and the short shorts in the same color blue from before. Then he glanced at the unpleasant-looking belt wrapped around her abdomen.

"The color is *Must be Rusty*. Funny, huh?"

"I don't get it," he said.

"Don't they do second belts where you stay?"

He should not have talked. To correct his mistake, he waited for her to talk over her question. But when she didn't, he just slowly shook his head.

Her shoulders dropped, and she let out a frustrated sigh. Not at him, but toward the belt as she looked down at it. "Some of the mean kids call it a chastity belt—as a joke. Insulting us with such language around the archaic way of doing things. Now you know what I'm talking about, right? Yep, I'm in the low ranks of my batch right now. It's humiliating. All I can think is they do this to us to help motivate us, to try and get us to focus harder on our studies."

Yam had reached the storefront where he needed to pick up the supplies: some bolts of fabric, a list of clothing supplies, and a couple of shoes for Mum. He had plenty of tasks for the day's events and needed to begin tackling the list soon. He edged toward the doors, to indicate his priority. But Aria just kept pace with him and continued talking as if oblivious that he couldn't seem to follow what she was saying.

"Not only am I falling behind in my studies, I told them I wanted to work in clothing once I graduated. Like here." She held the door for him as they entered the building. It had a spiral staircase in the center and white rooms that ran the circumference of the store. He had mistaken them for dressing rooms until he'd heard someone refer to them as EnRapture rooms while soliciting an exchange with another customer.

Yam's usual routine was to get in and get out. Just like Baba had instructed. Lately, since he looked old enough, he had to decline the levels of payments. *"An EnRapture experience?" "No." "EnRapture pills?" "No."* Just regular bills which seemed to be frowned upon more and more these days.

He had his hair down to cover an early prototype of the Fluid Interface Device. All he wanted to do was be able to think clearly, so he could activate the shopping list and be guided through the most efficient path through the store. But beside him, Aria said, "They don't think I'd do well as a clerk here. Instead, they think I should focus on being a leg model."

Yam couldn't concentrate enough to activate the device. Instead, he fought the desire to look down, to inspect those legs as she stuck them out, one at a time. "They say these are my best features. That I could be a leg model, and an instructor."

He made the mistake of looking. "An instructor of what?"

She laughed at him as if he were teasing her. "I could instruct at the school, after I graduate, help other batches learn how to benefit from what they want to do with their legs. Accessory-based or not, these can be purposeful as an asset within exchanges, you know?"

Yam turned away. At the moment, he needed to not look at her legs. Or her eyes. Or hear her speak. But it was too late. She was diving further into EnRapture. The parts Baba said Yam didn't need to know more about, just that it existed and he was to stay away from it.

"They think I'll want to keep my legs as is. No additional work will be needed on them. I'm very lucky in that way. My breasts, well, we'll see." Again, Yam fought against the desire to look at her, but based on what he saw out of the corner of his eye, her palms had pressed against the frilly camisole. "But not a big deal," she said. "I'll just accessorize them out."

Yam took the bait. Against what he knew would be Baba's wishes, he asked, "What does that mean?"

She cocked her head to the side. "My breasts. Out?"

"The accessories?"

She stepped close, super close, so close Yam felt

all queasy inside like he wanted to step away, but he remained planted in place.

"I've started to wonder about you," she said. "You aren't part of the batches, are you? Tell me where you came from."

# TWENTY-TWO

## FOSTER

"It worked," Ashyr said as he withdrew from his place near the couch. He strode past Foster and Mariana. As he looked to their handholding, his volume increased. "What I built is a world of order."

He reached the back of the room only to speak calmer, "Come with me and see."

Foster rubbed at his forehead, still feeling the pain from the split. But the look in Ashyr's eyes suggested he had recovered. "It's okay," he said to Foster. "Everything's okay."

"Hardly." Foster said.

"It was tense during the war. A lot of hiding. We were no longer United. We were just individual states. And as each state tried to deal with the catastrophes, infrastructure instabilities, high mortality rates, and a collapsed economy, state governments soon disbanded too. Then the fear set in. We, as a people, were broken. Everyone was broken, all of us just trying to survive. But EnRapture saved us all! Once the worst of it was over, at least within my society, we used the unknown as a new beginning to build an incredible place." The smile returned. "I think you would find parts of it beyond fascinating.

You too, Mariana."

She dropped Foster's hand and folded her arms. With a furrowed brow, she looked at Foster. "What did he do?" Then she spun toward Ashyr and tilted her head. "Am I hearing you right? You stopped procreation?"

"Hardly," he said. "We created a fair society, where gender, sexual preferences, biological defects, and personal ambitions do not segregate any minority from the majority. It was absolutely the right thing to do."

"By whose standards?" she asked.

"Don't worry," he said softly, almost disturbingly sweetly. "There are regulations. The tribal government has a firm hold on the situation."

"Oh, Ashyr," Foster whispered.

"Don't you see what we've done?" Ashyr's smile only expanded. "We've given society sex without the sex. We've given them uniqueness without the gender differences or offensive labels or any type of suppression. We are all equal individuals."

"This makes no sense to me!" Mariana said. "It doesn't even sound possible."

"Oh, it is! It so is."

"Ashyr. . ." Foster said, but Ashyr made no effort to look at him.

Instead, he kept looking at Mariana. "Let me illustrate to you all the issues we've eliminated with this fix. We've eliminated sexual diseases, broken homes, a lot of heartaches, crime as you knew it, and we've completely revolutionized entertainment. Through a few tweaks to Em-Path, which brought us our earlier versions of EnRapture, we've truly changed *the world* as I promised you it would."

Mariana shifted to meet Foster's eyes. "Yes," she whispered. "It appears Ashyr has."

"We. All of us have." Ashyr waved his hand at the three of them.

"Stop!" Mariana said. "No. Foster did not create that. I didn't either. Don't include us in any of what you've done."

An awkward laugh spilled from Ashyr. "You don't want it?" He shifted to a pacified tone. "You don't want credit for making the world a better place?"

"So. . . you said it was a choice." Foster rubbed at his beard while peering at Ashyr. "People could choose this lifestyle you offer. But what if someone chooses not to follow your altered path?"

"The traditionalists," Mariana said. "The ones who want children and family and a life that is normal."

"Careful," Ashyr said softly. "Your terminology of normal is considered offensive. For us, this is the new normal."

"Ashyr." Foster heard the strain in his own voice. "Life is about making peace with the truth that surrounds it. Not about rewriting truth."

"You are trying to become a god," Mariana said quietly.

Ashyr released an angry laugh. "Here you are criticizing my greatest work. And what about you? Living in your little ecosystem in the sky. How is what I've done any different than what you've done? What? You're not playing like gods, too, lounging around up here in the clouds?"

Foster stepped back; his arms folded.

Mariana moved to his side. She touched his arm.

"We're fine," she said to Foster. "Don't let him upset you. He wants to mess with your head."

Ashyr expelled another laugh. But his eyes had shifted to Mariana's hand that touched Foster. "Wow! If I'm able to mess with Foster's head, then I am underestimating my abilities. Perhaps I am a god."

Her hand fell to her side. "Don't flatter yourself, Ashyr." She moved to the side of the room then pulled out a little stool from under the corner table and sat diagonal from Ashyr. "So, what happens to the ones who don't want to join your party?"

"First, we collect their contributions—"

"Serious?" Foster stared at him. "You control their ability to reproduce, and you call it a *contribution* to your society?"

Ashyr waved his hand as if to brush off Foster's look. "It's like a tax. We collect eggs or sperm from each individual. You should know the procedure is free of charge. The tribal government offers this procedure to everyone with the criteria that they pay their tax before they reach adulthood."

"How thoughtful of the government," Foster said, "offering what will lead to their free sterilization."

"Not necessarily," Ashyr said.

"But what if they don't want the procedure?" Mariana's face appeared tense like she was really trying to understand Ashyr. "They don't have to pay the tax, right?"

His voice was low and calm. "Everyone pays a tax. It's either through the procedure, which is their donation to the bank and then they're given their first official EnRapture kit. Or, it's their trade-off, their thank you to us as they choose to relocate, to exist with another tribe at another location."

"Where?" Foster asked.

"Australia."

"Is it safe there? Last I'd heard from Brody, after the nuclear warfare subsided, humans couldn't even dwell on the eastern hemisphere."

Ashyr quickly cleared his throat and then waved his hand as if giving a lecture. "It is far enough south and enough to the west, it's fine for them. But yes, geographically, Europe and Asia are still unhabitable locations."

"And there, in Australia, they can live a normal—I mean, *traditional* lifestyle?" Mariana corrected herself.

"However they choose." Ashyr smiled at her.

"Sounds lovely." She rolled her eyes.

Ashyr leaned against the wall, directly between the doorframe and the birds of paradise painting, and folded his arms. "Sadly, you aren't allowing yourself to see beyond all you think you know. What is traditional to you," he nodded toward Mariana, "is no longer the traditions of this new band of children. Instead, we are getting rid of the outdated traditions of the so-called fathers to build a new, more free generation."

"How?" she asked.

"The consequences of infidelity are removed. The consequences of divorce—removed. Rape? Gone."

Mariana raised an eyebrow at Foster before looking again at Ashyr. "How?"

"Because everyone in our nation has traded in the traditional methods for EnRapture. It's our new sex, our new drug, our new labor exchange, our new currency, our new way of living."

# TWENTY-THREE

## YAM

### Travel log

July 3, 2050
5:21 p.m.

*I'm hearing noises upstairs. That's a good sign. For a while, it'd been so quiet, I wondered if everyone had gone home. Had that been the case, I think I would have ended up here through the night. Like maybe they forgot about me.*

*But with noise, there's still a chance.*

Yam remained silent against the wall and listened to the sounds coming through the vent above. He strained to make out the words.

It was a deeper voice. "Serena. It's Ashyr . . . wrapping up a youth issue here. And then I need you. I never ask you to come. But . . . let's just say that for a day like today, you're the best elusion. So, as soon as you can be here."

Relief and concern rushed through Yam. Of all the people who could attend to him, they called in Ashyr.

*In. Out.* He could almost hear Baba's words.

Still, this all was a simple misunderstanding.

It happened when he had spotted Aria on a basketball court today. He had passed by a youth center. She had been outside with other teens. Although she looked different, Yam had felt a sense of pride that he recognized her.

Really, it was curiosity that had done it for him.

It was he who had approached her this time, moving around the large group, slipping in on the side, stepping up behind her.

"Hey," he said.

"Oh." She was wearing shorts not as short as she had worn before, but her legs were still long and graceful, even against the gray loafers she wore.

But now that he stood close to her, he noticed her pink lacey short-sleeve top was practically see-through, and she wasn't wearing a bra. Yam tried not to look toward the sheer material.

"Haven't seen you in a while," he volunteered, keeping his focus on her face. Her dreadlocks were gone, replaced by platinum and golden-brown sweeps of hair which were pulled up into a sideways ponytail at the crown of her head. Her skin color had changed from bronze to a peachy crème look. "You look different." He nodded at her face.

"Well, if it isn't secret boy." She gave him a wink. There was no EnRapture mask on her face, just pink, thick-rimmed glasses. "They are going to want to talk to you." She nudged her head in the direction of the other teens who had all turned and were watching him. The whole crew stared at him as if he were out of place.

In. Out. He had clearly made a big mistake.

"I don't want to get in trouble," Yam said softly

while a teen with beefy legs, a layered lacey skirt, a letterman jacket, ruby stained lips, and an afro approached him.

"You won't," Aria said just as softly.

# TWENTY-FOUR

## YAM

## Travel log

July 3, 2050
5:40 p.m.

*I know that I am running out of time. But I am still hoping.*

*I will only be a little late. Maybe more than a little. But I haven't given up hope yet.*

The biggest mistake Yam made was going out of his way to talk to Aria. Before he knew it, he became overloaded with information.

When they asked who he was, Aria had answered for him. He was also third batch, Ashyr Order, like her.

Aria gave a general introduction to the others. They were first batch, some second batch, and they were currently consoling her after she'd received a bit of bad news.

The instructors were advising her to wait even further after her graduation, to delay her full transformation. She should maintain her femineity features even though they weren't currently the vogue fashion.

"Don't let it get you down." A lean kid stepped forward. A hoody, covering most of the face, raised toward Yam. "I'm Wyatt," he said. "I'm almost done with my transformation." The voice sounded high; the hands looked strong and thick. An elastic back brace covered his waist as if supporting a recent injury. When Wyatt tugged on it, Yam caught the tattoo of a flower bracelet around the wrist. "Aria. You know none of that matters. Gender stuff is just for show, it goes in and out of style fast. It's all about fairness, what you know inside your head."

"It's about picking your accessories and enjoying the other person's experience." Another youth came over. Large hoop earrings danced around the head, while the jeans appeared practically painted onto the body. The clothing emphasized the groin area, the zipper protruding, the fabric a neon orange. "How much pleasure can they transmit to your neurons? That's it."

"So, don't worry." The hooded kid, Wyatt, continued. "Listen to them. They are training you. Meanwhile, your question is only relevant today. Within the moment. We have the freedom to change as we choose. Once you get a strong enough registry, and you have enough experiences, you will thrive, and then you select whichever path you choose."

Aria nodded. Yam nodded, too, unsure of what else to do.

Suddenly, others surrounded them. Words came at Yam from all directions.

*You can be anything. What's on the outside, none of it matters. All of it can be changed.*

"But for today . . ." the large-hooped earring youth nodded at Wyatt.

Against his hood, Wyatt lifted his head and repeated the words loudly. "For today . . ."

All the other youth joined in. "For today . . ."

Then all of them continued into a chant. "For the moment. Our future is free and undetermined. So, for today, we are content to learn. To be where we are, in the present, learning to live in the moment so we can truly channel our focuses, our energies, our minds into the ultimate exchange."

Even though the FID was nearly invisible and extremely lightweight in Yam's jacket pocket, he slipped his hand near it and felt a heaviness there. The device was turned off, his communication needs suspended. Still, Yam almost felt Baba trying to communicate with him, telling him to get back to his mission, to focus, to get away from the distractions, and accomplish his specified task so he could get home.

"Give him some air," he heard Aria say as if he had zoned out, as if he had stopped following the chants around him. "He's coming with me," she said. "Right now." She broke out of the crowd then gave him a look to follow.

As soon as he did, a catcall bellowed behind him. "Go. Go!"

"Exchange time." The youth with the orange groin area started dancing in the background.

"You look different," Yam told her again while trying to sound calm, quiet and reserved.

The calling continued behind them. "Go to your pod."

"Or use mine," another youth called out.

"Come on." Aria motioned him toward a small building in the distance.

Yam froze, finally cluing into what was happening. "I don't want to."

"Look," she whispered near him. "It'll be easier to talk. They will leave us alone."

"I don't want them to think . . ." his words trailed off.

"I don't care what they think." She moved quickly, turning around often to make sure he was keeping up, while sirens of warnings kept telling Yam to turn around, to head back to the path he had been on, and to focus again on rounding up the supplies.

Instead, Aria disappeared behind a tree, the building still a few yards away.

"I want to come with you," she said as soon as he stopped near where she was.

"To where?"

"To where you live."

"You can't." His mistakes were growing around him.

"I can't stay here," she said, pleading with her eyes.

"Aren't you about to graduate? In like some cycles or something?"

"One more annual retrieval of my donation," she said mockingly.

"You have changed. You look different." It was the third time he had told her this.

"My colors." She folded her arms and gave him a frown. "My hair color is slate—*It's Getting Slate*. As in it's time to go, okay?" She gave a quick, firm nod. "And the color of my shorts, they are *Dill With It*. Get it? 'Dill' like the color. And get it? I'm coming with you, so deal with it."

He didn't have to respond because she kept right on talking.

"I don't get to be a color wardrobe coach because my legs are my best feature. And I should consider, strongly, training others on how to get the most of either authentic or plastic surgery help to their legs. A model of legs like mine will enhance the pleasures of their exchanges. Like you already heard, my instructors are recommending I hold on a little longer to my feminine look. Even though it makes me feel like a failure. But for now, my top, it's the color *Oh So Pretty*. And looks come and go. Accessories change. Right now, I have options. And this is what is necessary, doing my prep work, so when I do graduate, I can have some really great exchanges."

Her tight exposed belly danced back and forth as if inviting Yam forward. He felt dizzy. "It's all a race," she said. "Our registry. Giving others an experience around my own pleasures, exciting their neurons. The higher the ranking, the hotter one is, which means they draw more partners of other higher ranks to them. I want out of this. And you can get me out."

Suddenly, the kid with the hoody appeared. "What are you doing, Aria?"

"Talking," she quickly said, her face appearing a bit flushed.

Wyatt looked at Yam. "I saw you touch her."

"He didn't touch me," her words came out fast.

But Wyatt's eyes remained fixed on Yam. "What are you going to do with Aria?"

Yam pulled back. "What do you mean?"

"Back there, you acted different than us. Like

a stranger. Like you have no right to be here. And then you touched Aria."

"He didn't!" she practically screamed.

"This is dangerous, Aria. You know that," Wyatt said.

"He is harmless."

"Let me see your registry." Wyatt pointed at Yam.

Aria stepped forward. "Leave him alone. We haven't graduated. We don't have our registries."

Wyatt rolled his eyes. "Training registry. Let's see it." He folded his arms. A look covered his face as if representing a powerful authority.

"I need to talk to him," Aria said.

"I don't think that's a good idea."

She shrugged. "Sometimes we all have to learn from our ideas."

"Let EnRapture teach us. That's how we work around here." Wyatt looked at Yam as if he had transformed into a dog. "If there is no training registry on you, you had no intention of doing what was right. And I am going to report you."

"Please don't," she said.

"Be smart, Aria." Within his hood, Wyatt lifted his head, signifying a final warning.

"I will," she said.

# TWENTY-FIVE
## LEILANI

As I neared the house, I paused to catch my breath. Once I had control of my heavy exhales, I carefully made my way inside, back through the house, and onto the roof just in time to see Mom clutching her head and saying, "I so don't get this."

Both my parents sat on the couch. Ashyr stood above them like he had just given them a presentation. And my parents seemed engrossed in his words.

"Rape can't happen," he said. "Because we control what we give another. We control the experiences we share. If we share bad experiences, no one wants to share with us again. We have a registry, a database of feedback, and everyone can access that registry. We know who has the high marks and who is still developing their skills. Sure, we often lower ourselves to help the learners, but those with high marks are sought after, craved, if you will."

I was lost, but as my parents said nothing, I could tell something big had gone down.

Ashyr continued. "No one wants to break code, to commit a crime, to lose out on the privileges that come with one's registry marks. You cross a line and it will destroy your chances of surviving in our society."

"So, you have no criminals?" Dad's face looked so intense, like he was trying to absorb everything Ashyr was saying.

"Sure. We still have a little, but the consequences are severe. So severe that no one wants to take the risk. If they do, we ship them away."

"To where?"

"To Australia?" Mom said. Sarcasm was in her voice.

"Yes. Actually, we do. It's a big place. The beaches are reserved for the traditionalists. The criminals are dropped in the center, in the heart of the outback. Not only must they face the ruggedness of nature with no viable supplies, but they must survive without their fixes of EnRapture, which I hear can be insanely brutal. Once the mind has separated like that, to not have some reprieve, to have to slip back into the archaic way of thinking, it can be the most excruciating form of torture, mental torture, that we don't have to administer. All we do is take away the gift that they'd been given, and the punishments take care of themselves."

"Very humane," Mom said, the sarcasm still there.

Ashyr shrugged. "It's better than the alternative that our ancestors saw, all the horrific history we heard as children. This is their choice. And very few make it. Because the truth is, everything they need can be found in these EnRapture experiences. Complete and utter entertainment, in any form they wish, whether it's a thrill from an athletic game, extreme sports, passion, adventures—it's all right there and they can access it all through a registry directory. If a partner accepts, they can have new thrills, new highs, new fun without hurting another person, no negative consequences, complete and utter freedom. Why would anyone want to leave that?"

Dad looked around the room. "Yes." He let out a loud sigh. "Why would anyone not want that?"

"EnRapture is amazing. One of man's greatest inventions. I helped it become what it is today, and I'm proud of that. You both had a part too. So, there's always a place for you within our nation."

Dad shook his head while Mom watched Dad. Then she stood up and said, "It'll never happen, Ashyr."

"Well, you should try EnRapture before you're so quick to judge." He faced Dad. "The freedom is all there. All you do is find someone on the registry and then you're able to do what you want, anytime, anywhere."

"It sounds like the downfall of mankind."

Ashyr chuckled. "You sound so removed from the world, Foster, like you have no idea what it's really about. The physiology of human beings has changed. We aren't what you are. You limit yourself. You put on blinders and live a life that doesn't exist anymore."

Dad stood, too, and put his hands on his hips. He looked angry again. "Then explain why you are here."

Ashyr moved away from them, close to an end table, and leaned against the wall. He looked back and forth between Mom and Dad. The whole room seemed to pause. At last, he said, "I want your help in finding a solution."

"Seriously?" Mom said. "Why are you here? Just say it."

"What are you looking for?" Dad asked calmly.

Ashyr shrugged. "I've been exploring ideas." Still leaning against the wall, Ashyr crossed his right leg over his left. "If we pulled Brody back, with all our great minds, we could figure out a necessary cure to get over a small hiccup."

"That's not going to happen." Mom gave Dad a look that I knew well, one that said her word was final.

"Well," Ashyr said. "I've been contemplating another idea. Perhaps ... maybe your daughter Leilani could come ..." I should have stayed in place to listen, but I was already bounding toward the house, while catching him say, "to help us out, to give a contribution—"

As I darted through their room, protests came from my parents below. I scrambled down the stairs, barely processing the words I had just heard, while overhearing Dad's, "Absolutely not!"

Out of breath, I ran through the kitchen to hear Mom, "And now, Ashyr, Foster and I ask you to leave. No. We demand you leave."

"But I want to go," I said, halting in the archway.

Dad's eyes grew huge. "Where did you come from? Upstairs?"

"Why aren't you at Kate's?" Mom asked.

I walked right past them to face Ashyr. "I want to go where you live."

A grin spread over his face. He looked past me at both of my parents.

"No!" Mom said directly behind me. But I

would not turn around.

I stayed focused on Ashyr, who sent me flashes of smiles while watching the scene that must have been unfolding behind me. Mom's feet retreated. Then came her tense whisper toward Dad. "What did she hear?"

I whirled around. "I heard enough to know that you both lied to me my entire life. That this isn't an island. Not a real island. But a little science experiment."

"Floating along in the clouds," Ashyr added.

I twisted back and Ashyr nodded at me.

I spun back to look at Dad. His mouth had fallen open.

"Really?" I whispered. My body felt like it was going to go into shock again. I just stared at my parents.

"Guess the cat's out of the bag," Ashyr said. "Too bad, mate."

"Get out." Mom stepped forward, almost passing me, to point at the door. "Ashyr, just get out!"

Dad grabbed Mom, pulling her back. "Hold on."

She spun around to face him. "Don't you see what he's doing?"

"Yes," Dad said quietly. "He's turning all of us against each other."

"Am I?" Ashyr folded his arms and leaned against the wall again.

I tried to keep my eyes on him, and to keep it together while everything around me had changed. "How long will we be gone?" I asked.

"For as long as you'd like," he said.

# TWENTY-SIX

## YAM

### Travel Log

July 3, 2050
6:01 p.m.

*I've been notified by an officer that Ashyr would like to speak with me. In fact, I hear noise at the door now. Got to go.*

Yam pulled off the stickers quickly and shoved them in the inner, lined pocket of his jacket. He stood up, clutched his hands together, and waited until the officer opened the door and stepped aside to reveal the infamous Ashyr standing before him.

Bright blond hair swirled out. "I have an EnRapture marathon party that I will be heading to shortly," Ashyr said. He wore shiny, tight black clothing, a fiery orange-patterned cape, and a mask around his eyes. "A pop-up one is being coordinated right now. I need it desperately. The sooner we can get it underway, the better. It's been one of those days for me, kid."

Yam just stood in the doorway, not quite sure what to do or how to respond.

"So, this," Ashyr pointed directly at Yam,

"wasn't exactly on my schedule. Every once in a great while, bad news slips in. Difficult news when you're in my position. And today has been a tough one. Ever have one of those days?" He waited as his light blue eyes looked directly at Yam.

Obediently, Yam nodded, waiting for the right chance to ask about Aria, or to clarify he had not touched her, or just to take a warning and get on his way.

Instead, Ashyr took a step back. "Walk with me, kid. I'm throwing this party to de-stress. To get my mind cleared up from a heavy secret I need to carry right now. What about you? You got any heavy secrets you're carrying?"

Yam followed Ashyr down the beige-lit halls. The walls were bare. Besides their footsteps, the swish of Ashyr's cape was the only sound.

Getting out of this mess was supposed to be easy. Aria was to clarify. He had not touched her. He had spoken with her, but that was all. A simple misunderstanding. And Yam would be no further problems for anyone.

"I think everyone has some secret they carry," Yam finally volunteered as he continued to walk alongside Ashyr, hoping that they were on their way to retrieve Aria.

Instead, Ashyr paused in the hallway. "Is yours heavy?"

He was suddenly face-to-face with Ashyr. What would Baba think of this? Yam gave him the smallest of nods.

Ashyr shifted back half a step then leaned against the wall. He clutched his hands together as he looked over Yam. "Where are you from?"

Yam's heart beat quickly. The plan was set. Follow Aria. She would talk them out of this. He was a terrible liar. "Um . . ." he tried to remember Aria's answer. "Third batch. Where's Aria?"

Ashyr shook his head. "The reported crime is you went off with her, alone, not for an exchange but for other reasons. I've already dealt with her. She told me no touch occurred between you two. She understands what is forbidden, that only an EnRapture touch is allowed, especially while in training, before you undergo your transformation. And I assume you understand as well."

Yam quickly nodded. "Is she still here?"

"No. She has left."

Yam gave another quick nod. He hoped he, too, would be leaving shortly.

"You won't see Aria like that again, understood?"

He nodded, stronger, more definite. According to her, they would get a warning, that's all.

But Ashyr raised an eyebrow at him. "Whose order are you?"

Yam drew in a breath, the word falling out slowly as he again channeled Aria's response. "Ashyr's."

An amused grin tugged at half his mouth. "Mine, huh?"

Yam nodded slowly.

"How come I don't recognize you?"

Yam searched quickly. Aria would have salvaged this better. Now, he was digging a hole for himself. This was why Yam hated lying.

"I get sick a lot." Yam tried again. Then he quickly threw in a truth from his childhood. "Anxiety attacks."

Ashyr peered at him. "Where's your training

registry?"

"At home."

"Home." Ashyr nodded his head and rubbed his hands together. A small grin emerged from his lips. Then, in a serious tone, he added, "You need to get this under control, your anxiety. Otherwise, it will hurt your exchanges terribly. You get it fixed, kid."

He nodded.

"No registry. At home," Ashyr said. "What's your name?"

"Ashyr!" A voice, deep at the onset but escalating in pitch, came from behind them. Footsteps accompanied the sound.

Yam turned to find a woman. Her body was slim, her hair in dark curls on her left side and green-dyed spikes on her right. Her eyebrows were thick black lines. "Look at you." Something odd was going on with her voice; it started low then ascended into an odd sound, almost like a note of a cat's meow. "Dressed for a party. A spontaneous one. But you need me?"

"Yes," Ashyr said, his hands slipping into the pockets of his shiny black blazer. "I do need you. Embrace the rareness of this request—"

"I had important work at the lab," she cut in. "New accessories in the works. Nothing you've seen before. It's absolute brilliance."

"It always is, coming from you, Serena."

"I've got one to share with you tonight." Then she nodded toward Yam. "Who's he?"

"He's coming with us tonight."

Yam felt the shock burn over his face.

"One of your guests?" She lifted a thick, black-lined eyebrow. She appeared less than impressed with Yam as a scowl formed around her mouth.

"Yes. Yes, indeed. He's one of my guests. We just need to stop by his *home* to retrieve his training registry."

Serena's head pulled back. An unfavorable expression crossed over her lips. "You don't have time for this. To babysit like this." She threw a nod at Yam like he was now a problem. "Besides, it's too premature for me to take this new prototype accessory to your party. So, we need to run a test right now. And I want you to see it."

"Officer Ell," Ashyr yelled up into a device on the wall. "We will get this all taken care of," he said to Serena. "I need a de-stress to transition. See, kid?" He turned to Yam. "You've got to learn how to manage that anxiety. Maybe, if you're extremely skilled, you can have someone of Serena's caliber seeking an experience from you someday."

"I need funding on this one," Serena cut in. "Entire new production line. It will completely change everything."

Ashyr chuckled. "In a good way?"

"When have I ever failed you? You always said we need to be at the forefront of all this. Supply them with the next big thing. Keep the shock value there. Otherwise, the people will get bored. We can never lose the entertainment here, the thrill for the people."

"I did say that." Ashyr grinned at her.

"Well, this will be expensive. Crazy expensive. But you will get it all back and then some. Because this is huge—it's my best work yet."

"Dear Serena, your accessories have never disappointed." Ashyr turned to the officer now behind them. "Here, Ell, take this . . . I still didn't catch your name, kid?"

As all eyes turned on him, Yam knew the lies were about to be done with anyway. "It's Yam."

Ashyr's eyebrows pierced together. "Yam, huh? Interesting name. Not a common one, is it?" Then he spoke in a low whisper only for Yam to hear. "A bit unusual name for *parents* to give their kid, am I right?"

Yam pulled back. His breathing felt more and more unsettled. Ashyr knew. Nothing Yam said now could get him out of this situation. He had been caught.

"Ashyr, we don't have time for this," Serena said. "I need to get back to the lab. Finish up my work for the day. And maybe make an appearance at your party. But, since you insisted I come, you need to try this prototype. It's going to blow your mind."

"Let's hope not. I need this mind." He laughed at her, but he kept staring at Yam.

"Are you listening to me?" Serena stepped forward, nearly pressing herself between them. "I have something that is going to take everything to a whole new level."

"Sure, sure." He nodded in her direction but kept his gaze glued on Yam. Then he said, "Go back with Ell." His hand waved toward the officer. "Before we kick off the party, we'll pick up your training registry. It's going to be quite the night for you, Yam."

# TWENTY-SEVEN

## LEILANI

I met the firmness in Dad's eyes. "Come, Leilani," he said, positioning himself between me and Ashyr. "We need to talk."

I stepped toward the back door and shifted my weight closer to Ashyr. "I want to do this, Dad."

"You don't even know what he's asking," Dad said faintly. "Just come with me. Let me explain."

"What will you explain?" I put my hands on my hips. "That my whole life is a lie? That the world I thought I knew is fake?" I turned to face Ashyr. "It's time for me to see what's real."

"It's hardly real," Mom said.

"Please, Leilani," Dad begged. "Let's not make a scene."

"A scene?" I opened the door but hung back. Words came fast now. "Dad, I think a scene would be learning that I've been trapped on a fake land for what, sixteen years of my life? A scene would be knowing I'm a freak of nature, one of your silly science fair projects. And what, Mom?" I pointed at her. "Is this a social science project for you too? What will a human being be like if they're raised in a bottle and told that this is the only place in existence—and that the rest of the world was destroyed in a nuclear warzone?"

"Well," Ashyr said. "They got half of it right. Pretty much, the eastern hemisphere isn't really considered as 'existing.'"

"Shut it, Ashyr." Mom said. "This matter is between our family."

"Oh, I love that phrase." Ashyr grinned. "See, I'm practically family, because, in our world, you share an exchange and you become family. And here, I've done that with both of you. So, carry on. It's all in good company here."

Dad shut his eyes. "Ashyr. This is wrong. You know that."

"Leilani," Mom's voiced cracked. She looked up at the ceiling. "Listen to your father. You don't even know what he wants, why he's asking you to go."

Dad looked at Ashyr, then back at Mom. I kept my hand on the door and watched all of them. I was confused. I didn't know enough about anything right then. The only thing that was clear was what I had thought was truth no longer was.

"Wait, everybody. Just wait," Dad said. "Leilani," he said my name softly, "go to your room, please."

"You're sixteen, almost seventeen." Ashyr looked over at the open door, then back at me with a shrug. "In our world, that's quite close to being an adult."

"Stop!" Mom spoke with the sound of terror. "Ashyr! Just stop."

I bit my lip then scanned each face in the room. Mom's face matched the sound of her voice. Dad looked afraid. And, Ashyr smiled at me. "I want to talk to him alone," I finally said.

Like a gentleman, Ashyr waved at the open

door. "After you, my dear."

"Stop!" Mom approached us. "Ashyr." She pointed back to the couch. "Go back and sit. And shut up!" Then she turned to me. "You want to talk to Ashyr, fine. We'll all talk together. All of us. But not right now. You don't get to talk. And you don't get to listen. I don't want you in this house. I don't care where you go. Go down to the beach. Yes, go down to the beach. Your father will come get you when we're ready."

"No." I folded my arms and stared at Mom. I was so done with her trying to control me. Telling me what to think. What my actions needed to be. I was glad Ashyr didn't obey her either. We just both stood there, his eyes moving back and forth between mine and Mom's, as if waiting for me to do something.

"Please," Dad appeared, reaching an arm to steer Ashyr away from the door. Then he stood close between Mom and me, forcing Ashyr out of our circle.

On his way to the couch, Ashyr paused. He snapped his fingers at me, gave a confident grin, and nodded. "We can accommodate their wishes. Go ahead." He waved his hand out past my parents. "Head on down to the beach. Since you're planning on joining me, I won't be going anywhere without you."

I looked from Ashyr, to Dad, to Mom, then back to Dad.

"I'm going," I finally said to him. "I'll be waiting for Ashyr at the beach." Then I walked out the door.

# TWENTY-EIGHT

## MARIANA

Once Leilani was out of sight, Mariana hastened to take control. "I want to talk to Foster, alone. So just sit," she ordered Ashyr. "Just sit. And don't touch anything. Don't think. Don't be! Just sit."

"She's a beautiful girl, Mariana," Ashyr said calmly as he resumed his spot on the sofa.

"Shut up!" Mariana roared. "Don't speak either. Foster! Upstairs."

Foster obeyed. Neither of them spoke as they weaved through the kitchen and up the stairs, slipping into their bedroom while the curtain blew through the opened window.

Foster shut the door while Mariana exploded. "What are we going to do?"

"I don't know," Foster said with a tense calmness.

"She can't go. She just can't."

"I know," he sounded too calm.

"And yet I can see it. I can see it in your eyes. That *science* look. Well, this is your daughter, and I don't give a damn about your science right now. We didn't create Ashyr's world. He did. And we deserve to have nothing to do with it."

Foster scratched at his neck.

"Stop, Foster!"

"I didn't say anything."

"You don't need to. You're not taking my baby."

Foster raised his hands as if in defense. "She's my baby too."

Suddenly, giant tears rolled down Mariana's face. She hadn't even known they'd surfaced until she swiped at one. Then she didn't even bother to fight the rest as they rolled down. "The difference is she'll listen to you. She likes you—she hates me."

With one arm, Foster reached for Mariana and pulled her into a hug. His fingers brushed away a tear. "Right now, it doesn't sound like she'll listen to either of us."

"That girl! Do we even know that she actually is down at the beach?"

As if taking in the validity of her question, Foster released her. He headed to the window, and from out on the roof, he retrieved the absent screen.

"I want to ground that girl. Take away all her privileges."

"She's down there." Foster nodded out the window toward the beach.

"How long was she there? Listening to us?"

"I have no idea."

"I didn't hear her. But, I . . ." the words were hard to say, "I don't always hear everything as clearly as . . ." She let the words fade away. Instead, she picked up new words. "Does she even know what Ashyr wants?"

"Do we even know what Ashyr wants?"

"Does it matter?"

"Yes. It does."

"No, it doesn't matter. She's not going."

He nodded while they both looked at each other, waiting, as if one of them could solve this problem.

"This is horrible. I hate it, Foster." She looked to the ceiling, batting her eyes to stop the tears. She wasn't a crier, but the more she thought of how strained her relationship was with Leilani, the more the moisture surfaced. "I just thought it would end. I thought she'd grow out of not liking me. That, in time, we'd find something to relate to, talk about, something, anything, like when she was a little girl. Or maybe, we'd hit that moment, you know, when we'd finally talk like . . ." The tears forced her to stop talking.

"Like the adult she's becoming." Foster finished with his own words.

"Don't."

He released a laugh, but it sounded broken.

She let him wrap his arms around her again. Her wet face pressed against his soft Hawaiian shirt. The tears soaked into the cloth. "I don't want to hear about choices," she said. "About her needing to experience things for herself. Or that maybe we protected her too much. You always said at some point we would need to face what was ahead. Whether that was returning to what was left of the world, or that the rest of humanity would eventually find us someday. That this couldn't last forever, being here with all of our children, and their families, and us believing we were entitled to this paradise forever. And I don't want to hear it. Or blame us, Foster. I don't want Ashyr to do what's he's doing to us. I just want him gone. And I want my baby to stay here." Tears kept rolling down her cheeks, and she still couldn't find the will to stop them.

When he spoke, his voice, too, sounded caught in emotion. "I don't want this to be happening either."

"But you're going to let it," she mumbled into the shirt.

"Do you think our one Justice of the Peace can handle Ashyr?"

Suddenly, Mariana laughed—a real, deep laugh. "Ashyr would corrupt Tony before he even made it off our property."

"He'd convince Tony to try one of his pills and then send Tony off on some synthetic experience— and all we'd have done is introduced the island to what we'd left behind."

"I hate Ashyr!"

"I know."

"Why? Why would he do this?"

"Because he's desperate to save what he created."

"Let's call our kids." Her crying had stopped. "Let's get all of them over here." She wiped away the remaining tears. "A human wall of all our family, where we could march Ashyr right off the island. Force him out into the lagoon. And leave him to drown out there."

Foster let go of her, leaving her to see a distant, deeply troubled look on his face. "You do that," he said softly. "Call them all. Tell them what's happening. But first, before you do that, I need to go talk to Ashyr."

"Why?" Her anger returned. "Nothing good has ever come from talking with him."

"I need to know some things."

Mariana shifted to stand in front of the door to

block his path. "It's a mistake."

Foster reached for her hand, and held it for a long time. "Even if it is, I need to. And I need to alone."

Before she could argue, he kissed her on the cheek then gingerly pulled her away from the door.

Before she fully registered what had happened, Mariana was staring at a closed bedroom door. Foster had just slipped out, leaving her alone so he could talk to Ashyr.

She yanked open the door—to find him there, standing in front of it, as if expecting her.

"Mariana. You're right." He offered her a smile full of love. "It's not about science. But this is about humans."

She held her breath, still processing the strange moment, trying to comprehend how it could seem like they were on the same page—only for him to slip out away from her.

"I need to know what we're up against," he continued. "And what's being asked of our daughter. But right now, Ashyr's feeding off our anger. Leilani's angry too. And we could lose her. We don't want that. This is extremely serious. You know that. I hate Ashyr too. But I need you to keep that anger inside this room."

"And then I can come with you?" she asked, perplexed. "To talk to him?"

"Right now, I need to do this alone. Just trust me, okay?"

# TWENTY-NINE

## FOSTER

When Foster returned to the living room, he found Ashyr sitting on the sofa staring again at the framed family picture. When the icy blue eyes met Foster's, a grin spread across Ashyr's face.

Foster couldn't tolerate looking at him. Instead, he reached for the photo and took it from Ashyr's hands. He held it tightly and worked on controlled breaths, on not releasing the roar that circled inside him. He headed to the end table and returned the frame to its proper place.

When he turned back, Ashyr had twisted ninety degrees to stay connected with him. "What have you done?" Foster finally asked. "Really, Ashyr! What have you done?"

The grin was gone. Instead, a stoic face met Foster. Followed by a series of nods. Ashyr spoke calmly, "I did what people wanted. I gave them a fair world. Where things are equal for all of us."

"How?" Foster rubbed his forehead, working overtime to keep his tone even. "How could it have gone this far? Really, Ashyr!" he repeated. "Did you stop and think about the consequences?" His reserved tone, which he'd laboriously worked to keep, broke. "There are always consequences, in everything. Either you are going to pay those consequences, or your children are! But you won't be able to escape the consequences of what you've done."

"I don't have children, remember. I'm not Foster. Or Mariana. I'm fair—that's what I am."

"Liar!" Foster slammed his hand on the nearby table, causing the framed photo to topple backward. "You're now the father of a nation! You took this invention and you fathered it in a way that you control and manipulate life for, what, thousands, Ashyr? Maybe more?" He looked down at the floor, unable to process the extent of what had been done. "One invention should never have led to—"

He stopped himself, pausing to breathe, to fill air into his lungs, to work at controlling this anger he told Mariana he had under control. When he lifted his head, he spoke slowly, working out each phrase as it came. "One thing about science, about inventions, once it's there—once the technology is there—you can't return to how things once were."

Moving past Ashyr, Foster slid back into the wicker seat and the words slowly repeated themselves. "There's no way to go back and restore what once was."

"Which is why I came to you." Ashyr repositioned himself on the couch, tugging on his suit jacket, folding his arms, then unfolding them, finally clutching his hands together in his lap. "They're dying." He leaned forward, his eyes set on Foster. "This next generation within the tribe—it's a form of liver cancer. Ironic, huh?" He tossed his head back as if he could lessen the impact of the words just shared. "The thing that almost did me in is now spreading through the youth of my people."

His voice broke, revealing emotion outside his control: a side of Ashyr Foster had never seen before.

"But it's a new strand." His voice regulated again. "Nothing we've ever dealt with before. And all of this, the concern, what we are up against, it's a relatively recent discovery. Just a small band of doctors and myself know about it."

"And the patients? Those who are impacted, I assume."

"Yes, of course." Ashyr leaned against the sofa. "We examined twelve teenagers who had noted symptoms. That's what started all this. And for each one, we found cells mutating, attacking the liver, toxins unable to leave the body.

"Yes, Foster," his voice suddenly sounded distant, his eyes no longer focused on Foster. "I am a father. That's how this began—it is how this works. Our mandate. Our laws. Every adult invests time and participates in caring for the young housed at our Children's Centers." His eyes shifted back. "Hours of contact with these children. Adults offering parental care, educational training, essential needs, whatever is required based on their skill sets and interests. The service hours are in trade for each adult's monthly supply of their EnRapture pills. It's worked beautifully. No one misses their dosages, everyone volunteers, each child benefits from the variety of love and knowledge that's showered over them in their upbringing.

"This next generation of youth, they were to be the most complete human organism evolving from a foundation of fairness. The best of the best, truly on the brink of coming of age within our society. And not only do I know these children—I love them. I am a father to each of them with my care and attention."

Foster remained quiet and observed Ashyr's movements: his shifting focus, the fluctuation of his tone, a tenseness emerging in his shoulders.

"We just finished the genetic testing on a large pool of our batches, from the newest infants to the original test-tube group, who are currently in the process of graduating into our society. What we found is every single tested individual shows the same mutation in their DNA."

"Are you seeing the same symptoms in all of them?" Foster's question was quiet, as if wanting Ashyr to stop revealing the rest of this reality.

"No. It's a dormant disease, hibernating inside until the symptoms appear. From what we've found so far, we believe there is a connection to the maturation hormones. As these children reach puberty, as more of these hormones release and the teen reaches a certain level of activity, the illness turns active. And once active, the body holds onto the toxins and refuses to release the bad inside them. It seems there are no visible symptoms until it's too late and the cancer has taken over."

Foster blinked three times, his mind trying to process the news, the details throwing him into a sense of overdrive to comprehend the meaning of it all. How could Em-Path have had any correlation to a rising population that would now suffer as his first wife Haizley had? "So, what are the next steps?" he said cautiously.

"Of course, the plan is to find a cure. To create a vaccine against this. Then we get the vaccine administered and remove the disease before more symptoms surface in our youth."

"Until then," Foster spoke firmly, "you stop the lab fertilization. And the sterilization, I would expect."

"It's more complicated than that. It's now part of the drug, the culture, the transformation, the full process." Ashyr shrugged. "We start out raising the youth to learn techniques to stimulate their mind for their own creations of euphoric magic. Throughout their training, while they provide donations, we train them with controlled low dosages of the drug and, bit by bit, give them access to EnRapture experiences until they're properly prepared to graduate into society. Then we complete the transition process, wrapping up the sterilization by letting them use the full-strength drug, and remove their born gender if they choose, as they graduate into society."

Foster grabbed his head. The crisis kept growing worse than he could comprehend.

"The sterilization started out as a partial side effect, now we view it as part of the procedure. We call it our trade-off. It's the way we regulate who's chosen to take part in our society." Ashyr produced a signature grin, as if back to self-indulging in his own perceived triumphs. "It all came together. The tribe. The industry. Our government. Our regulations. The entertainment. The experience. The people crave all of it."

Foster looked up at the ceiling and shook his head.

"It was working." Ashyr shrugged as Foster looked back at him. "As I said, what I just shared with you, this is a rather recent development. The tribe isn't aware of any concerns yet, and it needs to remain that way. Deviations would send a message of panic."

Foster looked across the room, out toward the window that faced the beach. He wanted to speak out, to lecture Ashyr, to say that humans were too broken to ever correctly control the advancements of science. Instead, he listened as Ashyr continued.

"After the big earthquake, we lost a lot. My greatest mentor, A.J. Stone, he died in that quake. A lot of people died. But we got through it because I tried to think like A.J. *What did the people need during this time?* That's how I figured out what to do. How I fixed things. It came down to building up the good and not throwing out what had great potential. Our tribe, our society, it is now working, Foster. But that earthquake, the wars, the calamities, all those things that destroyed our world . . . another change at this point would stir up hysteria.

"So, first, there has to be a corrective solution underway. EnRapture has always been a source of comfort for the people. We can't let it become a source of secondary fear that ripples through them instead."

Foster leaned back in his chair, processing more, placing it into his context of meaning. "Just so I'm clear, after the quake, after all that broke, EnRapture was used to replace fear."

"I believe it happened within the perfect timing. Circumstances allowed EnRapture to skyrocket. These were controlled experiences. And everyone wants to feel a form of control. And they did. Now, within our society, fear is only found in a simulated form through EnRapture experiences. We hone in on the thrill of fear, and use it to our advantage, in controlled environments. Then, when the exchange ends, the fear is placed in proper context, and it's gone again—there are no real dangers among us."

"Until this."

But Ashyr seemed to not hear him. "My people have come to expect safety, a fairness, a place of control. Not crisis. So, until we get this under control, they can't experience fear due to the unknowns."

"You could wipe out your entire tribe if you don't get a handle on this."

"Which is why I'm here, one step in working through a theory, which seems quite likely."

"What's the theory?"

"The problem is with our containers, where we have been growing the fetuses, incubating them, maturing them to infancy."

Foster leaned back. He folded his arms and shook his head. "Explain."

"Do you recall reading about the BPA theory, back in the early 2000s? Polycarbonate plastics leaking into our systems, disrupting hormones, and stirring up numerous health concerns? Well, either our cryopreservation method of storing the donations has contaminated the gametes and embryos, so right out of the gate, or the containers themselves that handle the gestation process of the organism is causing the contamination. Basically, it seems that through some equipment used, a toxic leak is happening early on and causing this DNA alteration."

Foster nodded, at last getting a clearer sense of the proposed solution. "So, you are looking to start over in how you preserve the gametes. Or at least, find a control group, one separate from your current preservation environment."

Ashyr nodded. "At the test level, we start over. New DNA. New everything. We get healthy fetuses, and we have lots of possibilities to work with to counter the broken DNA in our children."

Foster shut his eyes. He couldn't look at Ashyr. It was hard enough to process his words. The moment felt like an assertive wasp hovering in front of Foster's eyes. A swat would not resolve the issue. At this stage, any attempts to remove the issue would only result in a painful sting.

So, Foster stood up and walked to the other side of the room, back to the end table, and lifted the family photo from where he'd knocked it over, again restoring it to its rightful state of order. "We negotiate," he said calmly.

The wasp buzzed back. "Sure. Just like we've always done."

Foster kept his focus on the photo. It'd been taken less than a year ago. His thumb stroked over the image of his youngest daughter while he tried to silence the approaching sting. "Leilani stays here," he said.

"Well . . ." Ashyr gave off an unnerving laugh. "I'm not sure where's the negotiation in that, mate? From what it sounds like, she's already planning to go. Regardless of whether you and I work out our own agreed-upon conditions."

Foster studied the face of his daughter in the photo, seeing her clearly, Leilani—on the brink of adulthood. "She doesn't understand the request."

"So, we ask her. I have a hunch she'll still want to join me." The triumph in Ashyr's voice was unmistakable.

Foster pressed on while his eyes remained fixed on his daughter's carefree smile. "If she still wants to go, I go with her. And we, together, decide what happens next. Once I have a better chance to assess the situation."

When he finally turned back, a large grin covered Ashyr's face. "Anything else?"

Foster nodded. "We go see Brody first."

"Deal."

# THIRTY

## YAM

## Travel Log

July 3, 2050
6:39 p.m.

*I'm back in the cell and I need . . .*

He pulled off the device. His heart was racing, anxiety seeping in and around him, an attack underway just like those he'd had as a kid.

He struggled for air. He tried to control his breathing, but it was too late. There, in the corner of a cell, his body sweated. His breathing falling out in short gasps as if he had just been running from something.

Baba needed to know! But Yam had waited too long.

If he couldn't get himself under control, his call for help would be a call of panic.

While he sat crouched in the corner, with his jacket draped over his knees, he closed his eyes and tried to pause everything, to shut out all the noise and find a space of grounding.

Bit by bit, he used the breathing techniques from

his martial arts training to work around the fears which had taken over.

As he exhaled the last breath in his rotation, he reached inside the jacket pocket for the stickers again, but stopped. There was movement outside the door, then it swung open.

Officer Ell stood there.

"You're free to go, kid."

*What?* hung on Yam's lips, but he held it in. Instead, he smiled to hide the sense of surprise and relief.

"No pass to the party tonight. Ashyr just says to get on . . .home."

He nodded, quickly grabbing his jacket, then gave the room where he'd spent the last three hours a surveyed farewell.

"Thank you," he said as he walked out.

"But if Ashyr sees you here again," Ell said, "or hears you're stirring up trouble somewhere, you'll get a one-way ticket to Australia. Understood?"

With the strongest of nods, Yam hastened down the halls toward the exit sign. Hastily, he moved through the nearly empty streets. Some people rushed past toward an EnRapture club. A few yells called out into the night, people spreading the word that Ashyr was launching a spontaneous party.

In the darkness, Yam didn't know his way out. But the FID would guide him home. He secured the stickers. Before using the device's input mode for navigation, he mentally switched it to output mode. Then he worked through his thoughts, even and calm.

*Baba—I ran into a small incident out here. Nothing too critical. Or overly urgent. It's all been taken care of. It just put me back a few hours. I'll wake you when I get back. And you can track my progress. I will be loaded up and in-flight soon.*

Then he broke with a quick, *I love you, Baba.*

# PART TWO

# THIRTY-ONE
## LEILANI

From the porcelain coffee table, a vase of flowers stared at me. Full circles of white petals fanned around brown gumdrop-like centers, stirring a memory from a year ago: Violet and Grace walking toward the house after school, me trailing behind on the dusty island road, Violet explaining to Grace how some girl, in some romance she was reading, figured out whether the boy liked her or not by pulling flower petals out, one at a time, assigning each petal to: *He loves me, He loves me not.* On that day, I had to stifle laughter over Grace's questions. *"Did it really work? Did the petals tell her if he really liked her?"*

Such a memory felt like it had happened so long ago. Simple and silly compared to the confusion erupting in my mind over all that had occurred just within this one day.

I twisted against the couch onto my knees to look out the airship's lounge windows. My breath caught as I peered through the airship's mesh covering. Blue skies with hazy white clouds outlined the spectacular globe, the grand planet Earth below.

I struggled to breathe.

Each time I looked, I had to twist around and

tuck my elbows into my stomach, press my fist against my knees, and find a safety there within the sofa until I could calm my breathing.

And I had to sort through the lies.

I stared again at the vase and traced my eyes around the petals.

Around.

Around.

Around the brown flower head, until my rapid breathing subsided and my muscles loosened.

I reached for a single stem then slouched back into the sofa. Sunlight filtered through the window behind me.

I twirled the stem between my index finger and thumb and watched the bloom dance in front of me. Then I reached for one petal and plucked it free. "This is truth," I whispered and watched the petal float its way down to the coffee table.

The delicate whiteness lay against the marble tabletop until my eyes hurt. I shut them and pulled in another stabilizing breath. I thought back to hours ago, to when I first announced to Ashyr that I would come with him.

The joy on his face! The proud smile which offset Dad and Mom's scowls.

When I went down to the beach to wait for him, I realized how much the world around me had changed. The familiar and peaceful had turned unfamiliar and left me unsettled.

I gave the adults a while. Twenty minutes, a half hour, an hour, I don't know for sure. Everything now felt so disjointed. Eventually, I headed back up to the house and peered through a back window. Mom was again standing in the kitchen archway.

Everything about her looked tense: her eyes, her face, her body. Through the windowpane, she made eye contact with me.

Turning from the couch, Ashyr saw me too. He immediately stood, shifted his shiny blazer into place, and stepped past Dad toward our glass doors.

"Care to join us?" he said to Mom. But she only gave the smallest headshake then looked back toward the window to give me a final deep, disapproving scowl as if disowning me.

But it didn't matter.

After Ashyr joined me on the wooden deck, he hollered back toward the kitchen, "If you change your mind, Mariana, you can catch up with us down in your loading dock."

*Your loading dock*—my entire world was a façade. It was then I was ready to leave my parents behind.

Now, on the airship, I reached for another petal. My breath caught as I exhaled. "This is a lie."

The petal fell as I remembered my parents' loud voices over my choices. Their noise spilled from the house while Ashyr and I descended along the beach path.

"You will love my airship," he said as my parents' voices faded. "And while you're in my care, you'll be treated with the regality of a princess."

Another petal, another whisper. "This is truth." I leaned against the airship's sofa, feeling the soft fabric under my bare knees and the solid sway of the aircraft's movement.

For a moment, when it was just Ashyr and I on the path, I had felt uncomfortable. But he kept the conversation moving, talking about the wonders of his airship. Then he veered forty-five degrees off the sands, inland toward a small cluster of trees.

"A vehicle lighter than air with video displays to let me disappear . . . Twenty in the fleet . . . You get to ride Tear—our only raindrop shape in the group." His excitement had fed me, dissipating the awkwardness. Instead, he shared the adventures that awaited me. Flying in the air, leaving the island, visiting a new land, experiencing new opportunities. He spoke of concerts. Mass EnRapture rages. Marathon parties.

Then a twig snapped, breaking into our conversation. We turned to see Dad jogging to catch up. His breathing was rapid and jagged.

*This is a lie.* I ripped at another petal and let it cascade down with the rest.

That tree—Ashyr had approached it. His fist had leaned on the open bark as he asked Dad, "So how do we get in?"

Dad remained expressionless. Other than his tight breaths, the rise and fall of his chest, he made no sounds or movements for a long moment. Then he stepped toward the tree, lifted a low hanging palm leaf, and pressed his thumb into the bark.

Just like that—a portion of the bark folded up into the tree, revealing a four-foot entrance, and the movement ripped through my heart.

Dad disappeared into the tree. Then Ashyr.

And I stood alone in the woods, next to an imposter tree a quarter mile from my backyard.

Against the memory, I twirled the fragmented flower and watched the petal gaps as it circled. I wanted answers, clarity, truth. But the person I'd always sought answers from was the same person who had fed me a life of lies.

I pulled another petal. *This is truth.* Concert events, airship travels, life in Los Angeles. I planned to embrace whatever lay ahead.

Once I had decided to follow Dad and Ashyr through the fake tree, I descended a ladder to find an underground world of pipes, metal hallways, and concrete floors. It was then I made two critical observations. The first was that within that moment, Dad had killed the world I lived in. The second was that I would not allow him to kill the new life I was going to live. Now, in the airship's lounge, I renewed those commitments and ripped at another petal. *This is a lie.*

While I followed Dad and Ashyr through tunnels below our island home, I felt lost in the mechanical engineering forest before me: the beeping, the scales, the gauges, the heat so dry and different from the humidity above.

I tried to ignore the shift in my breathing, or the pit of sadness growing inside me. Instead, I moved, footstep after footstep, through the steel maze, in stride behind the adults until I gasped at the large tear-shaped ball that appeared.

Remembering that moment now, my fingers eagerly grabbed at a petal. *This is truth.* I looked around the airship's lounge. The little fridge, the two-seat bar area against the opposite wall, the vase of flowers in the center, still lit by the afternoon sun.

I was floating inside a tear-shaped flying contraption.

When we had first seen the airship, Dad had been mesmerized too. He had paused mid-step and whispered, "Remarkable."

For a few short beats, I stood next to him. Dad. Daughter. Looking at the colossal apparatus resting on its tripod legs before us.

It was Dad who walked forward first.

While he circled around the device, his head scanned upward. "What's it made of?"

I followed a fair distance behind him, peering at the miniature lights embedded in the faint colored, nylon-like fabric and listened to Ashyr explain it to Dad. " . . . a soft, flexible skin that covers the mainframe which is a hard carbon fiber honeycomb shell."

I bent down and tilted my head underneath the airship to spot the bottom which contained a glass-like floor.

"So, these LEDs make it so you can disappear?" Dad sounded so in awe.

"Yep." The two men's feet continued circling while I hunched down, moving through the tripod legs, to peek up into the glass bottom. "Covers the entire outer surface," Ashyr said. "Anything can be broadcasted. It's mainly used for marketing purposes, but I can use it to become invisible."

"Satellite images?"

"Yep. I send out the command, capture the surrounding images, the device broadcasts those images, and to the external viewer, I disappear."

"Incredible," Dad whispered.

A face blinked at me through the inside glass. "Ah!" I leaped back. My rear bumped onto the concrete floor. There, inside, a wide mouth smirked. Dark, round spectacle eyes stared at me.

My hand clutched at my heart. I scooted the few feet from under the airship to find Dad and Ashyr looking at me. "What was that?" I asked. "It's like a Cheshire cat in there."

Ashyr grinned and nodded. "You met Tear's pilot, huh?" With a fist, he lightly knocked against the structure. "Cap, we're ready to load."

I jumped to my feet while the tripod legs seemed to tighten and extend slightly. The circular glass bottom lowered, stopping one step below the ground.

"In the air, that's our observation deck," Ashyr said. "On land, it's our loading area." He waved his arm for me to proceed toward it as a round-faced man with large black spectacles plopped down into the loading area. I placed my hand back over my heart and looked at that same wide grin from moments earlier. He offered a tilt of his pirate-like captain's hat.

"You happy?" The captain tipped his chin toward Ashyr.

Ashyr and the captain shared some looks. Then Ashyr rubbed his chin slowly, "Getting there."

Something had him amused. I turned to catch the direction of his grin and I saw her too. She held the same glare she'd given me when I left her standing in the kitchen archway. "Ah," Ashyr said. "Coming with us, Mariana?"

Lies.

Lies.

Lies.

I pulled out six petals, two at a time, leaving the flower half plucked.

My breathing quickened. Inside the aircraft, with walls that separated us, I still had not escaped my mother's fury.

I looked up. The lounge had no ceiling. Instead, the outer honeycomb walls rose all the way up to form the airship's tear shape. Without a ceiling, I could still hear Mom's confrontational tone coming from the captain's station, speaking against Ashyr's light tones.

I didn't want her here. "Truth, truth, truth," I chanted under my breath, pulling out a fourth of the flower's petals. I drew in a breath and spun my body, so my knees rested against the sofa's softness. Again, I peered out the window.

As a child, I often would have reoccurring dreams of flying where I would flap my arms in bursts to get a small distance above the ground. It took a lot of effort in the dreams, but for just a short duration, I felt like an angel in my invincible moment.

Over time, I outgrew the dream and those flight feelings left me.

Until today.

When we had boarded the aircraft, Ashyr had directed the captain to lead Mom and Dad into the upper, circular region that ran the perimeter of the loading area. But he had me delay.

He spoke softly and quietly. "If you'd like a once in a lifetime experience, Leilani, stay right where you are. First, Cap will raise this loading area. Then once your dad gets us out of your island's belly and we have the all clear, Cap will lower you down in the observation deck, and you'll feel like you're flying." He gave me a kind lift of the chin, a fatherly look, leaving me with a smile, making me indeed feel for a moment like a princess.

Everything played out as Ashyr said it would, and when the observation deck lowered again,

I was surrounded by circular transparency. The invincibility of my childhood returned—the thrill of flying—the moment where anything felt possible.

I swam in a sea of open color. Against the soaring azure sky, I lifted my elbows back slightly, pressed my eyelids closed, and with an inner eye almost sensed the sun and wind kissing my face.

Less than an hour later, I now sat in the lounge, remembering the good of the moment followed by the bad. The discomfort caused me to grip the fragile flower stem tightly. With petals off balance, the flower sagged to one side. I lifted my head and stared out again into the blue sea sky.

While on the observation deck, my tranquility had been interrupted by Dad. I knew it was him from the smell of ocean, soap, and dirt. For most of my life, I had associated that scent with safety. Now, it left me with a resolve not to look at him.

"Leilani." Tenderness filled his voice. "Look down."

When I did, I gasped at the view—the curvature of a planet. Earth. Brilliant. Blue. Far below us, covered by a blanket of clouds. Whiteness swirled, cycled, and pulled me into a softness I'd never witnessed before.

Warmth filled me. A banquet of brilliance unfolded. The sun spotlighted the curve of the planet, a sparkling blue hue, a glowing aura of what I thought had always been my home.

"Amazing, isn't it?" he whispered.

Now, looking down again through the lounge's window, beyond the nylon film covering, I could still feel Earth's grandeur. It was slightly less intense than that initial moment, yet it still left me pulsing with eagerness.

But standing next to Dad on the observation deck crushed my recollection of childhood flying dreams. He knew all this existed. And he knew all the truths he'd kept from me.

To get away from him, I headed up the stairs away from the transparent cylinder I had been in.

"Did it make you sick?" Ashyr called out to me as I ventured toward the circular command station.

I nodded and glanced up at the computer monitors overhead which broadcasted the open sky. The movement enhanced my dizziness with my head spinning over my previous life and Dad's lies.

As if caught in a gag reflex, I pressed a hand to my mouth. Ashyr pointed down a small hallway. "There's a lounge area. Bags if you need them. Rest on the couch. Cupboards are labeled. Grab some crackers. That might help."

Mom stood nearby. "Do you want my—" But I shot her a look to stop her question.

In the quietness of the lounge, I continued to look out toward the wonder of planet Earth. While I watched my new home below, my fingers crumpled around the flower in the palm of my hand and I whispered, "Lies, lies. Truth, truth."

# THIRTY-TWO

## YAM

Yam fastened his hair into a snug bun at the crown of his head. His fingers massaged against the closely shaved portion of his scalp, right at the base of his neck and ears. While the afternoon sun's rays beat down on his face, a calming breath followed. His legs spread out into mountain pose on the grassy mound. He closed his eyes and rolled his neck from side to side. Next, his arms reached for the sky, then a torso lean to the left, where he paused to feel the pull of his stomach and back muscles, followed by a lean to the right.

When he arrived home, around two that morning, he had woken Baba briefly. The exchange had been quick, leaving Yam alone with his thoughts. From there, he wasn't able to unwind and fall asleep until after three.

Now he used his own choreographed ritual, a variation of Tai Chi, Aikido, and a little Capoeira, to transition away from yesterday's stress and refocus on the world he now was in.

"Yam!" Baba's voice broke over the island. "I need you." The broadcasting system invaded into his tranquil moment. "Out on the pier."

In slow motion, Yam pulled out of the stretch to

hear the husky voice again, "Sunny, you too. Both of you. Pronto. We may have an urgent issue here."

Without the meditation sequence complete, frustration stirred inside Yam's lungs. He worked through it with a huffed-out exhale. The rest of the day would be in a state of imbalance.

Most likely, it was some mechanical malfunction. Baba just needed Yam present, offering support and a little peace of mind while they fixed a minor deviation.

But calling for Mum too. That was unlike Baba.

With a steady jog, Yam headed down the gravel road, out into the clearing, toward the lake's beach. His father stood on the pier with a hand shading his eyes as he peered into the sky.

"Ah," he groused as soon as Yam approached. "Should have told you to stop at the house and grab some of them prism nocks. Maybe I can catch her in time."

From the bib of his Dickies overalls, he pulled out the antique 2001 Motorola phone, converted into his own inner island dispatch device. "Sunny. Sunny, stop where you are. I need you to turn back. Go to the house and round up as many of the high-powered binoculars as you can, as fast as you can."

The broadcasted command bounced round the transparent dome. From the pier's location, Yam disdained that hollow sound quality—audio waves intersecting, springing around, deflecting off each other, creating their own noisy chaos, reminding Yam they lived in an upside-down punch bowl.

Another indicator that if he'd completed his day's meditative sequence, the island's sound quality would have skimmed over him. He would have breathed in with an open heart, felt the gratitude, and noted the miracles they lived in.

But the 2 a.m. return from yesterday's supply run, followed by his long morning nap, had led to a delayed afternoon start to the day. And now, Baba was reliant on him. Which meant Yam had to keep it together so his father could keep himself leveled as well.

"What's up?" Yam's lean-poised posture brushed up against his father's lumberjack shoulder. Although the two shared little in genetic similarity, fortunately, Yam was tall like his father, and not like his five-foot-two mother.

Baba rubbed a large palm across his auburn-brown beard. When he shaved, he appeared more on the presentable side of sanity. Not that he was insane, more like a bit eccentric in his own passions and hobbies.

"Here." Mum came traipsing toward the pier. Flowing folds of her dandelion-colored dress wrapped wildly around her. Her yellow heels paused their gravel crunch as she fought to calm the fabric tornado. When she resumed her march, the three sets of binoculars, fastened around her neck, jostled against each other.

"Here," she said again, deflecting her dress away from herself as she headed up the pier. "I got the 12x one for you, dear." She bowed her head to lift the straps off her neck then handed the highest quality set to Baba. Another pair, she handed to Yam while offering him a tender little smile. She had given him a truly long hug when he had returned from the late run. Now her smile felt like an extension to that hug. Then she peered into the remaining pair of binoculars. "What are we looking for?" She scanned across the lake toward the mural backdrop of a façade mountain.

"No." Baba tenderly touched her shoulder then lifted her chin heavenward. "Up."

"Oh!" Her voice turned giddy. "Up." She craned her neck forward, lifting her magnified eyes. Then she gasped. "What is it?"

"I don't know," Baba's gruffness resurfaced. "Wally sent out the notification. I'm hoping between the three of us, we can figure it out."

Yam was the last to look into his pair. He searched the blueness, scanning hard until he could almost convince himself he could detect the glass-like shield which surrounded them.

Earlier yesterday morning, when he'd left for the supply run through the belly side of the island, he briefly headed upward to enjoy the outer view of their home. Always, in those moments, Yam marveled at the wonder. But while living inside, the dome's atmospheric separation was nearly untraceable from the true sky. Such seamlessness had always helped Yam, giving him a stabilizing peace, an awareness that they all were still part of a greater whole.

"Are you seeing it?" Baba grumbled again.

"I sure am," Mum cooed back.

"Yam? You?"

Still trying to fill his meditative void, Yam held his breath a little longer. He didn't want the lack of its completion to surface in his voice. "No. I don't see anything."

"Try . . ." Baba paused. "Uh . . . try your one

o'clock." Yam felt his father's sturdy hands turn his body slightly to the right. "For you, it might still be a little speck in the sky. But it's growing, I tell you. That speck—it's growing."

Back and forth, Yam shifted his binoculars, slowly, intentionally, until suddenly he spotted it, a blackness, small as a pinpoint, descending toward them.

A breath felt trapped between Yam's lungs. "What is it?"

"Here." His father nudged the more powerful eyewear toward him. "See if you can tell me."

Yam swapped, only for the breath to lodge deeper inside. His heart sprinted. "Baba! It almost looks like a man."

"Floating, right?" Baba's shoulder nudged against Yam's. "It looks like a man is floating down in our sky."

"Not in our sky, honey." Mum corrected. "Clearly, that thing, whatever it is, can't enter our little quadrant of sky."

"But he, or she, or it, or whatever it is—tell me it's not looking like it has every intention of coming right at us?"

"Well, it can't be too dangerous. It's just floating along, just that little small gnat of a thing."

"Here. These are a little better than those. Tell me what you see."

Yam kept his eyes on the falling figure while his parents switched out lenses. "Hmm," he heard Mum say." Then after a long pause, she gasped. "Brody! It's a man all right. And I think . . . oh my, I think it's Foster coming toward you."

Yam dropped the binoculars to squint up bare

eyed into the sky. Baba grabbed the higher-powered set from his hands and peered into them. "Can't be!"

After a few silent seconds, Baba handed the 12x device back to Yam. "What do you think? It's a man, all right. Would you recognize Foster? When was the last time you saw him? Is that him?"

Looking through them, Yam gave his eyes time to settle on the debated subject. Sure enough, although it'd been well over a year since Foster had been on-site at a drop-off, Yam thought he could make out the slightly moppy island hair, the beard, and beach attire.

"Pretty sure that's him," Yam said softly, only to feel the binoculars being pulled away again.

"What in heaven's name is Foster doing floating in the sky?" Baba said. "Toward us. Without a warning. Without a reason. Using some . . . what . . . some apparatus to float . . . how can he be breathing up there . . . this is all preposterous."

"Honey!" Mum drew in a breath. "Look. Look closer. Do you see it?"

She slipped between both Yam and Baba and pointed to a small section of sky that almost looked like a repaired page of a book, like a taped rip in the sky.

"What the—"

"Follow it down," she ordered.

Yam followed this rip, which offered the slightest variation in the sky, almost like a wave of heat was playing tricks on the mind, adding dimension before them. And then, he knew.

"It's Ashyr. His airship. He's digitally imaging the sky to make it look like he isn't there."

"Ashyr?" A silence trembled through Baba's lips, the gruffness missing from his tone.

"I've never seen his airships, only heard about them," Yam added.

"Why would Ashyr be coming here?"

"Because he missed us," Mum said so sweetly both Yam and Baba couldn't help but look at her. She shrugged at their looks. "Looks like he found us."

"How did he find us?" Baba's large arm suddenly wrapped around Yam's shoulder. "Did we underestimate the trouble you ran into down there?"

"Maybe." Yam's heart raced with a panic he wished to abolish.

"So, did he follow you?"

"Not that I know of. I dropped off Foster's delivery then headed straight back here."

Suddenly, Baba handed Mum his binoculars. "We don't let him in." Then he headed down the pier toward the house.

"Brody!" Mum's voice was sharp. "You can't not let him in."

"I sure as hell can keep him out. We're a tight dish and we're going to remain that way."

"You have to let Ashyr in."

He turned back. His grizzly hands wrapped around the steel handrails. "Sure don't." His chin lifted toward the sky. The speck of the floating man was now clearly visible to the naked eye. "Nothing good will come from letting Ashyr onto our land."

"Brody," her voice was soft, almost pleading. "Who do you see up there?" She pointed her finger to the sky but kept her eyes on Baba.

When he answered with silence, she continued.

"There's a reason Foster's visible for you to see him. He's sending you a message. If he wasn't, he wouldn't be there for you to see him. Foster isn't sneaking up on you. Foster's telling you clearly that he's coming. We don't know he's with Ashyr. But if he is, I trust Foster. And if he's with Ashyr, he has a very clear explanation why, and you owe it to your friend to find out that why."

Baba stared at her. Then he looked at Yam. Finally, his eyes looked up at the sky. For a very long time, he stared toward the ripped portion and the descending man.

At last, he looked again at Yam. "What do you think, son? What should we do?"

# THIRTY-THREE

## MARIANA

The airship swayed back and forth like a lullaby, calming and soothing, moving them along the tranquil sea. The vast lake of external placidness was a direct paradox to the internal chaos erupting inside Mariana.

Everything had turned inside out so fast.

She glanced toward the lit boardwalk that led down the short hallway to where Leilani rested. It was her right to check on Leilani, ensuring she was okay. But fear lodged deep inside Mariana, telling her that if she said or did anything wrong at this moment, she'd only drive her daughter further away.

She looked down into the center of the airship. Foster stood alone in the descended deck area. His elbows rested in opposite palms. Occasionally, he would lift a hand and his fingers would tangle around his beard. He stared out, his mind appearing lost in thoughts, worlds away from her right then.

So much of her wanted to join him, to ask what the plan was. How would he fix this?

Or they? How would they, as a team, regain control of their lives, their family, of all that was happening?

But again, fear kept her from moving anyplace

other than where she stood.

Near her, a large leather chair with a saddle seat and spindle armrests offered her a place to sit to observe the spectacular scene before her. But with Ashyr so near, she couldn't relax.

Past him, the captain sat in a half-arch station of computers. Large earphones covered his ears. His round spectacles angled down as he scrolled back and forth between monitors as if engaged in an eager hunt.

Her arms crossed over herself, squeezing her body into a hug. If she could not control anything outside of herself, she needed to at least control what was happening inside.

She closed her eyes and listened to the swaying of the ship. Her exhales felt trapped, caught against the lumps inside her throat, turning the simplest task of breathing into something difficult and laborious.

Again, she focused on the ship's movement, letting it work a soothing motion on her heart as if the craft offered to cradle her through the vast blue skies.

When she felt the slightest sense of composure, Mariana opened her eyes to find Ashyr looking at her.

"Ashyr," she said his name calmly.

He nodded, giving her a simple smile.

Since Foster seemed unable to deliver them out of this mess, perhaps it was Mariana who would save their family. Perchance, if she appeared pacified, less volatile, she could create her own negotiations with him.

She used her mothering firmness, which had worked numerous times with her older children especially during their teenage years. "Ashyr," she repeated his name, observing her sound of sanity, the monitored anger, the controlled tone. "You won't be able to win this."

"Win?" He let out a charismatic laugh, his eyes dancing in play at her. "Is that what you think this is? Some game between you and me?"

Her gaze locked on his light blue eyes. She felt a pull from him, calling her back to a time so awfully long ago. To a place she had no desire to revisit.

Quickly, she laid out the boundaries. "Foster will stop you."

Another vibrant chuckle issued from his grinning lips. "Ah, a game between Foster and me. Is that what you're wanting? A masculine ritual of honor to win the maiden's love. I would have done it for you." He tilted his head as if beckoning a reminiscent flirtation between them. "Gladly. Back then, if Foster would have been man enough to state his intentions with you." His head straightened, so did his shoulders. "Instead, he snuck around with you. Treating it all like it was some underground separate life he could live with you while we all slaved away at the lab."

"It wasn't like—" She cut herself off, the control in her voice clearly absent. True to Ashyr's nature, he'd distracted her, thrust her again toward a defenseless state of mind.

To counter, she churned over her words to justify her and Foster's actions.

Wasn't it just enough that they were in love? Couldn't Ashyr have just been okay with that? Couldn't he have accepted their love wasn't personal, no hit against him?

But it was different for Ashyr. She knew it then, and she was reminded of it now, just as he vocalized such words, "You were my family. And I loved you."

"It was a platonic love, Ashyr," she said, quietly.

He nodded at her. "It was love."

She turned away, unable to look at him. It had been a safe working friendship—until it wasn't. Until she had let feelings emerge.

Twenty years, and she'd still never shared the true events with Foster. That entangled situation, which she had caused. The confusion of Ashyr thinking a relationship could possibly unfold between them.

Before there had been Mariana and Foster, for one brief moment, she had considered Ashyr.

Then the big fallout over Em-Path happened. And everything turned so incredibly complicated.

"None of it matters anymore, Ashyr." She sought for control again in her voice, but it was gone. Broken, desperate justification oozed out. "The past is the past. And we're living in separate futures now."

Those blue eyes remained on her, taking her back. Even with all the changes he'd made to his exterior—his eyes, his body's stance, the angle from which he looked at her—it all triggered the past for Mariana.

"You meant everything to me," he said. "You. Foster. Brody. We had a good thing. All of us. And then you left."

She wouldn't listen to this. She would stop looking in those eyes. Twenty years, and she would not house the guilt he wanted her to carry.

Foster carried guilt. Not Mariana.

Instead, she looked overhead at a monitor. Against the blueness, in the left diagonal of the screen, a clouded mass surfaced with the smallest speck of land peeking out from within. A tumultuous reality around their current situation caught in her throat. "Brody won't—" She paused, regaining mastery over her tone. "He won't let you in."

"Really?" His question held enough hurt that she turned back to still see a glimpse of the pain in his eyes. "It's been a mighty long time since I've seen him. Almost as long as it's been since I last saw you and Foster." In contrast to his sadness, the right portion of his lips curled upward. "I'm looking forward to catching up with him too. A big reunion for all of us."

"It doesn't work that way." She spun around. The past was the past. And no matter what, she was not letting him take her daughter. "You snuck into our space, in through our back door. Our home. So, guess what? Foster's now leading you straight at the front door of Brody's dome. Directly on top of it. To be seen. Ringing the doorbell like an unwanted solicitor. You're not wanted, and you will be refused."

The left side of his lip rose to even out his smile. "I've missed that about you, Mariana. How you try to appear so confident, like you know how everything will turn out, like you are the author of your story—the author of all our stories. But then you bounce your curled knuckle against your lips, like a ritual, like now that your wishes have been spoken, you can make them fact. It's endearing. Something I love about you."

Mariana paused the knuckle bouncing against

her lip. Had she done this before? She'd never been aware of it.

The pale blue eyes gave a simple lift before he left her to peer over the captain's shoulders.

"Now that I know what to look for in the sky," his mouth tilted in the direction of Mariana, "I feel confident about this visit. And any other future visits. See?" He pointed at an overhead monitor. "I just need to look for that little entrance knob. Right there on top of your island's glass cake tray display. That little handle. Quite clear on the sonic radar."

As if on cue, a large monitor above them displayed the sonic readings, the vibrations bouncing off, revealing the shape of the dome as Ashyr had described: the knob followed by the curved covering with a tray-like bottom.

Memories filled Mariana: memories of Brody, Sunny, and the special time during which their families worked together to ensure the safety of both environments. All their efforts. Their worlds. Now with an invader at their door.

She clasped her hands behind her back, raised her small stature as tall as she could, then spoke with all the confidence she could find. "It still needs to open. Which Brody will not do for you."

As if on cue, the captain hollered out. "First pod entrance, opening."

And sure enough, on the monitor, the shape of a clam appeared, opening as if ready to eat them.

"Look at that." Ashyr winked at Mariana. "Like the Red Sea parting. What a welcome."

"Damn," Mariana said. She spotted Leilani out of the corner of her eye, heading toward them. Although she didn't need to hear the snicker from her daughter, she could sense it from the glowing triumph in her daughter's eyes.

"Foster won't allow this." Mariana twisted between Leilani and Ashyr, her voice cracking, a panic shattering inside her. "You can slip into this small trap, but that's all it is. Brody's trapping you. He'll never open the real entrance."

From the overhead monitor, the airship maintained a steady descent, floating softly, tenderly into the orb. Above them, a low hum sounded, followed by a hollow sound. Although the outside noise already revealed it, the sonic wave reading now showed the clam shutting around them, leaving them encapsulated in its center.

"Brody won't let you in," Mariana repeated. "Foster will stop you."

"I think . . ." Ashyr spoke smoothly, calmly, almost with a caring coo towards her. "Foster knows what he's doing." He extended his arms as if reaching for a hug, only to drop his hands toward the open floor below where Foster stood in full view to anyone watching from Brody's island.

The captain announced, "Second pod entrance, opening."

"Wonderful." Ashyr's hands interlaced behind his back mimicking her stance. A victorious smile creased his face while the tear-shaped airship descended. "It'll be good to see Brody."

# THIRTY-FOUR

## YAM

Once inside the island's atmosphere, a magical tear-shaped airship materialized. Foster stood in an encapsulated area which rose into the craft. Then three legs extended until the device landed gently on the lake's sandy bank.

Baba stomped powerfully across the pier. Yam gripped a steel railing to steady himself. Foster stepped out, heading straight to Baba. Mum followed Baba.

"What is this?" The fury in Baba's voice was clear.

Mum reached out and hugged Foster. "Welcome."

"Hello, Sunny," he said then nodded at Baba. "Walk with me. Ashyr surely will be catching up."

"So, you did bring him here." Baba led the way inland. "Unbelievable!"

Suddenly, Mum squealed, "Mariana." She ran as fast as her dress would allow, nearly entering the airship to greet her friend, hugging her near one of the craft's extended legs.

"I so didn't want to come," Mariana said, wiping at her eyes. "But it's good to see you. Really good to see you."

"Of course, it is," Mum said, wrapping an arm around her and leading her in the same direction as Baba and Foster.

But Yam hung back to study the airship, feeling great concern that yesterday's supply run, and his mistakes, had led to this. He worked at stabilizing his breathing as he headed off the ramp, following his parents only to hear light steps behind him. He spun back to catch a sight worth remembering.

Dark curls flowed around the girl's face, waving in a carefree rhythm with the lake's breeze. She was dressed in a teal tank top and cutoff jeans. Her shoulders were pulled back, her skin bronze and beautiful.

She smiled directly at him.

Leilani? It had to be.

All these years he'd heard about her, the other baby born nearly the same time as him. Both serving as the initial "motivators" for the Air Island life. Of course, others were motivators too, but not how Mum told the story. She always made it sound like everything had sparked into action because of the two babies, Leilani and Yam.

And now, a reunion at last.

Except a sudden shyness choked him as she said, "Hi" as she walked past. She followed the others up the small sandy path, but he couldn't muster out a reply in time. Such a fool.

He was acting as if he'd never seen a girl before. But it didn't help who this girl was. Growing up, Mum would create stories about Yam's future with this mysterious Leilani, as if they were meant to be. The stories only stopped because his sisters started teasing him as if he had some pretend girlfriend.

Now, with a quick exhale, he trailed behind her, watching the dark hair sway back and forth down her back.

Mum paused and turned around. "Leilani!" She extended her free arm, wrapping the girl into a linear hug: Leilani, Mum, Mariana. "Haven't seen you since you were two years old. You look just like your mom."

"Um, thanks," Leilani said.

"I'm Sunny." She let out a happy little laugh. "Since you surely wouldn't have remembered me." Yam caught up to the ladies just in time for Mum to nod her chin in his direction. "This is our son, Yam. You were toddler-play-buddies a long time ago."

He gave her the largest smile, a way too strong of overcompensating for his missed *hello*. When she offered a soft smile back, his cheeks burned.

"And that's Brody up ahead." Mum chatted away. "All the treasures you'll encounter as you enjoy our island are his pride and joys."

"Yam!" Baba turned back, his large beard lifting in the direction of the airship behind them. His stern eyes said enough. While Mum gabbed away, spilling happy introductory chatter with Mariana and Leilani, and Baba carried on his urgency with Foster, Yam needed to attend to the rest.

He turned back to see the exact need. The man emerging from the airship looked like a cross between a 1980s politician, seeking to wave to his constituents, and the old AI personality Max Headroom.

As Yam returned to the scene, his delayed *hi* for Leilani finally emerged as he met Ashyr.

"Huh!" Ashyr nodded at Yam with a large grin.

"So, we meet again, kid."

Yam opened his mouth, wanting to know how his mistakes had led Ashyr there, but no words came. Instead, Mum took the moment.

"Ashyr!" She had turned back, breaking away from the others. With open arms it was as if she beckoned Ashyr into a hug. "Welcome to our home."

He moved swiftly toward those arms, sharing the embrace while a soft smile painted across his face. Then he waved a hand across the spanning horizon. "You and Brody have done well."

"Oh, well, let's take you up to tour the place. You've seen nothing yet. Brody's got his fair share of gadgets here, which I'm sure you can imagine."

Ashyr shared a chuckle. "I'm sure he does."

With free arms, she waved the group forward. "We'll find some food for all of you. Make up some of my famous limeade. Let you see what Brody's been up to, his current pet projects."

Mum was good at this; she would tease Ashyr with just enough answers that he would have no clue to seek out more. Still, Yam struggled to compose himself over the shock. His breathing had turned jagged from those brief words with Ashyr. Plus, his heart refused to slow down after finally meeting Leilani.

He held his position on the bank. How he needed today's meditation.

Perhaps a short one could help. He took his chance, inhaling and exhaling rounds of breaths as he circled the airship. A hasty attempt, but enough to help calm him slightly before he followed the group toward the house.

# THIRTY-FIVE

## FOSTER

How far Ashyr had taken everything still seemed difficult to comprehend. With only short seconds to explain it to Brody, Foster's sentences didn't come quick. The only word that clearly prevailed was *danger,* and right as more words formed, *Ashyr is here because he created a path to extinction and needs our help*, the noise of the group surfaced.

Ashyr walked near Sunny while Leilani and Mariana stayed on opposite ends of the pack.

Leilani gave Sunny a short remark then veered away down a different path.

The rest continued up the gravel drive. Foster vaguely heard Brody and Sunny exchange directions, but his attention was on Leilani. She disappeared past the metallic gate and through an arch which appeared as if it had once belonged to some small town's fairground. The arch's lettering was long gone, replaced instead with some white hockey puck devices which flashed green and red lights across the top.

Under other circumstances, Foster would be intrigued, anxious for Brody to share the arch's purpose. But the weight of the day's events tanked such joy.

Instead, when Foster turned back, the group was disappearing through the house's front door, once again leaving him alone with Brody.

"Finish what you were saying." Brody hunched over, stepping closer to Foster.

But before Foster could pick up where he'd left off, Brody raised a silencing hand as Yam came up the way.

"There's a driver still in that thing," Yam said, pointing toward the lake.

Brody grunted. "Don't tell your mum. She'll ask him up. It's bad enough we've got Ashyr loose. If I had it my way, that thing would already be back in the air and out of here. I expect your support with that, Foster."

Foster nodded, capturing half of Brody's words while looking at a quick fix solution in front of him.

"Leilani," Foster said to Yam. "Um. Any chance you could help me—us—out?" He pointed toward the arch.

"Sure." Yam turned, looking along the path beyond it. "What do you need?"

"This is your home. Your island. Just help her. Show her around. Make sure she's smart and safe and okay. She's very angry at me right now."

"Sure. Sure."

"I really appreciate it."

Yam gave a quick steady nod. "No problem."

"She went that way." Foster kept pointing toward the arch, as if, at that moment, this was his greatest way to protect her.

When Yam looked back, Foster saw his willingness, a readiness on the boy's face as if happy to come to his aid. "Yeah. Got it." Then with a slight jog, Yam headed toward the arch. Foster felt an inner smile form over this potential lifeboat of hope.

"Nice." Brody's low voice spoke nearby. "Thanks for sending him along. Now, finish explaining why you brought Ashyr here. Just me and you. Let's get this cleaned up."

Foster nodded. "Can I trust your son?"

Brody offered one of his very rare smiles. "Absolutely."

Foster twisted back, giving the arch another glance. He needed to stop looking at it. What was done was done. At this point, what he thought he controlled was gone.

He faced Brody. "It may be imperative that I trust your son."

"I've placed my own life in his hands. You can trust him. Now spill. Why did you come—with Ashyr? Let's deal with it so we can get him out of here."

# THIRTY-SIX

## LEILANI

For my first adventure off the island, I really didn't want to be on a second island. The mere thought of being trapped in a fishbowl was more upsetting than helpful in my current situation.

Besides, I didn't particularly care for this island. There were fewer plants, and the place had a rundown feel, like a junkyard of scraps, metal, noises, and smells.

I needed some quiet time away from my parents and their island-making friends. So, I found a quiet clearing surrounded by a grove of large trees with big leaves. I tried to place the type of tree, but I'd only seen it in books before.

Tree stumps and a log bench formed a half-circle. I sat on a tree stump and looked at the trees wishing them to offer some ease over my disquieted sadness. Instead, I picked up a stick and started drawing circles in the sand. I kept wanting to ask Dad questions about the science behind all he had done, except I no longer had a relationship with him.

My stick slashed through the circles. I worked against my drawing until it all was just a scribbled-out mess. I made my pact: I would have nothing to do with my parents.

With my foot, I brushed through the sand making sure my drawing had been eliminated. When I stepped from Ashyr's airship, onto the real Earth, that would be my moment, my separate life from my parents and the confines of the island.

"Hey."

My hand flew to my chest. The voice startled me.

"Sorry," the voice continued. "I was trying *not* to scare you."

From my line of sight, I caught the boy who had been near the lake when we had landed. "Well, you did." I tried to cover myself with a renewed confidence in my tone.

"Mind if I sit here?"

I just shrugged. "It's your island."

"I hear it's been a rough day for you." He sat on a neighboring stump.

He was tall and thin, like me. Possibly taller than me. The pigment of his skin color was more yellowish than I'd seen before. His hair, although dark, had shades of auburn highlights. He wore it in a bun that twisted up near the crown of his head. The top half, anyway. The rest of his head was almost shaved.

He was different. Not like anyone from our island. And other than the muscles that protruded from beneath the sleeves of his t-shirt, and the outline of a tight chest under the fabric, I wanted to stop looking at him.

I just wanted alone time. Or to be back in the sky, traveling somewhere. But when his hazel eyes met mine, I noticed the specks of yellow and brown and those eyes did something to me.

They caused me to open my mouth and speak. "Yeah, it's been a rough day. I sort of believed my parents, like for my whole life." I let out a hasty laugh, only to cover it up with more words. "I kind of feel dumb right now. Like maybe I should have questioned them or something. I just never thought I needed to."

He watched me. "Yeah." His voice was soft. "They should have told you."

Then it hit me, another spear at my heart. "You knew. For how long? When did you know the truth?"

He reached back and pressed against the tree stump. He let out a long exhale like he was pondering my question. "I don't know. I guess I just always knew."

Such an isolating moment. First new person I meet, close to my age, who also has been caged up on an island, and he knew.

Quickly, I crunched the numbers of our island's residents. I was the first born *after the world ended*. At least, according to the stories they told me. Between my half-sister Caroline who was the last of the *before* group and then me, I was the divide. Surely, all the other *afters* were as clueless as I'd been?

"Have you been there?" I asked anxiously. "To Earth? Have you seen it?"

"Oh yeah. Lots of times." His bottom lip pulled over his top as if he wanted to take back his answer.

I picked up my stick and stabbed at the dirt. Poke after poke. Lie after lie. My family kept all this from me while *he* got to see Earth. He'd even experienced it *lots of times*. I took in a big breath. I let it out slowly to calm down. It wasn't *his* fault they'd lied to me.

"So, you like it?" I paused to look at him, meeting his golden eyes that had been watching me, which surprisingly made me smile. "I mean . . ." I aimed to recover from a slight warmth in my cheeks. "You've gone back. Lots of times, you said."

He shrugged. "It's okay." He now sounded all nonchalant, like the information he shared suddenly carried no real value. "My mum calls me Hermes. My baba calls me the Supply Boy for the Air Islands."

"Wow." I tried to lighten my tone. "Got a shirt for your company, Supply Boy?"

"If I get one, want to be my assistant?" He held a little smirk on his face like he was flirting with me.

"Why?" I aimed to sound cocky, to put him in his place. "Are you that busy?" Instead, I caught the rise in my tempo, like I was flirting back.

I leaned back against the log and tried to quickly, urgently, assess the situation. I wasn't quite sure what was happening here.

"Well . . ." He shrugged. His eyes offered a playful look. "I bet we could use your help. Baba's always putting together a shopping list for me. The best runs are when I'm out scavenging some resources left over from the destruction. You'd be surprised what he considers a treasure. And whenever I'm out, Mum wouldn't mind if I picked up some shoes for her. It's a small addiction she can't quite get a handle on."

I looked to my left, past the clearing, to a mountain of metal junk off in the distance. When I looked back, I tried to keep my smile in check.

"She's the one with the addiction, huh?"

"Oh, yeah!" His eyes lit up and he leaned forward. "Be sure to ask about her collection. She loves to show it. But make sure you have time on your hands. Like a couple hours. It takes *some time.*"

I couldn't stop the smile. In fact, it grew into laughter. "Sounds excessive."

He shrugged. "Not if you like shoes."

I looked at my feet. He did too. I wore my favorite pair of flip-flops. Within my seven-pair collection, they were all I needed. But maybe it'd be different once I got to the real world.

"Those, I picked up for her, but she didn't . . ." his voice trailed off.

I glanced from my shoes to him then back again. "She didn't what?"

He tried to shrug it off. "I'm the Supply Boy for our Air Islands."

Another realization hit me. I tugged at my tank top. "My clothes?"

He shrugged again. "You look great in it."

I looked from my teal cotton top to my cutoff shorts. My toes wiggled in my simple flip-flops. Then my face began to burn. My hand flew to warm cheeks as I thought about my bra and underwear.

# THIRTY-SEVEN

## ASHYR

The odd living space resembled a metallic workshop. Shades of iron, steel, and pewter surrounded Ashyr as he nodded absently along with Sunny's chatter. He sat on a large chair with legs made from gears. Behind his head, a loud clock, with hands made of unwound springs, ticked off the seconds. Ashyr could scarcely believe Brody's fate.

They could have worked side-by-side in changing the world. Instead, Brody chose to construct a flying scrapyard. Unbelievable.

Occasionally Sunny shared a warm smile with Ashyr, but the bulk of her attention was clearly focused on catching up with her bestie. Once she started sharing details with Mariana over a memory of her oldest daughter's first period, Ashyr cringed inside. Within his society menstrual cycles were part of a countdown, a retrieval process, a crossing the threshold to reach a better way of life—and a way to contribute to an entire society. But this was archaic, nomad, regressive talk.

"Poor girl," Sunny shot Ashyr another quick smile before turning back to Mariana. "It's been years since, but when it happened, we played the whole excited act. The 'she's growing up' card. But she cried like a baby. At the time, she asked if she could still play with dolls now that she was grown up."

Ashyr's hand wrapped around the sofa's aluminum-framed armrest. It was time for his reunion with Brody. "Excuse me," he said. "I have some details still to finalize with Foster."

Mariana shot him a chilled look while she spoke to Sunny. "Our children are still children."

"That's right." Sunny placed a hand on Mariana's, pulling her gaze back. "They will always be our babies. And I told my darling that she didn't need to grow up any sooner than she was ready."

Ashyr slipped out the front door to be greeted by a similar cold stare from Brody. "Quite a steampunk palace you got in there, kid," he said as he stepped off the porch.

Brody's eyebrows furrowed.

"Trying to catch Brody up," Foster said stiffly.

Brody grunted. "How's that all going, Ashyr? Your new generation?"

Foster rolled his eyes. "Yeah. So, I was just getting to the part about why you're here."

"Well," Ashyr looked down at his now filthy alligator loafers. His feet felt in desperate need of a soak, a soothing pedicure to recondition his skin after stepping onto Brody's island. When he looked up, he spotted a wrought iron bench. He approached it with a laugh. "Where did you pick this one up, Brody? Looks like something I sat on clear back when I met you, Foster. Some sturdy stuff just ages better in time. Kind of like all of us, right?"

He took a seat and brushed off their cold stares. "How's it going, Brody?" He looked over the large man he had once mentored in his youth. With his overgrown auburn hair and overalls, it was nearly impossible to believe Brody had ended up like this. Still, he pressed forward. "I've been dying to ask the question."

Brody shook his head. "Don't ask."

"Foster achieved his impossible, I achieved mine, what about you?"

Brody looked Ashyr directly in the eyes and firmly said, "Nope."

Although Ashyr felt the chill in the response, he chose to respond back with sincerity. "I'm sorry to hear that. The world could have truly benefited from what you wanted to give it."

"Just tell him why you're here," Foster said.

Ashyr raised a hand to pacify Foster's earnestness. "Well, first, can I just say, we all had a part to play in the development of Em-Path. Brody and I were introduced to it nearly at the same time, me a bit before him. So, had you both stayed with it, you all could have enjoyed the playing field, been part of something big. Instead, Em-Path flopped." He quickly raised his index finger to silence any potential comments. "But it set the stage for EnRapture. Em-Path led the way for EnRapture to thrive." He gave them both a grin, a willingness to share his achievement, but when neither seemed to respond to his kudos, he carried on.

"What was important to realize, because it didn't take long to see, is that the more experience one had with EnRapture, the more desirable, more sought-out as a partner they became. So, with a new and upcoming generation, when they were ready to have a go at EnRapture, they didn't have a fair shot.

Unless there was some proper training. The solution worked right alongside modernizing the family unit since it was outdated." He gave a quick shrug. "We implemented a new plan to support human growth and development from infant to adulthood where this new group could thrive within our society. We gave this new generation a fair beginning from the start."

With eyes fixed on Ashyr, Foster folded his arms and said, "Ashyr, our good buddy, found a way to destroy the entire human race."

Ashyr shook his head, then spread out, kicking his feet up onto the bench. It wasn't comfortable. The grated slots of metal pressed into his skin, stacking more discomfort as he stared at them.

One-on-one, Ashyr could handle Foster. But with Brody there, his intellect felt outnumbered. Still, he crossed his legs and let his alligator loafers dance back and forth as if he were listening to gleeful music. He let his words almost sing out as if he were unaffected by Foster's words. "We came across one issue. We have revolutionized our society, and you're harping on one small issue. Still, a somewhat," he shrugged, "speculative issue, too, mind you."

Foster turned to Brody, his tone a bit softer. "Did I mention he needs our help?"

"Of course he does. Just like he always has."

The alligator loafers stopped their swaying. A little fury pricked at his heart. Only Brody and Ashyr's own mother had a way of using words that pierced right through him. And Brody had done just that.

"After all we've been through." Hotness, deep within and unrestrained, shot out from Ashyr. "I invested a lot in you, Brody Daniels!"

A smile broke over Foster. He used the back of his palm to hide it. As if Ashyr coming unglued had given Foster some type of victory. As if the three of them couldn't just put their brains together and fix this one upset. Perhaps, even discover future efficiencies within Ashyr's brilliant society. If they would just see it—what he had accomplished while they'd been away. They weren't the only geniuses. He was too!

"He might want your son," Foster said, grinning directly at Ashyr. Then he stepped back to lean against an empty flagpole near the house.

"Stop." Ashyr threw his legs to the ground. He sat upright. "Enough, Foster! Brody, it's not like that at all."

"He wants to borrow," Foster said a bit softer. "No, not borrow." He scratched at his beard and cocked his head to one side. "What was the term? Ah, yes. He wants your son's donation."

Brody stepped forward. "Donation?" Gravel crunched beneath him.

Foster tilted toward Brody and, with a smirk, added, "A sperm donation."

"Foster!" Ashyr said.

"Assuming he's not already EnRapture infected. Ashyr, what age do you introduce each child to your process? When do you start them on your time-bomb experiment?"

"Stop!" Ashyr rose to his feet. "I don't have to take this." He threw his arms down. His bracelets clang together. "Foster, I don't need Brody's son. I can find a solution to that."

"Where?"

Ashyr shrugged. "Your island." He used his tone to remind Foster he had the upper hand. "I'm sure there is another willing person there, just like your daughter."

Brody's eyes grew huge. "You're letting Leilani be a part of his mess?"

"Yes." Ashyr stuck out his chest. "It's a simple mess." A smile of satisfaction surfaced. "And yes, she's practically begging me to be part of this solution."

"No!" Foster no longer leaned against the flagpole. Instead, his palms pressed together as if in an act of prayer. "She agreed to help you so she could do some traveling beyond our island."

"And has agreed to be a donor for us." Ashyr slipped his hands into the pockets of his slacks. 'Sweet girl' rested on his lips, but he held them in place as he watched Brody nod, taking in what Ashyr had just shared. The icing on the cake—Ashyr had just victoriously silenced them both.

Foster's head remained down; his eyes nearly shut. Brody's eyes still appeared huge, as if his brain had grown lost in system overload. So, Ashyr began to walk around Brody, listening to his own softer crunch of gravel underfoot as he sought to educate this small group. "A wonderful opportunity is here," he said. "Build the next generation, a clean DNA ready to take mankind to a new level."

Like a student, Brody raised his hand. "Count me out. Yam's not going."

Ashyr shrugged. "Not a problem." He'd never wanted the kid. He certainly didn't need him. "It's like the old days." Ashyr walked between Foster and Brody, making a loop around the wrought-iron bench. "Back then, sperm donors were a dime a dozen. The real worth was always the eggs. So," he shot Foster another victorious grin. "The hardest part is taken care of."

Suddenly, Foster's laughed. The sound, deep from his belly, caused Ashyr to stop his stride right in a bed of weeds. Hay-like bristles scratched against the exposed portion of his foot, right below the hem of his skin-tight tailored pant leg.

But the more Foster laughed, the less Ashyr felt he could move.

Instead, he watched his former friend wipe at his nose through the haunting laughs. The teaching moment was gone due to this disruptive student. "What?" he asked.

"Go ahead, Ashyr. Go pick up some pure DNA from the sperm banks walking around my island. Other than fourteen of them, all the males are related to Leilani. How's that for your pure next-generation DNA? Nothing like a little inbreeding to kick it off to a great start."

"Just like Adam and Eve's children." A trace of a smile emerged on Brody's lips. "Have to make it work where you can."

Foster appeared to be choking on a suppressed laugh. "Yep. Seven of them haven't hit puberty yet. So, as long as you aren't in any type of rush." Eyes watered with amusement. "As for the other seven," his voice softened, "one we think has Klinefelter syndrome. If that's the case, due to the extra X chromosome, he's likely sterile and unable to assist you. Oh, and the other boy has cystic fibrosis. Absolutely great kid. I'm no genetics scientist, so your call if you want to gamble with a hereditary disease. But, suppose you want to look elsewhere." Foster shrugged his shoulders. "Where does that leave you? Oh yes, Pedro, Pablo, Pax, Pancho, and Pepe, that band of cousins from the exceptional Saco families. Take just one of those boys with you, and Leilani will immediately bow out. In fact . . ." The laughter had started again. "I need something to write this down with. What do you have handy, Brody? I don't want Ashyr to forget this." But Brody remained frozen in place, so did Ashyr, as Foster chortled his words out. "For sure, oh my!" He wiped at his eyes. "Let me get you Pedro's address. First, you seemed able to find my house, so from there it's three roads down. Fifth palm tree, house on the right. Leilani adores Pedro so . . ." He couldn't finish his sentence. As if he was intoxicated, the silent laughter had taken over his speech.

All Ashyr could do was ignore the spectacle. Instead, he stepped out of the weed patch and directed himself toward Brody, standing closer to him than he had since his arrival. "What about you? Got any other boys hanging around this place?"

Brody's eyebrows raised, making Ashyr feel like he'd just asked if he were an alien.

He shook his head at both Brody and Foster. "It doesn't matter whether Leilani likes any of these kids. This isn't the dating game I'm running here. I just need a good kid, decent physique, clear head on his shoulders, and healthy. Not a hard request, mates."

Foster's shoulders softened. His finger wiped again at both eyes. He pulled in a loud breath then stated clearly, almost somberly, "Brody. Ashyr's right."

Brody's entire body twisted to face Foster who stood behind him. "What?" he said quite loudly.

"It needs to be Yam."

"What?" Brody's voice roared. Ashyr stepped back against the sound.

"He fits," Foster said solemnly.

Brody shook his head. He twisted around, creased his eyebrows, then gave Ashyr a grunt. He turned back and gave Foster another look. Then his boots stomped across the gravel toward a grotesque, old-fashioned arch with circular gadgets sticking out of places where the lettering once was. His mouth muttered undecipherable words.

Suddenly, Ashyr jumped at Foster's voice right beside him. "Yam's the right one for this.

# THIRTY-EIGHT

## YAM

He liked Leilani's eyes, the soft gray coloring against their dark outline. He especially liked it when those eyes looked at him. In those moments, he could forget how she got there.

But when she looked away, he remembered his mistakes. "So, when I pick up supplies, I try to get in and out." His words shifted, sounding apologetic in tone. "I don't sightsee while I'm running supplies. Just in and then out."

When she looked back at him, she was smiling, like she didn't associate the day's problems with him. "Well, I'm going there. With Ashyr."

"Say what?"

She avoided his eyes. "I'm going to help him with an experiment, a science experiment, something he needs help with."

"Huh." He let the vagueness hang there. He had no idea what to say. When she finally looked back, he raised his eyes at her. "Really?"

"Yeah." She nodded. Then she sat up tall. "I don't know if it's top secret or anything. Otherwise, I'd tell you."

He shrugged. Then he tried to mirror the matureness in her tone. "Have you been sworn to secrecy?"

"Well—"

He waved his finger quickly in the air toward her lips. "Well, if you're sworn to secrecy then don't say anything. I don't want to know." He lowered his hand. "I don't need to know. We all have our secrets." The words hung there. *Secrets*. Not telling Baba he was in trouble. Ashyr talking to him about secrets in the hallway. Yam trying to protect Baba. Leilani's parents keeping secrets from her. He didn't want to think about any of it anymore, so he focused again on connecting with her eyes. "So, you're going there, huh?"

She rubbed her lips as if words were buzzing inside her.

He was curious. But anything Ashyr related would leave a bad taste in Yam's mouth. And he didn't want a bad taste tied up with Leilani. Certain things are better left unknown. Yam would take that cue.

Which worked in his favor, because by not pressing her to talk, she instead shifted to the seat closest to him and then leaned in his direction. "So, tell me more. What's it like out there?"

"Out there?" he repeated her funny use of words.

"Earth." She answered as if he was the clueless one.

He scratched his neck, then tilted his head. Meanwhile, those soft gray eyes looked intently at him, leaving him with an inner smile.

"Tell me about it."

"What do you want to know?"

"Everything."

"The food is horrible," Yam said lightly, not that

he had tried much of it.

"What do they eat?"

"They'll tell you they don't have time for food. EnRapture experiences provide them with whatever *yum* factor they're seeking. So, for their nourishment, it's energy drinks, power shakes, meal wafers. Whatever they can eat fast and on the go."

She tilted her head as if trying to process what he'd shared.

"It's crazy," he finally said. "Absolutely crazy there."

Her face broke into a smile. "You excited to go back?" She had missed his warning.

He tried again with his tone. "After yesterday, I'm not sure if Baba will send me out again."

"Why?"

While he observed her, he debated over his answer. She seemed so happy and excited over something she knew nothing about. Finally, he opted not to dwell on the problems he'd stirred up. "We'll see." He shrugged. "If I'm there, while you are, I'll show you around, if you want?"

Her smile only grew. "Deal."

"Yam!" An overhead speaker crackled. Leilani jumped at the noise.

He stood and looked at the speaker. "Yeah, Baba."

"I need you now. We need to clean up after the pigs. ASAP!"

"On it," Yam responded, his breathing catching a bit over Baba's words. There was so much she did not understand.

He tried to recover as he turned again to face her. "I got to go." He lifted his hand in a slow reluctant wave.

"You take care of pigs on your island?"

He shared an amused smile. "No. It's my Baba's acronym. Stands for: People In Gears or Something. Silly, I know."

She looked perplexed. "I don't get it."

"I don't think anybody really does. It stands for my Baba's robots. They're everywhere. You aren't seeing them because he doesn't want Ashyr to see them. But they pretty much run this island. And that's a secret I'm not really supposed to share with you. So, don't share it with anyone, okay?"

"I want to see them."

"Not with Ashyr here." He wasn't quite sure why he had told her. The words had just come out. But they were still innocent enough.

"They sound interesting."

"They're amazing." More than showing her Ashyr's L.A., Yam truly wanted to show her Baba's PIGS and all they did around the island.

Such a dream began circulating in him, this idea of showing her around, sharing his world with her. He soaked in her smile until his cheeks began to burn.

Unsure of what else to say, he finally ended with, "Be sure not to leave here without saying bye to me."

"I won't."

He took a step backward but kept his eyes on her. "Promise."

"Sure." She nodded.

With that, he turned around and took off running toward the PIGS pen.

\* \* \*

After the last supply run, Yam appreciated the light and cheerfulness he suddenly felt. But his strong smile faded as he approached Baba.

"Let's do this quick." Baba thrust his thumb into the fingerprint scanner, and the side door opened.

Inside the barn, Yam whispered, "Do you want to deal with this right now? Wouldn't it be better after our guests leave?"

"One of those guests won't be leaving soon enough," Baba grumbled.

"I'm sorry." Yam frowned. The weight of Ashyr being here, spurred Yam into a further apology. "I didn't mean for him to . . ." but he didn't finish, because Baba wasn't listening. Rather, he was busy retrieving an oil can. Then he was already starting down a stall.

Besides, what had been shared through the FID. on the route home, as well as a few brief words when Yam arrived at 2 a.m., Baba appeared not interested in any further discussion about yesterday's disaster.

Until, from behind a stall, Yam heard Baba's distinct growl. "Mistakes happen."

Yam grabbed another oil can and entered the stall next to him. He didn't really wish to talk about it either. What could he say beyond what had already been said?

Baba had warned him. Yam had listened. Until he didn't. Until he did talk to a girl. And then, the teenagers in her group. And then a youth corrections officer. And then Ashyr.

And now Ashyr was here.

So, what more was there to say?

He focused on tending to Nellie. He confirmed that her hard drive was busy with the latest reboot then he lubricated her gears for mobile efficiency. After he finished her maintenance, he passed his dad heading to the next stall. Even though Yam didn't want to, he couldn't help himself. "I really messed up, didn't I?"

"No. Not yet. But you might be about to." Baba turned to Fredrico. Rusty springs coiled around the robot's head like a woman in curlers. Yam hung close to the stall, watching Baba fire up Fredrico's stomach, the updating process underway within the computerized system.

As Baba stood, Yam quickly said, "What I did, it wasn't on purpose. None of this was."

Baba moved to the next stall only to delay. "What's done is done. Ashyr's here now. At this point, it's what's about to happen that's our bigger issue. It won't be your fault. It'll be Ashyr's. Maybe even Foster's. I can't believe I'm saying that. Here I'd have given my favorite supercomputer for that man, and he's asking for more."

"What does he want?"

Baba's scowl broke. A harsh laugh came. "Oh, Ashyr will come to find you. Figured he can ask. Doesn't mean you'll say yes." A firm look followed. "You shouldn't say yes."

"What's he going to ask me?"

The question just hung there while Baba worked on Bentley's reboot. When he stood, he let out another harsh laugh. "To help save the world."

Then, he stepped around Yam. "Why would we help them?" he called out over the beeping updates from Nellie, Fredrico, and Bentley's stalls. "They brought this on themselves. It's their destruction."

"You mean Ashyr's world, right?"

Baba paused at the next stall. His hand slapped against his forehead. "Even my own son sees it as Ashyr's world. Ashyr sure thinks that. Well, he's been playing the great Creator enough with his world. But what do I always tell you? Go ahead, make choices, but then stand up and take the consequences when they come. That's what these Ashyrites need to do."

"Ashyrites?" Yam offered Baba a smile to lighten the mood.

"All his little followers. All his minions that follow him around with his lies, and his fancy promises of nothingness. All the people who now are in this mess. Of their own doing. As Foster said, the world was once a place of order, and bit by bit humans have been destroying that order. Ashyr has no concept of why that order was in place to begin with. Stupid human."

"You said he wants to talk to me?"

"Yeah. He wants to talk to you. Try to persuade you. I told him good luck. I was pretty smart when I was your age, but you're not just smart, you have some solid wisdom in that head too. That's a whole lot better than just being smart. Must have got it from your mum, certainly not me. I had to do a lot of stupid, cocky things before I figured out the best place, the safest place, for me is right here on this island."

Yam nodded as if Baba had just wrapped his arms around him, pulled him into a hug, and shared that what happened yesterday was okay, that Yam was forgiven.

"Brody One." Fredrico had wheeled out of his stall. "Where would you like me to go?"

"Back to sleep," Baba commanded. "Can't have you smarties roaming around while we got a snake on the loose."

"Snake!" Nellie shrieked. "I hate snakes."

"You don't even know what a snake is. Unless it's a plumbing snake." Baba called out at her.

"Seen one on the telly," she announced.

"Well, shut your eyes and watch your telly. Keep updating your intelligence while we wait until you all can get back to work."

"Will do, Brody One." Federico rolled back into place.

Before Baba could make it to the next stall, Yam met him at the entrance. "Whatever Ashyr's request is, it's clear you don't want me to do it, so I won't."

Baba folded his arms and heaved out a huff. "Any way I look at it, it's all wrong. All of it. Where's WatSiri?" He walked away with hunched shoulders. When he returned, he held the smallest PIGS of the lot in his hand.

"Let me take care of him." Yam reached for WatSiri.

"You can't fix it." Baba wasn't even looking at his outstretched hands. Instead, he spoke openly to the barn. "Foster wants us to fix it." He let out a scoff. "If we can, he says. He seems stuck, thinking we played our part in this horrid mess."

Baba huffed out another sigh. He set down WatSiri without conducting any maintenance before moving on to the final PIGS in the row. "We gave them the seed," he called out. His hands seemed to fiddle around the neck area of the latest addition,

AlexB, before finding the update switch. "Those idiots watered it, nurtured it, and let it hit fruition to feed their glutinous appetites. But we still gave them the seed."

"You taught me each person needs to carry the consequences of their choices," Yam said as he handed Baba the oiling can he'd left in WatSiri's stall.

"Exactly. I think Foster's got it wrong. We created a tool. It's not our responsibility how they use that tool."

"We don't control people," Yam said. "Each person chooses their own fate."

Baba heaved out a long breath of air like Yam had either said the right or the wrong thing. Yam wasn't sure. "Okay," Baba said. "You got to go find Ashyr. Avoid his stupid charm and just tell him no. That he can leave this island. Well, better yet, just tell him you're not interested! Then I'll tell him to get his brainless rump off our island."

# THIRTY-NINE

## YAM

**B**efore Yam reached the house, he spotted Ashyr sitting in front of their home on the iron bench, legs kicked up, face directed toward the lake, a corner of his airship visible behind one of Baba's granaries.

"I hear you want to talk to me," Yam said, watching as Ashyr turned those intense icy blue eyes to meet his.

"You don't make as much noise around here as your father. Didn't even hear you come up. But I guess that fits your job description, doesn't it? Still . . ." He swung his legs off the bench and stood to face Yam. "Nice of you to come find me. Very accommodating, you all are here."

"What did you want to ask me?" Yam folded his arms as if forming a shield that would protect him against Ashyr's enchanted words.

Ashyr shook his head and released a soft chuckle. "That's funny," he spoke as if more to himself than to Yam. "See. The easiest way to approach this would be to show you. Through EnRapture. Let you experience what I want you to understand." His eyebrows lifted, as did his grin. "You up for that? Let's give you an experience."

"Not on my land." A voice boomed from an overhead speaker attached to the house.

Startled, Ashyr spun around, scanning the skies for the camera. "Cute, Brody. Glad you got an eye on your kid." His finger pointed upward. "Just keep controlling his every move."

Silence responded.

Ashyr conducted another spin around, looking to the sky and all the neighboring structures. "Glad he's watching you, kid." Then he shrugged as if the surprise was simply an inconsequential defeat and resumed his seat on the bench. His eyes shifted to Yam. "Let's follow your father's wishes. And I'll explain the old-fashioned way." He patted the bench. "Here, sit. Man to man. Let's talk."

Yam looked toward the arch. On the pucks that lined the arch, a purple light glowed. It was WatSiri. One of the PIGS was now live on the island, hidden deep around them, carrying out Baba's commands. At the moment, as Yam sat as far away from Ashyr as he could, he felt a sense of safety. WatSiri providing the help, Baba watching over him.

The task was to say no to Ashyr. Easy enough. And the sooner the better.

Yam leaned his elbows onto his knees and clasped his hands together.

"Okay, kid . . ." Ashyr waited until Yam glanced at him. A scowl crossed Ashyr's face. "Let me give it to you straight. Last night, I was dealing with a heavy secret. Pretty sure I mentioned that to you." Yam looked away, but Ashyr kept right on talking. "Well, I can tell it to you now. We've got a problem, and you can offer a simple fix."

Yam didn't want to talk about last night. He

didn't want to remember any of the details or listen to Ashyr longer than he had to. The simplest plan was to say as little as possible, just let Ashyr get out what he needed to say and finish this up quick.

"Remember your friends in L.A.?"

Yam wouldn't call them friends, but his lips remained pressed together, determined not to slow down the conversation. He simply gave a nod.

"Well, yeah." Ashyr heaved out a sorrowful sigh. "Our Wyatt . . . based on the rumors I've heard circulating, pretty sure you've met the kid before."

"Maybe."

"Well, he's getting sick. Quite sick. Sicker every day. I mean, it's rough. Extremely rough."

"Not interested."

Ashyr pressed his hands over his heart. "You could see what this kid, and others, are facing if we had an EnRapture experience. But you—or your dad—don't want that. Fine." Ashyr rose for another brief circle. Again, he appeared to be looking for a hidden camera. "But not interested in hearing about a kid like you, fighting a tough fight." His eyes locked on Yam with a penetrating look. "That's harsh."

From the bench, Yam maintained the stare, looking up as Ashyr towered above. Finally, he shot back, "You want me to feel empathy."

Ashyr glared back as if a legitimate nerve had been pricked. "If you could see what this kid is facing, I don't know how you could not feel sympathy."

From the history Baba had shared, the original plan for Em-Path was to help with human connections and the understanding of others. But Ashyr had changed that. Yam pressed his lips together, again bracing himself, ready to protect himself against Ashyr.

"I just want to tell you about this kid." Ashyr rolled his shoulders back. "Show it, let you see it, experience it would be better, more real. But just trust me, what I'm about to tell you is sad. Very sad."

Ashyr lowered himself down onto the bench and gave Yam the softest, most sincere, look. A huge resemblance to all the propaganda EnRapture media Yam had seen displayed of Ashyr while in L.A.

"The kid's about the same age as you. Maybe a year off, maybe not even that much. He's a special kid. I mean, they're all special." Ashyr broke his focus from Yam. Instead, his eyes drifted in the direction of his airship, and his voice took on a distant tone. "But this one is really special. Went to visit him last week, and he told me about the pain in his back. Well, guess what? I know what that pain is. I know what it means. It doesn't get better. It doesn't go away. You don't just rest and find relief. You can't go to a doctor and they solve it. About the same age as you and he has a back pain that will grow, in depth, in intensity, in anguish. Because it's not his back, it's the organs pressing against a tumor. He's fighting a war. That tumor will win. And it will destroy him."

Still determined, Yam kept his lips tightly shut.

"It's putting pressure on his vertebrae and wreaking havoc in every part of his body. And as it grows, food will lose all taste. Life will lose all meaning. All he will be able to do is pass each day knowing how real the pain is. How it is always there. Now his sole companion. Unable to leave him until it takes him."

With a far-off stare Ashyr didn't say anything more, so Yam finally did. "Why are you telling me this?"

"Because we need to fix it," Ashyr said softly.

"Explain the *we*."

The cool blue eyes turned back. "It's time to start over."

Yam shifted, looking instead at the dirt than at Ashyr. From all he knew, from that which he'd heard, seen, and witnessed about this EnRapture icon, "starting over" didn't match. These were words of defeat, an acknowledgment that his society needed a reboot.

"You can help," Ashyr continued. "You can do something for this boy, and for thousands that are on track to experience his exact pain."

"Thousands?" Yam pressed his hands against his forehead.

"You can give him hope—all of them hope."

"Explain."

"Well, in two, quite powerful ways, you can help. For the future, you share a beautiful message that life will go on. And, even better, you offer hope through the possibility of stem cell surgery. Assuming we get enough healthy embryos from you and Leilani, we not only address the future, we actively work at saving the present too—we heal them."

Yam's breath caught. "What are you talking about?"

"We want you to donate your sperm."

Yam's fingertips pressed into the crown of his head. With crouched shoulders, he stared at Ashyr, trying to take it all in, now understanding why Baba had expressed so much fury.

"Can you do that? Take something from me and . . . and . . . fix what?"

"We need to do something." Ashyr stood then stretched his hands toward Yam. "We need to give these kids, like Aria, a chance to survive."

Yam didn't like how Ashyr said her name. Like he was using her as a draw to make Yam agree. Even so, it had a definite effect.

"Aria will get sick?"

"All of them—that's the current issue."

"So, what are you asking?" Yam needed this explained again. "You want my help to do a do-over. A new start and a solution?"

"It's a big maybe—the solution."

"Of what? I don't follow you."

Ashyr's gaze was back toward the airship. "It's a risk. All of it. Plenty of unknowns. Some giant hopes. But what's the alternative?"

"What if . . ." Yam still struggled to grasp what was being asked. "Leilani and I aren't able to give you enough of what you need?"

The question produced a pleased smile across Ashyr's face. "Yes. So, Leilani and you. You are our top aides in all this. And, so yes, we start with you two. We get what we need—some healthy embryos—and then we explore from there to gain a better sense of what our options are."

Yam took in a short breath then phrased his words firmly. "Sounds like a lot of maybes." He placed his hands on his hips, preparing himself to say the *no* Baba had instructed him to say.

"No matter what, I'm confident you would be

helping others. To what extent . . . well, we can only find out once we try. And," Ashyr paused, straightening his suit coat, pulling it down so it fit snuggly again around his chest, before speaking again, "that's what life is, filled with uncertainties."

"Start a new generation," Yam stated the requests clearly while the words ricocheted like obscenities in his head. "And, hopefully, save the current generation of teens."

"Yes."

"It's a tall order," Yam said dryly.

"It's just a request for your sperm," Ashyr said flatly.

"Used to save your science experiment—maybe."

"But maybe you know it's the right thing to do."

"Maybe," Yam said softly.

# FORTY

## YAM

As soon as he walked into the kitchen, Yam spotted the heavy grinder on the countertop. Fresh flour laced the counter and floors. His mum poked out behind the grinder, her apron soiled with oil and flour. From a bowl, she raised her hands where dough was entwined around her fingers like glue.

"Been a long time." Her voice revealed a hint of panic. "Mariana's headed off to find Foster. And, well, your baba said to leave all this alone." She tried to wave across the counter, but her hands were too attached to the bowl. "But how can I? He says no Nellie, no Bentley, no Fredrico until Ashyr's gone. But we can't just send our guests off without food, especially not without some of our bread. Your baba's signature wheat. Our special recipe. Plus, his heirloom jam. It'd just be rude." She lifted her hands again and when the bowl followed, she groaned. "Oh, it's been so long. This is hard work. I'm not sure I'm going to be able to pull this off." Her voice cracked slightly.

Yam pulled an apron off a peg and slid it over his neck. "Let's do it together." He fastened the strings behind him. "Like we did when I was a kid."

She laughed. "Start over. Start over with you, my partner. Before we had the PIGS. So . . .you make the bread, and I heat up the preserves."

"Exactly." He smiled as he worked with her to detach herself from the bowl. Then he discarded the glue dough and gave the bowl a strong rinse while listening to his mum bang around in the pot drawer.

The familiar sound from his childhood, with a sister or two helping out, stirred a smile in Yam. He missed those days. But, for now, just being near his mum felt good, like her presence alone offered a hug of comfort, safety, and love.

As he dumped a new measurement of the freshly ground flour into the bowl, he felt her shoulder bump into his. Her mouth whispered close to his ear, "So, what do you think of her?"

"Who?" He tried to act coy. But Mum had moved on scattering the fresh berries across a cutting board to remove their stems.

A half cup shy of the necessary flour, Yam cranked the grinder, pressing out more fresh flour. But as soon as he paused, he felt his other shoulder touched by hers. Again, she whispered in his ear. "She's nice, isn't she?"

Yam pressed his lips together, then heard the added, "It's not enough that she's so pretty. She needs to be nice too."

His cheeks began to burn. With his head down, he added the water-yeast combo to the flour-salt mixture and stirred vigorously. His mum's fingers danced across his back as she headed for the sugar container in the pantry. "She seems like a sweet girl." She called over her shoulder. "From what I've seen."

A huge exhale deflated Yam, sending flour across the counter space. When she passed him again, this time her hand paused firmly on his shoulder. "You got this," she whispered. Then, she slid onto a barstool across the counter from him.

"I don't know, Mum." He met her eyes. "It's weird. All of it's weird. Do you know why they're here?"

Suddenly, her eyes danced across the room and her lips stayed pressed together. Movements that revealed the answer.

"So, you know?"

"Mariana told me about Leilani. Your baba told me what's being asked of you. Uh, Ashyr has not told me." She tilted her head as if that act had lost him a bit of favor in her eyes. "But it sounds like he's talked with you now." She gave him a warm smile, then added, "You okay?"

Against his mum's caring eyes, he could only shake his head. "Like I said, it's all just weird." Another exhale plummeted out. "His society is weird. Ashyr's weird. I don't see why I'd want to be a part of fixing any of it. Why I would want to help him out? But I do want to help. I want to help Foster, and Leilani, and those teens, even if they're an odd bunch."

She nodded, her smile and eyes told him she was listening, offering her compassion, with no judgments.

"Baba doesn't want me to do it."

She gave a carefree shrug. "I'm sure your baba will support whatever you decide."

"I mean . . ." Yam paused and stared at the dough in his hands. His fist pounded into it, and he watched it mold under his weight. "I just met her. But she seems nice. And I don't blame her for being upset. Her parents lied to her."

"Only to protect her." The words came out so strong Yam immediately looked up.

"It doesn't matter," he said cautiously. "Truth is truth. They should have told her the truth."

She tilted her head and gave him her loving non-judgmental smile. "They tried to do what was best. To which you can relate, because you're always trying so hard to do what you see is best for us too."

He went back to pressing down on the dough. His eyes stayed fixed there while he cautiously added, "I'm glad you and Baba were honest with me."

"So, how soon do you need to decide?" she asked, swaying the conversation from further judgments. She always tended to do that, whenever remarks hinted at bias viewpoints toward another's way of life.

"I imagine soon. Especially, so we can get the PIGS back up and running and for life to be normal here again."

She cast her hand over the dirty counter between them. "We can get by without their help."

Yam gave her a warm smile. "Thanks."

He returned his focus to the dough. But seconds later, his mum asked, "What does Leilani say? About you coming?"

A shiver ran through Yam, his heart picked up tempo. He wanted to look at his mum but knew *truth was truth*, his eyes would reveal too much. "She doesn't know. At least when I talked to her, she didn't." He pressed open palms flat against the dough. It was malleable and ready.

"Maybe you should tell her," the whisper came across the counter. "Let you be the one. I think that would help her. She needs to trust someone right now. And it'd be better coming from you than her parents, and certainly this would be better coming from you than Ashyr. Oh, heavens!"

Yam shot his mum a glance. He couldn't hold back the smirk. His mum, who never said anything bad about anyone, ever, but leave it to Ashyr to find a way to break that streak.

"Go tell her." She lifted her head toward the outside door. "Looks like I can take the bread from here. I shouldn't mess it up too bad now." She gave him a thankful wink. Then, she rose from the stool and hurried over to his side to draw him into a hug. "I think it could help you both. Tell her you were offered this, and you are trying to decide what to do." She untied his apron strings, he lowered his head, and she removed it from around his neck.

"Thanks, Mum." He gave her one more quick hug. "You always seem to have the right answers."

A grin stayed on her face while her tone offered humility. "Sometimes. But your baba often does too."

He nodded. "I guess between the two of you, I'm in pretty good shape."

Her arm remained on his waist as she escorted him to the door. While she opened it, he paused in the frame. "Baba really doesn't want me to go."

"Yes." She nodded. "But I know your baba." She gave him another wink. "He will want you to make the choice. He respects you. And he wants you to do what you can stand behind."

Respectfully, he gave her a special Asian bow,

an act the two had exchanged ever since he was a young boy. Then he kissed the top of her head. "I'm lucky to have you both."

"I know," she said, then her hand pressed against his back, tenderly forcing him on his way. "Now go help her. I would think she really needs a friend she can trust right now."

# FORTY-ONE

## LEILANI

I stood between the airship and the pier. With folded arms, I looked out over the rippling water and felt the airship's shadow on my face.

"You lost?"

I turned around to see the same boy I'd talked to before approaching me. "Everybody's back at the house," he said. "Everyone except Ashyr."

I turned to the airship and let out a sigh. "Where'd he go?"

"He needed to rest," the boy said, then stopped next to me. "I think it's taken a lot out of him to be away from his EnRapture land for so long."

I bit my lip. I wanted Ashyr to come back to his airship and take me to that land he was missing.

I really wanted to get out of there. Too much time on my hands meant time to think. And it also meant I ran the risk of having to interact with my parents.

I wanted to be away from them and out of this—or any other fishbowl. I worked to contain the agitation by rubbing my palms against my thighs. "I didn't know we were going to be here so long."

He raised an eyebrow. "You don't seem to like it here."

I looked up at the sky. "Now that I know, it all just feels so claustrophobic. Like I'm a fly caught in a glass jar."

He shrugged. "Well, I can get you some wings and you can fly around here. Put on a show and I'll watch." Then he immediately stepped back. "Sorry," his voice was low and apologetic. "That sounded creepy."

I turned to look at him, holding back a smile. "Yes. It did."

"That was meant to be a joke." He still looked sheepish. "Just not a good one."

He had a cuteness about him, especially in his grin that sought my forgiveness. "What'd you say your name was?" I asked.

His face shifted. Like my question had offended him. "I don't remember," I said, sounding like the apologetic one now.

He did a super quick shake of his head, as if shrugging off any hurt from my question. "I don't know if I told you my name."

"Someone did." Oops. Wrong words again. The sadness in his eyes was back. Again, I tried to fix it. "I think your mom did. I've just had a lot to take in."

"It's Yam."

I stared back. I tried to put that name with his face, but it wasn't working.

"What?" he said. "And your name is Leilani. Nice to meet you?" He jokingly extended a hand, but I didn't take it.

"Your name really is Yam?"

"Yeah."

I lifted my eyebrows as if challenging him. I

tried again, "Like your mom's name really is Sunny. What's your real name?"

He shrugged. "That's what it is."

He seemed serious, but I still couldn't wrap my head around his name. "Short for . . ." I waited for him to finish my sentence, but he didn't take the bait.

"Yam," he said again.

"Okay," I finally conceded. I turned back to the water, not quite sure what to say next. He just stood alongside me, watching as little waves lapped at the pier and rolled back out into the lake.

But I couldn't let it rest. "So, if I were to ask your mom, what would she say your name is?"

Out of the corner of my eye, I saw him press his lips together. Then, I spotted his cheeks reddening. Caught him!

"Ha." I slapped my hands together.

He took a step back and cocked his head toward the house. "You going to go ask her?"

"Or . . ." I shrugged, facing him directly now. "You could just tell me."

"Yin-yueh-chih-yang."

I crossed my arms and let a finger tap against my lip. "Hm. You, shesh, chin, yang."

He rolled his eyes at my miserable attempt. "Something like that."

"So . . . how'd you get Yam?"

His fingers ran across the shaved part of his scalp. "My red hair."

I shook my head. "Your hair isn't red."

Comically, he lifted his eyes upward as if surprised by my statement.

"It's not," I declared with a short laugh.

"It is a little. More copper now, but it was red when I was younger."

I studied his hair until his eyes met mine. My heart sped up. Quickly, I asked again, "How did you get Yam from that?"

"It used to be Sweet Potato."

"Really?"

"Yep."

"Sweet Potato." I tried the name out.

I grinned, but he shook his head at me. "That was when I was like one, maybe two. I don't even remember it."

"Well, that's too bad, Sweet Potato." I winked at him.

"Stop," he said firmly.

But for some reason, that just made me laugh. "You'd rather I call you Yam?"

"That's my name."

"No, it's not. It's You-chin-chin-ee. Or something like that."

He pulled in a breath. It sounded sharp. "It's Yam. I've always just been Yam."

"Except when you were Sweet Potato." I couldn't help it. A smile was fighting against my lips.

He scowled at me. "Well, then . . ." His head motioned to the path behind him. "I'm going to head back."

"Sorry, Yam." But just by saying his name, I had to bite my lip to stop a bunch of laughter. I couldn't help it. My boredom had shifted to teasing this boy, but the remaining scowl told me he found no amusement in my words. I tried again with more sweetness. "Yam. Your name is Yam."

"Thanks, Leilani," he said. Then he shot the

airship another glance before looking again at me. He didn't smile while I smiled at him. Instead, his voice sounded stoic, "See you around."

He walked away, and I started to feel bad. Which made me feel sad inside. Quietly, I called after him, "See you around."

# FORTY-TWO

## MARIANA

When Sunny resurfaced through the front door, Mariana felt a wave of relief. For the last half hour, after demanding some answers from Foster, the two sat across from each other like expectant parents, waiting to see what unfolded with Yam's choices.

"Well, with Ashyr taking a rest, looks like you all aren't leaving anytime soon." Sunny smiled at Mariana. "Which gives us some time to catch up."

Mariana stood, extremely grateful to break away from the hideous wait. Anger still brewed inside her: at Foster, at the mess they were in, and that neither one of them seemed able to stop Ashyr from taking their daughter. "Let's go look at your shoe collection," she said to Sunny.

Earlier, they'd been headed that way when they were intercepted by a red-face Brody. He had needed to share with Sunny Ashyr's plan regarding Yam. Whether the news had ruffled Sunny, as it certainly had Mariana, Sunny made no expression of it. Instead, she now clapped her hands together. "Oh, yes, let's go look at shoes." But then she shook her head. "Drats. No PIGS." A few inaudible remarks fell under her breath before she tugged on Mariana's arm. "Can I ask for your help instead?"

"Please." Relief couldn't come fast enough. Any type of work would take Mariana's mind off the waiting; otherwise, they were just passing time until a ticking bomb went off.

Sunny led her into the kitchen and waved her hand around a counter of flour dust, fruit stains, and dirty dishes. "We've got a meal in the works, and honestly, I'm no cook these days." She let out a happy laugh. "I need help finishing this up."

"I'd love to help."

However, as soon as Mariana had cleaned up the flour spread across the island counter, Brody appeared. "I got WatSiri surveying the yurt tent. Any sign of movement from Ashyr and you stuff Nellie in the broom closet. Got it?"

Sunny clasped her hands together and pulled Brody into a strong kiss. "I love you!" She slapped his bum. Brody's standard scowl twisted into a smile.

"I love you too!" He pulled her into another kiss.

Mariana stepped away, strategically placing her back toward them.

Not until she heard the door shut did she turn back to see an out of breath Sunny. "Dinner is saved."

"Wow!" Mariana felt herself blushing for Sunny. "You two seem to keep your fire alive. Quite in love . . ." and then, Mariana couldn't help herself from stating the obvious, "even though he clearly runs this place. Doesn't that bother you?"

Sunny let out a playful laugh while she kept her hand over her heart as if now part of her was missing since Brody had stepped away. "Me and the girls moving to Australia hasn't been all bad."

"What?" Mariana stared at her. "I didn't know

this. You didn't tell me. You moved? With the girls?"

"Well . . ." Sunny shrugged. "Just with all our other catching up . . ." She rolled her eyes. "Ashyr's presence kind of dominated other conversations."

"Well, I just assumed the girls were . . ." Mariana paused, she had been so consumed, just assuming they were off playing somewhere. "Where are the girls?"

"With my sister. And I'm usually there too. But I make sure to return here often. It's that whole love affair with my hunky husband that keeps bringing me back." She grinned at the door he'd left from. A content sigh slipped out. She turned to Mariana and gave her a mischievous grin. "That and my shoes."

Sunny grabbed the rag in Mariana's hand and tossed it into the sink. "Come on. Let's go see them."

In a bit of a daze, Mariana followed her toward a cellar door which Sunny flung open then descended.

"Really?" Mariana said as she climbed down into the dark. "This is where you store them?"

"Oh, heaven's no!" Sunny paused to shut the cellar door behind them. For a moment, they stood in darkness. Then, as Sunny stepped forward, automated overhead lights triggered, displaying the maze and inner workings of the island. "I just like to use this short cut to get around."

After passing two rows, Sunny turned down a long hallway which allowed them to walk side by side. "Is it really working for you? And Brody?" Mariana asked. "Living such separate lives?"

Sunny's face scrunched as if she'd been asked the oddest question. "Every couple has to find what works for them." She wrapped her arm around Mariana's as they continued down the hall. "As your island's family therapist, you know this. One size doesn't fit all. We each have our own quirks, preferences, oddities. I just choose to love Brody, with his oddities and all. And he loves me with mine. So, now, you get to see my shoes!" She pointed to a ladder against the wall. "Ready?"

"After you." Mariana followed her up the ladder until her head poked up into a gigantic room. The shoes looked like fans seated inside a stadium. As the two women stood there, it was as if they were the athletes on the field, scanning the crowd.

Boots, loafers, patent leather, floral prints, sandals, booties, stilettos, flats, colors of the rainbow, gray sections, brown sections, red sections, an everything section. Mariana felt dizzy as she tried to follow the overhead lights spotlighted down and moving in a circular fashion, allowing different pairs to have their short moment of fame.

"Whoa!"

"Amazing, huh?" Sunny clapped her hands together.

"Sunny! You have two feet. A left foot and a right foot. And you have three hundred and sixty-five days in a year. If you were to wear a new pair every day, how long would it take you to wear everything in here?"

Sunny let out a delighted laugh as if she completely missed Mariana's hint at excessive.

"It's not about wearing all of them, it's about having choices."

"But are there ever too many choices? How do you keep track of them?"

She laughed again. "Brody made me my very own tracking system. It's one of his PIGS. She's all mine and her entire purpose is to catalog, organize, polish, and prepare them. I just ask Zappto for the ones I want for my next excursion to Australia and she gets me all packed up."

"How many shoes do you take at a time?" Mariana struggled to close her mouth over the abundance in front of her.

"Oh, about twenty for each trip."

"How can you pack that many? How do they all fit in the drone?"

"Oh." Sunny waved her hand at Mariana like it was an insignificant issue. "Brody built a drone just for my shoes."

"Unbelievable!"

Sunny shrugged. "They make me happy. I know most people can't understand, but my shoe collection is my generator for a reserve of smiles."

"Well . . ." Mariana shrugged. "You seem to have a lot of smiles, so it must work for you."

"Plus, it keeps me and Yam close. Since I'm now in Australia for a fair amount of the time, I don't get to see him nearly enough. But he's my buyer. And we have fun."

"Yam stays here with Brody?" Mariana still couldn't process her friend's life.

"Yam helps both of us. We couldn't do what we do without him."

"Are you sure you're happy with all this? You living in Australia, your family separated?"

"Here . . ." Sunny put an arm around her. "Let's go talk in my dressing room."

Sunny pushed a button that opened a hidden door in the stadium and waved Mariana toward it. With each step, Mariana saw other shoes she hadn't noticed in the crowd. Fuzzy slippers, a section of sneakers, a row of clogs. "Wait." Mariana paused. "Those are cute!" She pointed to a pale baby blue pair with a soft flower design impressed upon the leather.

Sunny grabbed them. "I absolutely agree. Let's go try them on you."

"Oh, no, no, no." Mariana pulled back.

Sunny reached for her arm and led her into the next room. "I remember from our pregnant days together you wear the same size as me."

"I couldn't." But before Mariana could protest further, she stood in awe over a large area that looked like it once had been part of a hotel lobby. A tear-drop diamond chandelier hung overhead. Rich purple velvet plush benches surrounded them. Gold embellished ornamental mirrors hung on the walls, some full length, some small and tilted out near the floor.

"I could live here," Mariana said while Sunny pointed to a nearby bench. "I wish Leilani could see this. She wouldn't believe it."

"Well . . ." Sunny said softly, then kneeled on the floor to remove Mariana's sandals. "I would like to help her find some shoes for her upcoming excursion."

Mariana shifted her feet back before Sunny could slip on the pretty clogs. "You don't support her going, do you? Or Yam for that matter?"

Tenderly, Sunny lifted a foot forward and slid the shoe on. A comfortable fit and despite herself, Mariana smiled.

"Other foot," Sunny commanded. "And to your question," she slipped on the other shoe, "all I have to say is that all three of you—you, Foster, Brody—you all seem to fear Ashyr too much. You give him power through your fear. Try loving him."

"Hah!" Mariana's face split between the smile induced by the adorable shoes and a sarcastic laugh. "There is no way I could *ever* do that."

"Fine." Sunny stood. "Don't love him. But don't hate him. Tolerate him. But don't give him so much power through your hatred. Now walk around. See if they will work. They look adorable on you."

Walking around, feeling the happiness of her feet, which still worked its way up to her face, Mariana tried to protest. "They are lovely, and I can't take these, Sunny. They are yours."

"And, clearly," she turned back to the room they'd come from and waved a hand at it, "I'm going to desperately miss those."

"Temporarily borrow," Mariana countered against Sunny's bright, encouraging grin. "You know I have no need for them."

"A woman always has room for shoes that make her smile. And to your earlier question, life sometimes gets overly complicated. And then, we just do the best we can do. Now, I need to find Leilani. See if, perhaps, we can help put a much-needed smile on her face too."

# FORTY-THREE

## YAM

Yam returned to the clearing where he had first talked with Leilani. He strummed his guitar and let the music soften his mood as he worked to clear his mind.

*Leilani.* She was beautiful. She seemed smart. But there was also something harsh in her. And Ashyr wanted Yam to create a new generation with her.

According to Ashyr, the request was simple, an impersonal way to create life—the fair way.

The concept still rang odd to Yam. Not even quite seventeen, fathering a child with someone he may not like.

He didn't need to like her. That wasn't a requirement for Ashyr's experiment.

But it mattered to Yam. He didn't even know Leilani—so how was he to know if he liked her?

As his fingers hit the chorus of his favorite song, he hummed for awhile. His thoughts took over. A stranger, and science, to blend DNA into a baby, for Ashyr. Could he do that?

It'd be more than one baby. It'd be babies and fetuses, and whatever they could use to fix something they had broken.

What science had broken.

And Yam maybe could help repair it.

Those who were hurting were innocent. Casualties of Ashyr's mistakes. So, who should pay the price to see if they could make things right?

All Yam's life, Baba had said *Each person chooses their own fate*. But did they? He also had said Foster was the one person he could trust.

But Leilani had said Foster had broken her trust.

And now Baba talked like Foster agreed with Ashyr, whereas Baba no longer agreed with Foster. Agreement and trust weren't the same things. But as a measuring stick, Yam needed something to go on, something he could hold to while making his decision.

He tried to release these thoughts. To forget about the visitors. Or the dream he'd momentarily had of someday kissing Leilani.

Instead, he let the chords pull him in. He returned to humming, which eventually became singing. A sense of order restored his soul.

Three songs in, the tall bushes moved and Leilani emerged.

He stopped mid-strum, catching his breath to stifle a laugh.

She was dressed in a flowing sundress, one he recognized as having picked up years before for his mother on a supply run. It fit Leilani better, like it'd been made for her, the seafoam blue contrasting delicately against her dark hair which fell around her bare shoulders. She wore gold sandals—his mother's too—as if his mother was sending him a message.

"You know there is a trail, just a little to your

right," Yam said, his fingers hovering over the guitar strings. "You didn't need to trailblaze through the bush." He wanted to add, *especially dressed like that*, but he opted not to comment on her attire.

"Been talking to your mom." She didn't look at him directly but did sit on a diagonal tree stump.

Yam nodded and kept strumming. At least the obvious had been stated.

"She told me more about your name."

He wanted to look at her again, but he refused to. Instead, he studied his guitar, picking up where he'd left off in the strumming. "Leave my name alone," he said, a bit gruffly over his own noise.

"She explained how to spell it. Yin at the front. Yang at the end. And Y-u-e-z-h-i in the middle, but it's pronounced Yueh-chih. She said it's a name of a people, like a real old group, nomads from China." She spoke louder with each strum. "And you also have in your lineage, all the way back, some relation to Genghis Khan."

"It's just Yam." He still didn't look at her, but he did soften his strums. His mum's message was failing; and her efforts were backfiring. Leilani's teasing at his expense was helping make his decision to stay far easier.

"She also told me that she's a *hapa* with her lineage." Leilani's short laugh stirred a smile inside Yam. He repressed it. "Then she had to explain to me what a hapa is. She says some don't like the term, but when they were all living in Hawaii while the islands were being built, it was a common term used. And she likes it. My mom's a hapa too," she added. "I guess that's why they've been such good friends. Your mom's multiracial. My mom's multiracial." She started singing her words against his strumming. "I'm a hapa. You're a hapa."

The painful singing caused his stoic face to break. He shook his head and quickly tried to restore the blank slate across his face. But the smiling kept breaking as she continued to sing against his strums. "Your dad. Mixed . . . with . . . German . . . Russian. Scottish. And a little Ukraine. My dad . . . well, he's a tough one . . . he only claims . . . to say . . . he comes from a long line . . . of Southern California beach bums."

He stopped strumming and just stared at her.

"What?" She tried to fight the smile that was emerging. Then she spoke very matter-of-factly. "You don't like my singing?"

He set the guitar down as if signifying it was his effort to make her stop.

Her smile only grew wider. "Well." She playfully rolled her eyes.

They both exchanged a humorous look.

Then Leilani's tone softened, the play gone out of her words. "Your mom says she loves talking lineage whenever she meets someone new. She says it connects her to the old world and the places that used to be."

Yam nodded, clearly aware of his Mum's nostalgia of the past.

"And she thought it was important I knew all this," she added.

Yam looked away, back toward his guitar, his mind revisiting the questions he had been pondering.

"Your mom also said that reddish hair," Leilani continued, "in a Polynesian culture meant you were a descent from high-ranked ancestors, and it carried a mark of rulership."

He looked again at her, in her flowery dress, and pressed his lips together, knowing clearly the stories his mum had shared.

"Pretty impressive," she leaned back and looked upwards. "Genghis Kahn, Polynesian high-ranked ancestor, your hapa lineage is looking *pretty good*."

He rolled his eyes, but let the humor come out in his tone. "My mom is pretty proud of her line."

"So, Mongolian nomad Yueh-chih, your mom says she has Japanese in her and some Polynesian." She raised her eyes and nodded at him. "What else?"

He shrugged.

"My mom," she volunteered, "is Puerto Rican, Dominican Republic, Italian, Hispanic, a bit of Native American, and German too."

At last, he took the bait and ventured down the taboo path. "Why are you telling me all this?"

She gave him a puzzled look. "What do you mean?"

"You . . . and . . . me. Leilani." He pointed at her. Then he hit his chest with a thud. "Yam. We go with Ashyr and what? Are we just trying to add up the lineage of the next generation from places that don't even exist? But really, what are we doing?"

Her eyes grew huge. "You're coming too? With Ashyr?"

He immediately looked at the ground. "I figured my mum said something to you. That's why you're saying all this."

"No."

When he looked back, she was shaking her head. Her eyes looked huge.

"Ashyr asked me to come," he volunteered. "So

did your dad. Mine sort of did . . . not."

She stared at the dirt. "My dad did?"

"I haven't decided if I'm going."

When he couldn't stand the silence any longer, he added, "What do your think?"

"If you come," a deep maturity filled her voice, "then maybe that was what your mum was saying. It's a new world. It all starts over. It becomes the Air Island generation."

He shot her a glance. Then he nodded. "The Air Island generation," he said.

"Yep."

"Yep," he whispered.

# FORTY-FOUR

## LEILANI

A calmness settled over me. All the fears that had been roaming inside over this plan to go alone with Ashyr were suddenly put to rest. "I hope you do come with us," I said.

"I don't know yet." He picked up his guitar again and strummed a few notes. Then he added, "My dad thinks it's a bad idea. And you have to admit, it's weird. Just like everything else that's part of Ashyr's world."

I just shrugged at his response. I didn't like how he talked about Ashyr. I tried to offer him perspective. "Well, you're just lucky you've already seen what's out there. I haven't. And don't worry, I get it. Your dad doesn't want you to go. My parents made it clear they don't want me to go either. But I think it's a good thing. I'm excited to go." I looked up at the overhead dome that I could sense now that I knew it was there. "Why do you think they didn't tell me . . . the truth about these islands?"

"I don't know." There was a strange solemness in his voice. "It's different. Where you're going it's very different than here."

"Well, I can't explain it. But it's important to me. I need to go."

He tilted his head at me but didn't say anything. He just kept strumming at his guitar.

So, I felt I needed to clarify better. "Do you ever just know there's something you need to do? Like an important task and certain people are just in your way. They are, like, holding you back. But you need to find out what it is. And just do it. Like something deep inside you just knows you need to do whatever it is you need to do."

I sounded like I was talking in circles, like I was trying too hard to justify what I was doing.

He stopped strumming. He shook his head like he was processing what I was saying. Then he spoke to the ground. "Doesn't matter what you want. Sometimes there are just certain things you have to do. Whether you want to do them or not."

"I don't follow."

When he looked at me, a sadness was there. "Doesn't matter if I want to go or not. This is just something I have to do. I can feel it."

"See?" Against his sadness, his words made me smile. I tried to get him to smile too. "Maybe you get what I'm trying to say. There are just certain things you know you need to do. And the more my parents are set on me not going, the stronger the feeling grows. I don't know if this makes sense. It's like in order to really be me, I need to get away. I have to take this chance . . . does that make sense?"

"I think I get it. You got to be true to who you are. Do what you need to do." The sadness was starting to lift from his eyes.

"Yeah. Something like that."

He started to hum something, then said, "Can I share a song I wrote?"

"You write songs?"

He shrugged and kept strumming. "I don't know if they're any good."

"I'll let you know." I leaned back on the stump. "Go for it."

He nodded. "I call it *Pulling Me Home*." Then he sang.

*It sure has been a while, the seasons have all changed.*

His singing was way better than my goofy attempt. His voice held a rich depth.

*The way I left last time, just made me feel so lame.*

*Prepared as I am, I would hate to worry you.*

*Take care 'til I get there, where I'll take care of you.*

He nodded at me while his fingers danced along the strings. Then he gave me a soft smile before he started singing again.

*Pulling me home, that's where I need to be.*

*Pulling me home, with my family.*

*Pulling me home, I've seen enough to see.*

*Home . . . is where I want to be.*

His voice seemed to connect with my heart, inviting me to feel certain things.

He kept strumming while the melody repeated itself. Then he started singing again.

*In this life so hectic, I need a chance to pause.*

*A time and place to rectify my flaws.*

I swallowed against a sudden lump inside my throat.

*Funny how in a big city you can feel so all alone.*

*Put aside my pride, strong as the tide pulling me home.*

My eyes burned as he repeated the chorus.

*Pulling me home, that's where I need to be.*

*Pulling me home, with my family.*

Now with Yam's voice and the music, I felt something breaking in my heart.

*Pulling me home, I've seen enough to see.*

Ever since I had learned my parents lied, it was as if a hard hurt had surfaced in my heart. Now in place of the hardness, I felt sadness. More heartache and breaking. A longing for my parents, a realization that I still loved them, even if they had hurt me as they had.

*Home . . . is where I want to be.*

Part of me wanted him to stop singing, to stop communicating with my heart. Another part of me just wanted the music to continue, for him to keep speaking this language of song that my heart seemed to understand.

He did keep playing and as the chords repeated, I tried to pull myself together. I didn't want him to see how his singing had affected me. Fortunately, his eyes remained looking at the strings as he repeated:

*Pulling me home, that's where I need to be.*

*I've seen enough to see, home . . . is where I want to be.*

As the strumming faded out, and he finally set his guitar down, I quickly used my thumb to jab at some moisture near my eyes.

"You have a nice voice," I said, unable to look at him.

"What did you think of the song?"

"Those are your lyrics, huh?" I gave him a quick, questionable look.

He looked back with earnest. "Yes."

I exhaled a sigh.

"You didn't like it."

"Pretty pointed lyrics. I got what you were trying to tell me."

"No." He shook his head. "I just was singing you a song."

I tilted my head at him. I wasn't buying it. "You didn't just write that song?"

Humor crossed his face. "You don't just write a song like that. At least, I don't. I wrote it for myself. A while back. When I had a choice."

"What was your choice?"

"Join my mum and sisters or help my baba."

"Where are your sisters?"

"In another place?"

"Where?"

"Australia."

"Oh." So many questions ran through my head. At last, I settled on, "What did you choose?"

His hands extended out. "This is my home."

I just stared at him for a long time, trying to make sense of his words, his lyrics, my own thoughts, and my heart that seemed to still be feeling too much in that moment. Finally, I said, "So. Do you think it's a mistake? Do you think I shouldn't go? Or that *we* shouldn't go?"

"No. I'm not saying that. I was just sharing a song," he repeated. "But if the song did say something to you . . ."

"What?" I pressed him to finish his faded words.

"I don't know. Maybe after all your adventures, after you've seen what you want to see, and done what you want to do, maybe you're going to find out it's okay to leave room to say that home is a really good place to be."

I stood and pressed down on the silky dress, working to straighten out the folds. When I looked at him, he was watching me like he was waiting for something. Finally, I said the words that seemed to be pounding in my heart, the defensiveness clear in my voice. "I didn't say I never wanted to go home again."

Instead of taking offense, he just offered a warm smile. "I never said you did either. But maybe that's what you heard." He gave me a soft nod. "Keep your option of home available. Even if you feel like, for now, you need to leave."

My shoulders softened a bit. "Okay," I said quietly.

He shrugged. "Okay," he said quietly back.

"Maybe you get me." I shrugged back at him.

"Maybe." He just watched me.

"Thanks," I said.

# FORTY-FIVE

## ASHYR

The EnRapture marathon party—he was dressed, ready for the spontaneous one he was throwing. The airship Tear—he had entered the craft, ready to broadcast the kickoff, to announce the evening events to his people. No. He was with Serena. An EnRapture experience with her—she was showing him a new accessory, one that would blow his mind. No. He had left Serena—she was angry. He was supposed to be broadcasting for the party. No. He was supposed to be de-stressing through EnRapture to counter the weight of the day. Bad, horrible news. Severe DNA issues with the young—batch one had the first symptoms which eventually would run havoc through all the batches. They all were going to die. Extinction.

It was a nightmare. He was dreaming. This was all a nightmare.

He needed something to latch onto and free his mind from this horridness.

A kid. A lean teen, light brown eyes, hair pulled up into a bun, the two stood face-to-face.

No solution. More trouble. The kid had stirred up an issue with other youth.

Words buzzed around Ashyr. The kid said

*parents.* He spoke of *home* like a societal unit, a family.

A puzzle piece . . . something from long ago . . . what had happened?

Ashyr had canceled his exchange with Serena. She had fumed at him, especially when he had made it worse, delegating the kickoff of the EnRapture party to her.

He had told her she would understand, soon, right as she had entered one of the spherical airships.

Then inside Tear, he had changed his attire, prepared himself and hoped for . . . a reunion.

While invisible, the pilot and Ashyr hunted the skies and at last spotted the kid. His drone was like no other—a direct indicator Ashyr was on to something good. High-powered, macro-strength, the drone hauled a large trailer upward.

Then a waiting game began. Watch. Follow. Stay invisible. Hitch a ride alongside the trailer as they moved into a cloud and then bingo.

The ride slowed down inside a large funnel. They had landed on a type of spacecraft. Next, the kid video chatted with someone's face projected onto the wall. Ashyr caught snippets. *Late night. In a rush to get back home.* The projected face said, *Drop the trailer in the reserve . . . Others would deal . . . in the morning.* And then the blessed phrase: *I will let Foster know.*

Foster!

With more waiting, watching, and following, he found his way through the spacecraft's underground maze to emerge into their upper-level paradise.

Ashyr's eyes opened inside a circular room.

Foster. Mariana. Brody.

The strange dream lifted. Bit by bit he tackled his disorientation. He had not had an EnRapture experience for a long time. A scream clung inside him, a hunger of the brain.

He worked through the pain by piecing together his thoughts. Something good was here—something incredibly good—and it was right in front of him.

From the bed, he observed his surroundings. The walls were a woven wood lattice covered by thick canvas. The top was a cone-shaped roof where a skylight shone down on him. Judging by the light filtering in, it was late afternoon. The sequence of events returned. He'd been on Foster's island. And now, he rested in a yurt tent on Brody's.

Ashyr grinned and arose. From a neighboring chair, he retrieved his filthy suit coat and slid it back on.

As soon as he stepped outside, he heard laughter coming down the path. Leilani and Yam walked close together.

"I don't see why you call me a kid," Yam said. "I'm six weeks older than you."

"How do you know my birthday?" Leilani nudged at him, but he jumped out of the way in time.

"I know the whole story. Same hospital. Our moms . . ."

Ashyr stepped away from the tent's shadow, placing himself in plain view with enough time to not startle the two.

"Just in time," Yam said to Ashyr, clear happiness on his face. "Mum just announced dinner is almost ready."

"They want to eat early to get us on our way." Leilani grinned at him. "Yam will be coming with us too."

"Marvelous." He'd gone from unsettling dreams to a real-life pleasant moment. The day would end on hope rather than sorrows.

Yam said something that made Leilani laugh. Ashyr didn't hear what had been shared, but he found himself grinning too.

Although Ashyr discouraged pairings among his society, as it limited registry growth, the charged energy between these two offered something satisfying to Ashyr's needs.

As he followed behind them toward the house, he felt a lightness in his step. Solutions were ahead.

From behind a branch broke. Loud steps pounded forward. He turned to see Brody running toward them, an old shotgun in hand. With his overalls pressed against his large build, he looked like he had burst right out of a twentieth-century farm portrait.

"Get off my island! Now!" He aimed the gun directly at Ashyr.

"Whoa. Whoa!" Instinctively, Ashyr raised a hand. "There, there old friend."

"Get out of here and never return."

"Is this about your son?" Ashyr looked down the lane, pointing toward Yam who seemed oblivious to the noise caused by his father. "He chose this," Ashyr spoke louder, hoping to draw Yam and Leilani back to the scene. "Free choice here. No coercion. Right, Yam?" he finally called out.

Thankfully, Yam turned. "Baba!"

Within seconds, Yam and Leilani were at Ashyr's side.

"Get him out of here," Brody growled at his son.

"He doesn't have any bullets," Yam said quietly to Ashyr. "Not for that antique."

"I might have me some metal scraps in here," Brody growled again. "I've got a fair amount of resources here, plus a little bit of homemade gun powder. Better that than letting him kill us all."

Ashyr raised his hands as if speaking to a hostile native. "I come in peace."

"Your airship doesn't." Brody raised his rifle toward the aircraft in the distance. "It's going to kill us all."

Ashyr sent a look to Yam, seeking support in the confusion.

"What are you trying to do?" Brody stepped forward, the gun nearly touching Ashyr. "Might as well chop off a segment of the sun and drop it right into our enclosed area."

Yam pushed Ashyr out of the way so that the rifle was pointed at him instead. "What's going on, Baba?"

Immediately, Brody lowered the gun. He spoke to Yam. "Damn levels are off. Since he stepped onto this place, couldn't have the PIGS operable to keep the peace around here."

Yam took a step closer, his voice softened. "Calm down. You aren't speaking at your best right now."

"Damn right I am. Thinks he can just parade in here. What do you have in there?" Again, Brody lifted the rifle in the direction of the airship. "Uranium, radiation, nuclear fission?"

Ashyr slowly, carefully, nodded, his eyes as much on the gun as Brody. "Correct. For our energy source."

Sure enough, the gun swung right back up to

Ashyr's chest. "Well, explain this to me. Nuclear fission creates havoc in an enclosed capsule. When I finally got my PIGS up and running, suddenly the atmospheric reading is looking like a carnival of chaos."

"Baba." Yam stepped around his father and placed a hand on his shoulder. "Surely we're prepared for this. Let the PIGS have some time to catch up and self-correct the levels."

"In an enclosed environment, they can manage just fine. But throw in this intruder, with his now unattached invaders roaming around, and I have no idea what the PIGS will be able to do."

"I take it," Ashyr spoke slowly and cautiously, "you don't have these pigs around for bacon."

"I want you off this island." Brody nudged his head in the direction of the lakefront.

Ashyr felt Leilani moving closer. "So we leave now."

He appreciated her even more at that moment. "Sure. Sure," he easily said. "We head out. Yam." He raised a nod at the kid standing close to Brody. "Grab what you need. I'd say pack for a couple of weeks, if that." His words lessened in strength as the rifle straightened in front of him. A bit quieter, he said, "We'll meet you down at the pier. Brody," he shifted his focus to the man whose eyes appeared crazed and illogical. "Someday, at a better time, we should talk about the farm you might be raising here."

"Get out of here!" Brody roared.

"Sure." Ashyr raised his hands again and stepped backward. "If you want to, send over Foster and Mariana. As soon as we have all our passengers on board, if you'd be so kind as to open your sky port, we will exit your premises right away."

"Not like that," Brody commanded. He took a step back. The gun lowered letting Ashyr breathe better. But Brody's chest continued to fire up and down. "We need to talk to Foster about all this. Make sure it's only this enclosed biosphere you've messed with."

"Mum put out the call for us to all gather at the house for dinner," Yam said, retrieving the rifle from his father's hand. "So, we can all talk there."

"No!" With the gun gone, Brody spread his legs wide. His burly arms folded against his chest. "I want your mum, Foster, Mariana, and you," he pointed at Ashyr, "on your airship now. We're going to get this figured out. And you," he swung the finger at Yam. "If you're going to fall for this buffoon's stories, and go rah-rah for his la-la land, then do what you're going to do. Go pack up, fast."

Leilani shifted between Ashyr and Yam, as if not quite sure where she should be.

"Come with me," Yam said.

"Go with him," Brody and Ashyr said in unison, only for Brody to grunt at their momentary agreement.

Then Brody stepped closer to Ashyr, his eyes wild again. "Let me make this clear. We solve this problem you brought with you. Together, we fix this. Then, from there, you never return here again."

# FORTY-SIX

## FOSTER

Noise!

From the moment Brody had corralled the adults together and led them toward the airship to gather around the captain's station, all Foster had heard was noise.

The impact of the roar felt like when he'd witnessed an F-22 Raptor jet fly by as a boy. The sky had been tranquil until, out of nowhere, the deep rumble had shaken the heavens then the ground beneath him. One hundred and fifty decibels. The loudest noise Foster had ever heard. And at last, a burst of the metallic bird, the stealth fighter, over-powered the sky.

Before Ashyr's shocking arrival, there had been tranquility. But then came the rumble, and now Brody's deafening blast, his words mostly flying at Ashyr, this grand disruption bursting into view.

Radio noise, waves of Mariana's communication, shook the airship as she bounced between stations, talking to Clark, then Rex, then back to Clark to assess the situation at home.

Sunny talked with the pilot, running through an endless list of questions.

Through all the noise, Foster tried to decipher

the real sound that needed to be addressed.

The details didn't add up.

If he listened to Brody, with the intensity sweeping through him so rapidly, myth soared over science data, facts stooped beneath fiction, and irrational thought exploded past logic, leaving Foster on unsettled ground.

And Ashyr, never had Foster seen Ashyr so quiet. Not countering, not trying to outwit. Instead, he took the blasting. Voiceless. Grinless. His face was as blank as Foster felt.

What Foster needed to do was speak to Clark and Rex, to tell them the next steps. Although he wasn't sure yet what those were. And he wouldn't know until he could hear past the noise to the single sound of what they truly faced.

"You're here to kill us, aren't you?" Brody continued throwing vitriol at Ashyr. "Splitting atoms, right? That's how all this is done? But what does that do for our enclosed environment? A nuclear reactor. It's going to react all right, going to ruin everything Foster and I have created. That's what you wanted. Really, that was your plan? This whole front. This sob story about needing our kids to help save your society while your goal was to come destroy ours. Sabotage us. Fools we are. Fools, Foster. I opened this thing up so he could ruin us. Ashyr, you followed Yam to find Foster, to find me. Destroy us all in one blow."

"Brody!" Sunny's voice practically shook the entire airship. All eyes turned. "Enough," she commanded.

"Do you understand what he's done?" Brody's voice turned softer as he spoke to her.

"You really believe Ashyr's a murderer? That he came here to ruin us?" Her hands were pressed against her hips.

"I don't know." He folded his arms and returned to facing his foe. "Ashyr, tell us, why did you really come?"

His reply was humble. "In hopes to find a solution to save my people."

"While killing us," Brody added.

"Brody." Sunny's commanding tone returned. "Decent people don't try to infect, contaminate, or destroy another person. It just doesn't work that way. Accidents, unforeseen circumstances, trade-offs arise."

"Decent? Trade-offs? A decent trade off—our lives for his people?"

"No. No." She waved her hand to clarify. "Ashyr, what, if any of this, was intentional?"

He sounded like a young, sorrowful boy. "None."

Against all the racket, Foster heard a strong note, something to lead to an answer. "I think you found it, Sunny."

"Me?" She hit her chest. "What did I say?

"Infection," Foster repeated. "Contamination. Bacterium. That makes more sense."

"No," the pilot spoke up. "We're not sick. We haven't been anywhere near that African virus. We follow all the health codes. We didn't bring—"

"No," Foster cut him off. For the note to grow, the excess noise needed to taper. "Brody," he said strongly. "When we built this, our team used Biosphere II's triumphs and failures as our guide. We made sure not to repeat their errors. And we

244

succeeded." His own words startled him. Of course they had succeeded. Years and years of success. The recognition caused Foster to break with a grateful smile. "Brody. Sunny. Mariana. We succeeded. Ashyr, you witnessed this—we succeeded. For all these years, the impossible was possible."

"Are you not understanding what's happening?" Brody roared as if the heavy jet decibels had returned.

"We had a perfectly balanced enclosed system," Foster said pensively.

"That's unbalanced now."

"Concerningly unbalanced," Mariana added to Brody's words, raising the radio to confirm the findings were appearing on both islands.

"So why the sudden spike?" Foster asked himself out loud.

Brody smacked a large palm against his forehead. "Are you with us, Foster?"

"How exactly was this danger introduced?"

Brody grunted at the question and waved an arm around the airship.

"We are two separate bubbles sealed and secured," Foster continued to speak out loud to himself. "Eight percent leakage a year, total, if that. But something is throwing off both our carbon cycles. We are slowly choking with too much carbon dioxide and nitrogen. We are going to see an increase of cockroaches and ants, and our health is going to be affected."

"So much for paradise," the pilot said, only for Ashyr to shoot him a look of warning.

"Part of your plan," Brody muttered to Ashyr.

*"If it's well, we are well, and if not . . ."* Foster quietly repeated the memorized quote from early

pioneers of enclosed structures. "How fast are the levels going to drop?" He looked to Brody.

"This morning, our oxygen was at the standard twenty-one percent. We're now at under nineteen."

"Can the bots give an estimate of how much time we have to stabilize the levels?"

Brody shook his head as if doing his own calculations. "I think we can have an estimate in an hour."

Foster nodded. "We may need to do an evacuation."

Mariana gasped. "To where?"

"Looks like you're coming home," the pilot said, getting another disconcerting look from Ashyr.

"We're not going back." Mariana stepped forward, practically pushing Brody out of the way to glare at Ashyr as if, in place of the pilot, he had spoken those words. "We will never live in what you created."

Ashyr raised his hands calmly. "We're just talking options, Mariana. It's an option to explore if needed."

"There's also where I am, in Australia," Sunny said. Everyone looked at her, but she only kept her eyes on Brody. "It's not ideal, but it's an option."

"If that's how it plays out," Brody spoke directly back to her. "We will work it out. Okay? We'll make it work."

Sunny nodded, the always present smile now gone. "It would be wise for Mariana to come back with me, to start making the negotiations, the plans if that's where the evacuation leads to."

Mariana shook her head, turning now to step closer to Foster. "This." She pointed down. "These islands. That was our evacuation plan."

"I think you are right," Brody spoke as if still conversing with only Sunny. "It'd be best for Mariana to go with you, to get things started. If it comes to that."

Foster reached for her hand and squeezed it tightly. "Could you do that?"

Mariana held his eyes for a long moment. She nodded, but her lips trembled slightly.

"Okay." Sunny clapped her hands together and let out a huge sigh. "We have one step toward a solution. Mariana and I will take the two-seat drone and head out to work on negotiations around an evacuation."

Brody cocked his head toward Foster. "We're not walking away from this."

"Absolutely not." Sunny quickly added. "We're only working on a backup, just in case."

"Brody," Foster said solemnly. "We don't have all the answers. We don't yet know why the levels are dropping."

"Or if they'll stabilize once we leave," Ashyr added.

"We've been watching this for sixteen years," Brody said. "But on the same day, on both our islands, we see this large of a drop? To get our atmosphere to its proper balance, our team invested a great deal of trial and error. Right, Foster?"

"Seventy-eight percent nitrogen, twenty-one percent oxygen," Foster said. "And under one percent for the other components, including carbon dioxide."

"Today, our oxygen is coming in close to eighteen percent, our carbon dioxide now reading close to three percent," Brody said. "When talking about the air we breathe, this is not something to treat lightly."

"No one is disagreeing with you, sweetheart." Sunny moved closer to Brody, placing a hand on his back.

"Foster." Brody shot him a look as if Foster had challenged him in some way. "Are you with me?"

"I'm just sorting through what data we currently have and trying to understand what would cause the sudden drop."

Brody clutched his hands to his forehead. "Are you hearing what I've been saying?"

"The nuclear fission may be emitting radiation here," Foster said.

"You are listening." Brody's shoulders heaved down.

"But it's only a small amount," Foster added. "I mean, it's a concern. Yes, it's a concern. But even within our enclosed environment, I think the risk we might be looking at is more a future issue of how the radiation might impact our health long-term."

"Fantastic! Two blows here. Can't breathe today. Tomorrow, cancer. Which is Ashyr's specialty." Brody glared at Ashyr until he turned away.

"I am not convinced the atmospheric unbalance is due to the fission," Foster added.

"So," Brody's large arms folded against his chest. "You got a better theory?"

Foster nodded. "No proof, just a theory. What if organic material was introduced? A bacterium that is consuming the oxygen and leaving us with its carbon dioxide waste."

"Hungry critter," the pilot added.

"Enough!" Ashyr said to him, then turned his full attention to Foster. "Are you saying we brought it in?"

"It's just a theory." Foster shrugged. "No evidence yet."

"What about your kid?" Ashyr spoke to Sunny. "Could your son have brought this in?"

"No," Brody said. "We have a process here. A way to counter against any foreign substances. But no plan in place for a parasitic invader to drop in on us unexpected." The glare went from Ashyr to Foster, twice.

Foster held his breath. "There was a lot to take in today. I didn't . . ."

"Yam has a process," Brody raised a finger at Ashyr, "which is not equipped for invisible hitch-hikers latching onto his trailer." When Ashyr didn't say anything to counter the accusation, Brody continued, "Sunny has a process!" He raised another finger. "My family is the only one who has come and gone. And Yam has only stepped foot on Foster's loading deck! So, I say again, why are our levels unbalanced today? This morning, all was well. As it's been continuously for the past years, day in, day out! Explain this, Ashyr."

"Quiet!" Sunny suddenly yelled. The rumblings of the jet ceased. Brody especially stared at her. She pointed at him. "Stop!"

"Sit, please," she said.

And he obeyed, slipping into one of the swivel chairs.

"Ashyr, you too. Sit."

He, too, obeyed.

"Foster, Mariana." She whirled her finger in

a circle, implying that the two needed to scoot together, that they all needed to gather around.

Then Sunny spoke like a drill sergeant. "We're done. Done blaming anyone here. What's done is done. Now, we need to focus like a team to get through this. Understood?" She looked around the room at every face until she got a solid nod.

"Brody," she pointed at her husband. "Why can't the bots tell us more?"

"They will." He raised his hands protectively. "For right now, for a little while, they're working with raw data. For us to get accuracy for what's happening here, they're going to have to test and filter through the input before we have a solid prediction. And from there, a solution. Now if Foster's theory is correct . . ." He shot Foster a glance, a more open look now on his face. "Eventually, we will know if he's right. First, we get their prediction. Then, based on what's already taken place today, they'll give us a model of what we can expect if there is a continuous decline. If the airship's energy source is the culprit, then we will eventually have a solid prediction of how to stabilize and work toward rebalancing our levels. But if Foster's theory is correct, for us to identify and isolate the oxygen-eating bacteria, that's going to take significantly more time. It's going to require work to build out an algorithm that will feed us back an accurate model. And once that happens, that's just identification. Then, we'll need to work to isolate the organism, while working to regulate and restore the atmospheric levels."

"Okay. So, in summary, you need to stay here to work with the bots." She turned. "Foster?"

He nodded at her.

"What are your next steps?"

He nodded again. "I need to figure that out. Organize priorities, decide what's most urgent here, especially if we don't yet understand the cause."

"I'll tell you what's most important." Brody stood up. "Once Sunny and Yam leave, it's just me on this island. Me, Foster. That's it. Me and the sinking percentage of oxygen that I can use while working with the data to get the answers we need. You. You have well over a hundred people dependent. Breathing in and out. Taking oxygen to live. Adding carbon dioxide back into the air, while more oxygen disappears. Your primary goal is to stop the depletion." Brody sounded out of breath as if he'd just run a fast race. "If we can cap the depletion at even just 14%, maybe even as low as 12%, we can buy ourselves some time. It won't be ideal. But everyone will just have to make do with a more sedated lifestyle until we get the levels balanced again."

"Or, everyone is able to relocate," Sunny said. "If required."

The noise had faded to a clear sound. "Okay." Foster said, knowing his next step. "I have to get back fast."

# FORTY-SEVEN

## FOSTER

The drone carried Foster and Yam deeper into the sky. Blueness darkened around them. Under the circumstances, the space felt like a black hole, absorbing them within the craft that carried them, enveloping them in their mortality. How fragile they were.

His breathing had become choppy, tight, as if consuming less oxygen in the drone would leave more for all those on the island.

The trip would take less than thirty minutes compared to the forty-two minutes in Ashyr's airship; and they would no longer allow him to land on the island. But Marianna was in it. And Leilani. Foster's family was spread thin like the oxygen he needed to restore.

Yam had not said much on the autopiloted drive. Still, Foster liked watching from behind Yam's hands encircle the driving shaft. Like he was ready to step in, ready to accelerate them forward to repair all this. It seemed like the young man wasn't feeling as helpless as Foster feared he himself might be when he arrived in front of the monitors to tackle the critical undoing of this.

"Is this the fastest we can go?" Foster had

asked. It seemed twenty minutes had already passed, but time also seemed trapped in a cycle. A round of twenty minutes, then the same amount of time repeating, only to discover the entire journey's duration had never yet reached twenty minutes at all. Racing against time, while chasing time, making the arrival home feel impossible. They would continue to lose oxygen until, eventually, it was all gone. His family. His life. Everything he had built to save them all.

Twenty minutes. Foster tried to not look at his clock. It still had not passed. Eighteen minutes and three seconds. He almost wished to count the seconds down, as if chanting numbers would challenge the time war they were up against.

Instead, he tried to speak to Yam, his words spilling out his concern. "I don't know if we can fix this, in time, in a way that actually repairs what the real issue is."

"I know," Yam said quietly as his fingers drummed against the driving shaft. "Baba explained a little to me."

As Yam shared this, Foster regretted he had confessed such huge concerns to a teenage boy. Immediately, he retracted his words. "We'll get it repaired somehow. Your dad and I have solved harder problems. We can solve this one too."

Yam nodded.

But when neither spoke again, Foster followed up with, "I'd appreciate it if you wouldn't share the details of all this with Leilani." Even as he spoke the words, he heard his weakness, his helplessness, how tired and afraid he sounded.

"You can repair it," Yam repeated the words

Foster had just shared as the long-awaited cloud came into view, still a small speck, but a necessary sign that home was approaching.

An odd yawn escaped Foster, a cry for oxygen, a gasp against what he needed to face. He thought about what Mariana had said, that the island was the evacuation plan. The moment he had launched it into its own gravitational pull within Earth's orbit, he had gambled all their lives. A risk taken.

And then they had lived among the miracles daily. The inconceivable had turned so regular now, it had become ordinary, as if it would always remain this way.

Over time, Foster had forgotten to fear the island's limitations, its own type of mortality. And now, both Foster and the island would need to face reality. The breath held tight in Foster's chest.

"Ashyr has what you need," Yam suddenly said.

Simple. Direct words. Clear and challenging. "How do you know that?"

Yam bowed his head as if possibly working through the words. "Baba told me. And he's right."

"What does Ashyr have?"

"He has tanks of crystalline compounds and filters to absorb and clean the waste he left us with."

Foster laughed. "He does, does he? Why did your baba not tell me this?"

"Here." Yam handed over a small device, built with Brody's modifications from an old smartphone.

"You've been typing on this?" Foster said in disbelief. The thing had an extremely outdated and tiny keypad.

"Not exactly," Yam said.

Foster pressed the up button, scrolling through

until he found the beginning of the correspondence.

Baba: May have a solution. Depending on the cause. Bots figured out a process to clean out the waste.

Yam: Great news!

Baba: Thinking Ashyr may have the materials I need. If he does, I can make up the machine to clear out the gas garbage Ashyr left us with.

Yam: What do you need?

Baba: The last time you were near Ashyr's warehouse, did you see anything like this?

A photo was attached that looked like a steel drum with a jagged circle label and the acronym UKrBa in the center.

Yam: I didn't make it into the warehouse.

Baba: Then outside, did you see anything like this outside?

Yam: I don't think so.

Baba: What about this?

Another photo followed, this one appearing like an ancient Connect Four game but elongated to a 20 by 6 grid with circular holes throughout.

Yam: Yes. I saw that.

Baba: Fam Dam Tastic!

Yam: What does that mean?

Baba: I'd bet that his warehouse has the rest of what we need.

Yam: So what does that mean? Repeated question intentional.

Baba: We're giving him what he wants. He damn well better fix the mess he created for us!

Foster reached the end of the messages. He released a huge exhale.

The belly of the island was approaching. "We

aim to save his world," Foster said quietly. "And now, through his help, we save our own."

Yam too heaved out a long breath. "Yep. So, I have Baba's blessing now to go with Ashyr."

"An *exchange*," Foster laughed out the word.

"Just not an Ashyr EnRapture-type exchange." Yam gave a tense laugh back.

"Definitely not."

"And I'll help Leilani out while I'm there."

Foster reached his hand forward and squeezed Yam's shoulder, appreciating this extended reassurance toward his earlier request. "That would be very helpful," he said as the cloudiness distilled and the drone slowed to a stop within the first panel of entry.

# FORTY-EIGHT

## LEILANI

While I sat in the main quarters of the airship, I watched our ascension into a cloud. The beeping, the pilot's focus, the grin emerging on Ashyr's face, plus Mom's hand over her heart—all this let me know we were approaching.

When we had left the other island, everything had been chaotic. I thought Yam was going to stay with me. Instead, his dad pulled him away and started giving him all sorts of instructions. Yam seemed to listen super intently.

Then it was Yam who told me what was going on. In real quick words, he said that he needed to get Dad back to the island before he joined Ashyr and me. That was it. Then Mom told me to follow her back onto the airship so she could get back home.

The entrance back in was way different than our exit. When we had left, we had been flying out toward the wide-open skies. Then, when we had reached Yam's island, it had been through the dome top, above the land. But now, we were heading through a large cotton cloud until a monster metal ship-like thing appeared. There was a funnel in the center of it.

The pilot dropped the engine and the airship glided toward the funnel opening.

"Are you ready?" The anxiousness in Mom's voice caused me to tense.

Without looking at her, I tried to nod, but I couldn't even manage that. I was extremely bothered by the earlier conversation I'd overheard between her and Ashyr.

They'd been speaking in really low tones, the kind that only made me want to listen more because they clearly didn't want me to hear what they were saying.

Their tones brought back my frustrations. So like Mom, still trying to keep things from me. But since she doesn't hear too well, their tones continued to rise, letting me catch parts of what they were calling *Leilani's procedure.*

Ashyr had spoken very kindly to Mom. "I wish you could be there, to help her . . . she'll have the absolute best support while she's in our care."

"Okay." Mom had sounded so subdued, defeated. "Thank you, Ashyr."

I didn't catch all of what he said, other than, "I'm sorry about all this."

"Me too," Mom had added.

I tried to stop listening and instead focus on the lowering sun. It would set within the hour. But then I heard Mom say it again: *Leilani's procedure.* I strained to hear the rest: *Will it hurt? Will you put her under?*

Ashyr's words did nothing to calm me: *medicine to stimulate a healthy harvest . . . shots . . . daily shots . . . someone to help administer, care and monitor during this time . . . make sure she doesn't overstimulate, which is very dangerous . . . never had a problem . . . if all goes well . . . back in six to eight weeks . . . maybe a little longer.*

His phrases wouldn't leave me. My mind got lost thinking through them until I saw the large chamber doors inside the funnel opening. Mom held a radio and was requesting entry. The airship came to a stop.

My oldest brother Clark's face projected onto the second set of wide doors in front of us. He offered no smile. At that moment, I wanted to hate him too. He had known the truth. It seemed likely all my siblings did.

When he spoke, he said nothing in the form of a greeting. "Instructions are to unload within this chamber. Mariana. Leilani. Mr. Harmon. The chamber doors behind you will close. Once the area is secured, the second set of doors will open, and you will enter the next chamber on foot. Once that area is secured, the main hall doors will open slightly for you to enter. After you are secured in the main hall, those doors will close. From there, the doors behind you, from which you just entered, will reopen, and we ask that Mr. Harmon's pilot remove the airship to at least five thousand meters away from our radius."

A puzzled smile covered Ashyr's face. "I'm to enter too?"

"My father requires it," Clark said.

Ashyr raised his eyebrows. "Requires." He shot me a look. I was glad to see a happiness appearing again in his eyes. Earlier it evaporated as we were shuttled so quickly into the airship to leave Yam's island. "Well let's go see about this requirement," he said.

But before proceeding to the exit, Ashyr paused and headed back to the pilot. I couldn't make out what he said, just that he whispered some directions to the pilot.

Then, at Clark's *all clear*, Ashyr stood beside me outside the airship.

While we waited for the next chamber doors to open, Mom clutched her hands against her chest. Ashyr's hands remained still in his suit coat pockets, but he did keep moving his lips as if counting off the seconds.

As for me, I just wrapped my arms around myself, trying to feel less lost in this giant chamber, trying hard not to think about this other realm that lived underneath what I thought I knew.

Soon, we were walking through the belly of my island home. Monitors, large flat screens, and visual tracking of beeps surrounded us. Pipes wore signs announcing they carried flammable gas. Digital meters and charts lit up in a range of colors against the wall. The island was a living thing, and I had been living within it.

Again, I felt this surge of questions to ask Dad, so much I wanted to know, so much I didn't understand.

As I just stood there, in the midst of all the information coming in, all that was flowing out, I was overwhelmed by this majestic wonder. This miracle I had walked on all my life.

How simple it had all seemed.

How complex it all was.

I just wanted to keep standing there, taking it all in, trying to make sense of each device and structure that kept the island working.

I felt the lightest touch on my arm. When I turned, the magic broke as I looked at my mom, her hand still cautiously near. "He did it all for you."

I shook my head, this wasn't for me. Not all this. The grandeur here was beyond anything I could compare it to.

I looked above. Pipes ran toward a large central unit, like veins and arteries sending nourishment in and out of the heart. Sounds triggered more sounds, like lungs, as if the island had its own respiratory system. A heat, a smell like boiling water, a purification process sharing more functions working around me. So much to take in. To comprehend. I felt lost. Mesmerized. But lost.

Mom and Ashyr navigated the maze around me, and I tried to follow. We rounded a corner, came face-to-face with Dad, and stopped. I wanted to say something, but I couldn't find words to express all I was processing. But he didn't even look at me. Instead, he reached for Ashyr.

"We need to talk." His shoulder breezed past me as he pulled Ashyr aside. Then, he glanced at Mom. "You too."

Suddenly, the adults stood in a line, only to pause in noticing me. Again, I was the kid. And all the secrets I now knew didn't give me the right to hear them talk further. It upset me more.

"You need to go pack," Dad, at last, said to me. "How fast can you be back at the tree?"

Here in the heart of his creation, there was so much to say, things that I really wanted to talk about with him. Instead, I rolled my eyes while I tried to mask the cut his words had just left. "Say again?"

Dad scanned the area around us as if looking for something. I couldn't tell if he was ignoring my question. Or maybe he was finally realizing I was completely clueless to where I was, of how to get out of the belly of the island and get to the surface to actually pack my stuff.

Nope. Dad was still clueless. He answered my question with, "Yam's there now. Waiting for you. We need you to grab your stuff and be ready to go asap."

I couldn't believe him. It was like he was in his only little world, oblivious to me and what was happening to my world. I looked at Mom. Now it was like Dad was kicking me off the island. Mom just shrugged. They were suddenly acting like my trip with Ashyr was now a school field trip, like I was just heading over to see Uncle Ed's farm on the other side of the island. What had happened to my parents?

"I'm not sure if I can . . ." I let the sentence drop, waiting for them to address my need.

"It's too late for that," Dad said harshly.

That really did it. I spoke back in the same harsh tone. "I'm not sure if I can find my way out of here!"

"Oh." His head pulled back, and he finally clued in.

Mom touched my arm so lightly, with no tension, it felt so foreign to me. Where had her firmness gone? She pointed toward a hallway. "All the way down. Then up the stairs. Through the door and you'll be at the tree. I'll be there waiting for you shortly. In . . ." She turned to Dad as if asking him to validate her words. "Twenty minutes?"

He nodded.

"Okay." The anger had returned. It was time to get away from my parents. So, I headed toward the hallway. But before I reached the stairs, I stopped and looked back.

They were already talking, totally lost in their own words, oblivious that I was still there.

# FORTY-NINE

## LEILANI

When I stepped out of the artificial palm tree, Yam turned around.

"Huh." I let out a sarcastic laugh as I looked from the sandy ground back to the tree. "I sure didn't catch this before. Right in front of me—this fake bit of nature right here."

The tree's door automatically shut. A locking sound followed.

"Did you know about that?" I pointed over my shoulder at it.

"Nope."

I walked past him toward the beach. He followed. His shoulder grazed mine. There was harshness in my whisper. "Are there more trees like that around here?"

When he didn't answer, I faced him.

He just stared back. There was a change in him. A fear maybe. A nervousness with his hands. A lightness to his breath.

"You okay?"

"I want to give you a hug," he said, but it came out like a kid wanting reassurance. And he didn't hug me. He didn't move.

"Why?" I asked cautiously.

"Baba has a plan." He exhaled a low breath. Like that resolved the need he had for a hug.

Then he turned out toward the water. He dropped his hands to his side and closed his eyes.

"Yam? What's up? What's going on?"

He didn't exactly answer me. Instead, he said, "I've been in the unloading dock of this island numerous times, more than I can count. But up to the top, this is my first time." He glanced at me. A stillness came over his face. A smile softened over whatever had troubled him before.

Then he looked to the horizon again.

I followed his gaze and for the first time, I hunted for it: the optical illusion that had been taking place. The spot where the horizon appeared to extend endlessly. Now that I knew we were encircled and floating within stratospheric air, I saw where the water reached its enclosure.

"It's beautiful here," he said.

His words sounded like he was working to manage the fear he'd displayed moments earlier.

I didn't like that he was afraid. He was supposed to be what took away my fears of the unknown.

I decided to help him. "It really is," I kept my voice soft like his. Then I kept looking, really looking at it, letting my gaze get lost in the reality I now knew . . . and the words tumbled out, "It really, truly is."

He reached for my hand. I let him take it. He kept his words very controlled as if it was no big deal we were holding hands. "Those waves just pull you into another form of space."

To my surprise, holding his hand did calm me too. "It's the pattern," I explained. "Us humans are drawn to patterns. And due to gravity, it's how this all works. Patterns are all around us."

He released my hand and turned from the ocean. "Can we sit?" He nodded toward an inclined patch behind us.

"I'm supposed to go pack."

"Okay. But I need to tell you something. Something your father doesn't want me to share. Or my father. Or anyone. There are just so many secrets, Leilani. And I'm just tired of them all."

I nodded, hearing the weight of his words and recognizing I could get real answers from him.

I headed up to the little incline. He followed.

I sat. He sat next to me on a small ledge. Our feet dangled down.

"What's up?" I asked when he didn't volunteer anything.

"I'm not supposed to share this with you. Or anyone."

"I can keep secrets."

"You are going to have to, because Ashyr can't know."

"Okay."

"The story goes like this. A long time ago, when your dad and my baba and Ashyr first started their business together, one day they all were sitting around and talking. Ashyr started it and said, 'Okay, if you had no limitations, and you could invent anything, whatever you wanted, what would you invent?' And your dad said, 'I want to live in the clouds, on an island. Away from the sorrows of life.' And then Ashyr said, 'I want to be invisible. So I can be wherever I want to be.' And then Ashyr looked to my father and asked him what he would do."

Yam paused and didn't say anything else.

"Which was what?" I prodded.

Yam inhaled a huge breath. "Singularity."

"What is that?" I asked. "I don't know what that means."

"Baba wanted to achieve the point when computers became more powerful than the human brain and operated on their own."

I just stared at him, waiting for him to say something else. When he didn't, I asked, "So has he done it?"

Yam shook his head and looked down at the beach beneath our dangling feet. "Not yet. But he's close. But for our family's safety, he has decided not to tell us exactly how close he is. He says it's bad enough just that we know what we do know."

"*For your safety?* I don't get it?"

He just shrugged. Nothing else.

"Why?" I prodded for more. "Why is it such a big secret?"

He kept looking toward the ground. "When it happens, it could become extremely dangerous if people knew. When technology becomes more powerful than humans, bad things can happen, really bad things, uncontrollable things, irreversible, unforeseeably bad if it gets into the wrong hands. So Baba says he wants to achieve this goal. And then he will destroy it. As soon as he succeeds.

"I don't know why I told you all this. I mean, I've promised to keep it a secret. But my mum thinks you'll be family someday, so . . . " his words trailed off.

While he looked away, my cheeks burned over the sudden smile.

Without looking at me, he touched my hand again. "It's my fault. All of it. Ashyr wouldn't be here right now if it wasn't for me. He wouldn't know how far Baba has come. He wouldn't know about the PIGS, and how we are going to have to lean heavily on these bots to save our islands."

"Save our islands?" I cut him off.

"It's the issue they're all talking about. It's okay," Yam exhaled a breath as if also trying to convince himself of this statement.

"How serious is it?"

"It's all going to be okay. Baba's been working on these bots for years. He started when he was my age. He knows what he's doing and they'll figure it out."

"Okay. My dad is really smart. Seems like yours is too, they'll work it out," I said, truly believing this.

"They'll get this fixed and everything else," he added. "But it's why Baba wanted his own island. It's the reason for everything in my family, in my life, in how we live. And it's not good Ashyr knows about the island and the PIGS now."

"That's a lot to take in," I said.

"I know."

"So where do we go from here?"

"I don't know."

I inhaled sharply. "Well, if it's secret time, then I guess I should reveal a secret too."

His eyes lifted as if my unload might help his unload a little further. "What's that?"

"This morning, I was on this beach, telling my dad I didn't want . . . " I couldn't finish it.

"What?"

"*This*" I looked at my hand intertwined in his.

"Oh." He released his hand. "You knew . . . that Ashyr would . . . " He struggled.

"Not *this*, like what's happening today. But *this* . . ." I struggled, too, and looked at his hand that had moved away. "I have never . . . " I pulled in a huge breath. I held it for a moment then released it. "Never wanted this."

I looked at him, but his eyes focused on the sand. "Okay." His voice lacked expression.

I released a huff. "You think I'm a bad person. Don't you?"

He shook his head. He again looked at me, but he still didn't say anything.

"What are you thinking?"

"Nothing." He picked up a nearby stick and started picking at the bark.

I let out a tense laugh. "Then, why won't you look at me?"

He shot me a quick look. Then he returned to picking at the stick. Then he paused as if reconsidering something. He set the stick down and turned to face me. "I'm just trying to figure out what to say."

I shifted so I could meet his eyes directly. "I know. I don't fit. It's what every girl on my island dreams about. Probably your sisters do the same too. It's what girls do. They dream about *this* and believe it's their destiny." I let out a huge sigh. "But I don't want it."

He changed his position, sitting cross-legged to face me. "Why are you telling me this?"

"Just . . . don't you think it's ironic?" I tried to keep my tone casual. "That you and I are about to go help Ashyr start a next generation, and I don't want *it*."

Yam gave me a puzzled look. "Then why did you agree to this?"

I looked away. I had a plan to leave, but my plan was starting to unravel fast. I suddenly didn't want to go. I wanted to be with my dad. And my mom. And learn more about the island. And be safe here. And I didn't want to go through the procedure I heard Ashyr talking about with my mom. I was scared. And now, Yam and this feeling when I was around him like I wanted a *man*. I was all confused inside.

But when I looked back at him, I found I couldn't say all that. Instead, I said, "Why are you doing this?"

He scooted back. His legs extended out, almost touching my knee. He pulled in a long breath. Then another one. When he spoke, he sounded very solemn. "I want to believe we're doing good for somebody. Not Ashyr. But we are offering hope to those who need hope. We might be offering them a future they wouldn't otherwise have."

I don't know why, but his words triggered something in me. A push I didn't want to feel. I immediately stood up.

He stood too. "You okay?"

But I couldn't look at him.

I didn't want to leave anymore because I was scared. But he was talking about hope and helping others. Of doing something good. Important.

Like I kept saying I wanted to do.

I folded my arms and stared out at the ocean.

"I think people are depending on us," Yam said,

standing next to me, rather close. "But things are very confusing right now. And it's a strange request. I know. You. Me. Populating a new generation. And us, maybe, possibly doing others some good."

"What if we don't do it?" The fear surfaced in my voice. "What if we still go with Ashyr, but we don't go through with the procedure?"

His eyes raised. "You wouldn't help him?"

"Yam." I grabbed his arm. This was a mistake. His face was close to mine. I wanted to say, "*Don't tell anyone, it's a secret. It has to be a secret.*" Instead, I said, "I don't know. I just have been thinking about my choices, but I don't know . . .but don't tell anyone, okay?"

His mouth hung open. He looked like he didn't know what to say.

I dropped my hand from his arm. "Yeah—I better go pack." Then I took off running up the hill toward the road above us, wishing I hadn't told Yam these thoughts that were running through my mind.

# FIFTY

## YAM

While waiting for Leilani to return, Yam watched the ocean. Before he'd found solace and peace in its rhythm. But now, as he watched the waves, he felt more turbulence. His breath felt unsettled alongside the continual crash of water. How had life become complicated so fast?

He had totally made a mistake. One mistake on top of another.

He should have never told Leilani about Baba's work. Clearly, she did not understand.

And Leilani's words now concerned him. Yam didn't want to go to L.A. with Ashyr either. He wanted to be with Baba, more than ever, helping him save their island.

He could be shuttling Foster back and forth. Together they could pick up Ashyr's supplies and then work toward rescuing them all.

He was the Supply Boy.

It was his job to gather supplies, especially during this time of distress.

Not create a disaster. One after the other.

Maybe he should talk to Baba through the FID. But not in the open. It was bad enough he shared what he had with Leilani. No one needed to see the progress of Baba's work. Especially those who didn't understand.

He headed toward the palm tree, ready to locate a safe place underground. Except he couldn't identify the right tree. All around him, they had the same rippled texture, the same wide bases.

The inability to find the exit stirred his anxiety. It grew in him just like it had moments earlier when Leilani had first emerged from the palm tree, when Yam was sorting through the state of the islands. The more he thought, the more he felt like his air passage was constricting, like he was starting to choke.

Until he heard her voice calling out for him. "Yam?"

From where he stood, lost in the trees, he could see her, but she couldn't see him.

She was dressed again in a tank top and cutoff shorts. Her hair bounced in its own pattern as she ran along the beach. "Yam?"

He stepped out to be directly near her.

"Hey," she said, her voice out of breath, her chest rising and falling near him. "I didn't know what to pack. I have no idea what I'll need while I'm there. But then, I figured if I need something, you can help me find it. Right, Supply Boy?"

A lightness was in her voice, a carefreeness as if she was ready to put behind them all the heavy secret sharing from before.

He felt his lips twitch, even though he fought against the smile. Instead, he decided to share his new plan. "I'm going home. To help Baba."

She flung her hair behind her shoulder. "What?" A questioning grin emerged as if she doubted the seriousness of his statement. "No. You're still coming?"

He stepped back and folded his arms. "And if you want my opinion, I think you shouldn't go. I think this is all a mistake."

She raised her duffle bag. "I'm all packed." The grin kept growing into a charming smile while she studied his face.

"If you don't want this," he bravely continued, "to help Ashyr, if you don't want to keep your commitment to him, I think you need to be forthcoming about it. Be fair to him." He stepped back, determined to not stand so close to her.

"I think you don't need to worry about it." She dropped her bag onto the sand. Her smile remained bright.

Meanwhile, Yam fought through his thoughts. His desire to communicate with Baba through the FID. His regrets that he hadn't just reached out to him at the very beginning when Yam knew he was in trouble. How different everything would have been had he just asked for help.

He relayed his lesson learned toward her situation. "You say you're angry at your parents for lying to you. What makes you any different from them if you're lying to Ashyr?"

In a coy manner, she tilted her head. "Maybe I'm not lying."

"But you talked about . . ." The anxiety returned. "Not doing *this* . . ." Yam felt a frustration growing, especially as he kept tripping over his words. "Whatever *this* is . . ." Awkwardness was taking over, leading him back down the dangerous path of his altered breathing, a hint of an anxiety attack forming.

He focused on his breathing. As soon as he got it regulated again, he would be okay.

In and out. In and out.

He chose his next words quickly. "This is different. What Ashyr's asking. . .we don't even have to like each other."

"Who said I don't like you?"

His breathing stalled.

"Yam." Her head tilted further, and her eyes gave him a chiding look. "I think you need to forget I said anything at all."

"I can't forget it." His folded arms tightened around his ribs. "I can't go with you if this is just a front. It's not right."

She shrugged and picked up her pack. "I'm going."

"Well . . . it's important." His words tumbled out as she walked away from him. He just wanted to get back to Baba. He wanted to start fixing things rather than keep seeing things break. "If you don't want to do this," he called after her, "let them find another person because it's important to Ashyr, and all the people it could help. And now, it's important to your dad too."

She stopped walking and turned around. "Explain this."

"Look." He approached her. "With the islands in trouble, we are helping them. Ashyr can save us. Just like we can help save him . . . his family."

She looked toward the water. Then she spun around as if searching for the fake palm tree too. "Then," her words came out like a whisper, "If it's important, I need to do this."

It was like the words were finally sinking in, like she was understanding how serious everything was for everyone. "I don't want them to find someone else," she added.

Yam's arms finally relaxed at his side. A huge gust of air exhaled out of him. "I don't want them to either."

"Then I do . . . I need to do this. We need to."

"That's what I keep coming back to too."

"Okay."

"So you are going to do *this*?"

"I think your *this* and my *this* are different."

"No, they're not."

"They are."

"You sure?"

She looked at him as if debating something. Then she nodded and stepped directly in front of him. "Come here." She motioned him closer. "This is my *this*." And suddenly she kissed him. Quick on the lips. Right there on the beach.

He felt stunned. Totally, absolutely, confused. She walked over to her bag, picked it up, and walked backward.

"Look I want to go. Like we said, we need to go. And I want you to go with me. So, let's go."

He raced to meet her, feeling speechless and blurry in the head. "Good. I'm glad."

She reached for his hand and he let her take it. A ginormous grin spread across his face. "I like you, Leilani."

"I like you, too, Yam."

"That's probably a good thing."

She tightened her grip around his fingers. "I don't know which tree it is."

"Me neither."

They both just stood staring at palm trees. Until Leilani said, "Come here. I want to show you something." She dropped her bag and then led him out toward the water.

"Stand here." She positioned him to face the land then she grinned. He grinned back. She leaned forward, appearing ready for another kiss. He leaned too.

Only for her to shove him playfully toward the water, right as a somewhat large wave lapped high up his shorts.

"You!" He called at her, but she was off running, laughing. "That was cruel." He took off after her.

"Living on this island," she yelled out while she ran along the sand, "I've learned to track the waves, and it was just too good a moment to pass up."

"You." He kept running while remembering the brief touch of her lips against his. "I'm going to get you back for that." He laughed boyishly.

She laughed back. "Oh yeah? Not if you can't catch me." She kept turning her head back, assessing his distance. Although he was fast, she seemed to glide effortlessly across the sand.

Eventually, he caught up to her, close enough that he scooped her up in his arms and carried her toward the water.

She was laughing, screaming. "Don't, Yam. Don't you dare. You just got a little wet, don't throw me in."

His legs were already in the water, his arms swinging back, in preparation to launch her out to sea.

"Please, Yam." Her laughter switched to giggling

pleas for mercy. "I'll be wet on the entire ride over."

"You have a decent point." He slowed down his swaying, and she sighed. "Although," he quickly rocked his arms again, ready to release her in mid-air, "I need a better reason than that."

"Like what?" she giggled her protest.

"Three." He started the countdown. "Two."

"If you throw me in," she started talking fast, "I very likely would catch a cold, and it could be a lingering cold, one that I'd pass on to your offspring."

He slid her softly down onto the sand. "You say you're a scientist," he said, holding her close. "But what you just said is purely nonsensical, and you know it."

She looked up at him, her breath still quick from their race. "About your offspring?"

"About them all being born with colds because you'd pass it on."

Her grin only grew. "But my clothes are dry."

Suddenly, Yam's mouth was on hers. Tender and gentle, as the wave softened around their calves. For a moment, it seemed like she was going to pull back, but when she didn't, he kissed her deeper and she returned the kiss.

When he finally released her, he felt the adrenaline racing through his heart. His head felt dizzy with a hunger for her.

"Wow," she whispered.

"Just . . . you kissed me first and, well, I thought it customary that I return that kiss," he whispered.

"Customary, yeah, right."

"Was that okay?" Yam asked, his eyes searching, all humor gone. "Did I go too far?"

Leilani glanced past him toward the trees, then she stepped further away. "Look," she said.

He did. Her mom was watching them. "Oh. I'm sorry," he whispered as if Mariana was already scolding them both.

"No. No." Her voice sounded confident. "It's fine. It just surprised me."

"Surprised me too." He chuckled. Then he tried to regain the moment of playfulness between them. "But I can still throw you in the water if you need another surprise."

His words did the trick and Leilani took off running toward the trees. "No. Don't you dare." She called out behind her.

He followed, toward the trees, feeling uncomfortable as he approached Mariana, well aware she had been watching them.

# FIFTY-ONE

## MARIANA

It came down to perspective. All of it.

As she watched Leilani approach, Mariana could not dismiss the smile behind her daughter's eyes. Under the circumstances, that smile, hidden yet emerging, meant everything to Mariana.

The moment came down to courage.

Courage to trust. Courage to say goodbye. To be okay.

"Leilani," she said softly, her voice cracking over the name. "Are you ready?"

Her daughter lifted the duffel bag, then slipped her head through it so the strap crossed over her chest. "Let's do this." Leilani glanced back at Yam, who lingered in the shadows, not quite making eye contact with Mariana.

And for some reason, Mariana was having a difficult time making eye contact with him as well. Before he surfaced out of the shadows, she turned to head down into the belly while her mind sorted through an assortment of feelings.

The first time her daughter kissed a boy, Mariana wasn't sure what she thought she would feel. Perhaps concern, fear, sadness to see her little girl no longer little. But Leilani hadn't been little for a long time. And now, circumstances required her to be grown up. Very grown up.

So, for some strange reason, watching Leilani and Yam kiss knowing everything that was stacked against them, Mariana surprisingly felt satisfaction. An absolute and complete relief over what had just occurred.

Foster had assured her she could trust Yam. That he was a good kid. More importantly, he was Sunny's kid. Because of that, she knew goodness dwelt in his heart.

And as much as Mariana wished she could change so many things, under the circumstances, this was the best the situation could be.

As she led the way, hearing Leilani and Yam's footsteps behind her, hearing their whispers and moments of laughter echoing off the metallic hallways, the young love made her already miss Foster. More than she thought possible.

Moments earlier, she had stood next to him in these hallways, her hand reaching to hold his. Grateful when he accepted it. A peace treaty offered, an olive branch extended, both parties letting go of any blame, any regrets, anything they could have done to prevent what they now faced.

A strange blanket-like sensation seemed to cover Mariana's heart. Comfort? Numbness? Gratitude? Reverence? Shock?

Thoughts ticked through her head. Had she known how all this would end, would she have done it? Taken the Em-Path job. Built something magnificently horrible with Ashyr, Brody, and Foster. Fallen in love with Foster. Married again. Had Leilani. Took her entire family into a new civilization. Left a broken world. Only now to see their paradise come to an end.

What would she have done differently? Which piece of the equation would she pull out, what would she omit? One tweak and the outcome would be different, the error perhaps even greater.

She didn't cry when Foster hugged her goodbye.

Even more surprisingly, she'd extended another olive branch to Ashyr. She hugged him, too, and tried not to recoil when his shimmering suit touched her skin or she smelled his sweat.

But she needed it, this effort to let go of the hate.

If any part of the plan that Foster had shared ended in loss, Mariana did not want to take such broken anger with her, not to her grave, not to whatever home was next.

# FIFTY-TWO

## LEILANI

While we followed Mom through the underground maze, I reached for Yam's hand. I needed that assurance. Like whatever adventures were ahead, it was good that he would be there. But as soon as Mom turned around, Yam dropped my hand.

A smile started to form on Mom's face, but she turned away.

"I hear you are going to take care of her," she said ahead of us. Yam and I both exchanged a quick look, not quite sure who she was talking to. But Mom just continued. "I feel better about that, you know? Sending her out into that strange place Ashyr's created. But you'll help navigate her through it. You'll keep her safe, won't you?"

When she turned, her eyes were clearly on Yam. Oh, those eyes. They could be so piercing. So commanding at times.

"Mom," I said softly, trying to remove Yam from her stare.

Her eyes shifted to me. "I love you." she said, a harshness in her tone with emotion cracking through. "Do you know that? Do you understand that? Do you know how much I love you?"

I stepped back, trying to distance myself a bit

from her intensity, feeling a bit embarrassed for how worked up Mom was getting in front of Yam.

But Mom just continued. "Your father would say something wise right now. Like, 'Leilani knows enough. And she will know more. And when she does, she will understand our love for her even more.'"

I could see moisture accumulating in her eyes. I had only seen Mom cry once, and right then, in that moment, in front of Yam, she was going to cry again. I just stood there, not sure what to do, trying to stop Mom with my eyes. Instead, my look only kept her going.

"When I saw you on the beach, laughing with him," she gave a quick nod toward Yam, "teasing each other, playing in the water, I saw you dear. I really saw you. The restlessness inside of you for these long months. Maybe it's even been years. I know this has been hard on you. All of it. But today, I saw some joy in your eyes, a small bit of peaceful-ness there."

"You're a good boy." She shifted to intensely look again at Yam. "But," her tone shifted to a warning. "Right now, she's too young to marry."

"Mom!" My eyes nearly popped.

"But," Mom raised her finger at me. Then she smiled at Yam. "She's not too young to start feeling some attraction. To remember she's a young woman with as many wants and needs as her peers."

"I . . . I . . ." Yam didn't know what to say.

I helped him out. I stepped a good foot away from him. "Mom, we just met."

"But, sometimes . . ." Mom turned away. She headed over to a finger scanner. Her hand hovered above it, before turning back to face us. "Sometimes things are outside of our control. All of it. Love and everything."

I had to stop this. I quickly stood next to her and spoke in a very low tone. "I'm not in love."

"Not yet," she said calmly.

"That's a lot of weight to put on me, Mrs. Grady," Yam spoke behind us with a forced lightness.

"Love is a lot of weight, period." Mom faced Yam again. "Someday, you two, it will be right." She looked directly at me. "Right for you to fall in love." Then she looked at Yam. "And if she does with you, under all this, so much the better." She looked at me again. I couldn't get my mouth to work to stop her. "So very much the better, dear," she said.

Finally, I broke out of my shock and embarrassment. "Where's Dad?" I scanned the loading area, hoping he would save me like he had so many times with Mom.

She exhaled a breath like she understood and would stop this awkward lecture she was giving me. "He's already left."

"What?"

"He and Ashyr are already on their way there."

"So." I grasped my hand around my shoulder strap. "We'll meet them there."

"Ashyr." Mom nodded as the chamber door opened. "Your father will already be on his way back before you arrive." Then she stepped inside the chamber. As did Yam.

But I just stood at the keypad, feeling lost as I processed the news. My first big venture away and he wasn't there. And I wouldn't be seeing him in L.A. "He didn't say goodbye."

Mom looked away as if my statement had distressed her too.

I was mad, hurt, sad, scared, everything that just being near Dad would help clear. I missed him. Right then, I really missed my dad. "Mom!" I stood next to her, feeling the pain cross my face, knowing I should pull it together with Yam right there, but I couldn't. "He didn't even say goodbye."

She nodded at me with a sadness. Like she understood. "He just wants you home. Safe. And back home."

The chamber doors suddenly closed, trapping all of us in the emptiness of the first chamber.

Mom reached for me in the darkness, and I fell into her sideways hug. She leaned close to me and said, "Once the airship enters the next chamber, and the all clear is given, our goodbye is going to be really quick, and I want you to know I am saying goodbye, dear. For both your dad and I."

My shoulder caved into her hug and my eyes began to burn. I didn't know if I wanted this goodbye, to leave, to be away from her, from Dad.

While we waited for the chamber door to open, I just kept my arm around her waist. She tightened her grip around me too.

"I love you, Mom," I said. But then, I got afraid that of all the times she never hears me, she hadn't heard me now. "Did you hear me?" I said it right into her ear. "Mom. I love you."

She didn't say anything. The quietness, the darkness, the moments of waiting. But I could feel her little body shaking next to me.

"Are you okay?" I asked, still close to her ear.

She nodded, then squeezed her arm around my waist a bit tighter. "I love you, too, dear. Intensely. And, yes, I'm okay. I've spent so long being afraid of all there was to fear. And fighting and fighting to not have to face all these fears. And in one day, that fighting has all changed." The second chamber unlocked. "Because, Leilani, everything that mattered before no longer does." The thick metal door opened to show the airship before us. She gave me one final squeeze then released her arm from around me. "Only one thing matters now."

Then, she stepped away.

*The story continues in LIES A PLACE,*
*Book 2 of The Existence Series.*

*Thank you for reading BEYOND THE END.*
*Please consider leaving an honest review on*
*Amazon.com, Goodreads, your blog, or another*
*form of social media. Reviews can dramatically*
*boost visibility for a published book, effectively*
*increase sales and allow an author to continue their*
*craft—and you to continue reading!*

## A SNEAK PEEK

# LIES A PLACE

### BOOK 2 IN THE EXISTENCE SERIES

## ONE

### LEILANI

I watched the nurse's thick, calloused hands intently. Her grainy, sweet voice sent an alarm to my head. "You'll need to give yourself a shot twice a day." With those hands, she produced a long needle. "When the calendar tells you to begin administration, you'll need to do this…" She inserted the needle into the vial, then filled the syringe to the 10mL level.

With her flowery scrub top raised, she pantomimed inserting the needle into her hairy stomach. "You understand?" Her head lifted. Her asparagus-colored dreadlocks nodded at me. Before I responded, she straightened and approached me with her needle raised high.

I pulled back. Sitting next to me, Yam placed his hand on my knee. I touched it, covering mine over his, and our fingers interlocked.

The nurse cleared her throat, a scold was there. Yam and I both withdrew. "It's okay," she said. I met her eyes and she nodded at our hands. "You can comfort her. I will allow that touch."

Yam slid his hand back into mine. For a moment, I closed my eyes, picturing his hand strumming the guitar strings, him singing, us laughing. Since our first kiss, back home on the island, I had hoped we might kiss again, but such contact was not allowed while we were in Ashyr's care.

"Leilani." I opened my eyes to find the nurse staring at me. "Can you give yourself these shots?"

My fingers tightened around Yam's. "I can."

Without asking, the nurse raised my tank top high, revealing my belly button and the lower edge of my bra. Yam turned away, as if giving me privacy. But as his hand felt like it might leave too, I gripped it firmly, leading him back to look at the large needle with me.

"You will go like this." With a mechanical motion, the nurse drew her arm back and then moved it forward toward my belly.

Unintentionally, I gasped. My body pressed against Yam.

The nurse laughed. "I didn't do anything."

I protected my belly with my free hand. "Well...I thought you were coming at me, like you..." There was too much panic in my voice. "Like you were going to do it now."

"I'm not." She laughed again. "But I need you to, so I know you can."

I closed my eyes, wanting the needle to disappear. I pictured myself back on the eighth floor of my secure living quarters. Since I'd been in Ashyr's care, each evening, around the same time, I watched the colorfully attired people on the gray streets below pairing up through some ritual between them. As night came on, they disappeared. Lights spread out like a fan through the city. Their ritual served as my daily entertainment, watching their bright specks dance below me. People living, while I waited.

Waited for this.

"Leilani." The nurse called me back. "If you can't give it to yourself, Jate will."

I realigned myself in my seat and tensely dropped my protective arm to my side. "Let me see it," I said strongly. While my other hand stayed locked on Yam's, I reached for the syringe. "I can do it."

My handler, Jate, smelled. On first meeting her, the foulness made me want to lose my first meal in L.A., a tasteless lunch of soda crackers and bland cheese. Yam had warned me that the food here was not good. What he hadn't warned me about were the smells.

I stared at the needle now. On that first day, when I had asked Yam if he had smelled Jate, or his handler, Kandi-Greene, who also made me hold my breath when we met, Yam had only grinned. "You'll get used to it." Later he explained, "It's the perfumes. Hairspray. Deodorant. Those are the smells."

"It's horrible," I said.

"It's how everyone smells here. You're going to see a lot of new things. Smell a lot of unique smells. Everything is different here. You lived in a bubble."

In my imaginary discussion with Dad...in a fantasy world where I had forgiven him for lying to me...where I magically *understood* why he had kept the truth from me, letting me believe the island we resided on was on Earth and not his invention floating in its own orbit in the sky, he would explain by saying, "We know how to keep clean with little impact to our sphere. The island has a huge impact on us and we on it." Something like that.

"Show me." The nurse nodded at the syringe in my hand.

Yam had explained I would get used to the smells but as I stared at the needle and thought of Dad, and the island, and what he would say about the smell, between the nurse's odor as she hung over me and the needle in my hand, nausea stirred up the bland roast beef sandwich from lunch. "I thought you said we weren't doing it now," I said, trying to push down the fear.

The nurse's eyes shifted to the hand-holding; a scowl formed around her lips. Then her eyes returned to the needle. A look of sadistic glee spread over her face. "Do it," she said.

Between the syringe in one hand and Yam's hand in the other, I felt she was now punishing me for our touch. "You said...." the fear kept resurfacing in my voice, "I needed to wait...until the time on the calendar..." I cleared my throat. "Wait...until I start this."

The nurse nodded. "That's saline solution." The gleeful look was still there, tight against the extra makeup on her face. "It won't hurt you. But you need to show me you can do this. Can you?"

I tried to laugh it off, like *of course I can*. But the sound, hollow and disgusted, turned against me.

"Do it." The nurse's large arm touched me, right around my forearm.

I pulled back from her, letting go of Yam's touch too. He shifted to look at me directly.

"Can you do it?" he asked.

"Sure. Sure." I couldn't quite meet his eyes.

His hand pressed against my knee. "I can come give them to you. Every morning, every night."

"So can Jate," the nurse replied.

"I can do it," I said, speaking to the floor.

"Then," the nurse cleared her throat, "go ahead."

I touched the spot directly below my belly. *Three. Two. One.* I jabbed it in and tried not to wince at the pain.

"Very good." She took the syringe from me. "Begin once the calendar tells you to."

TARA C. ALLRED is an award-winning author, instructional designer, and educator. She has been recognized as a California Scholar of the Arts for Creative Writing and is a recipient of the Howey Awards for Best Adult Book and Best Adult Author. She lives in Utah with her husband.

Her other published works include the *John Sanders* series, *Helping Helper*, and *The Other Side of Quiet*, a 2015 Kindle Book Award Finalist and Whitney Award Winner.

For more info, visit www.taracallred.net.